THE JOURNEY PRIZE

STORIES

WINNERS OF THE $10,000 JOURNEY PRIZE

1989: Holley Rubinsky for "Rapid Transits"

1990: Cynthia Flood for "My Father Took a Cake to France"

1991: Yann Martel for "The Facts Behind the Helsinki Roccamatios"

1992: Rozena Maart for "No Rosa, No District Six"

1993: Gayla Reid for "Sister Doyle's Men"

1994: Melissa Hardy for "Long Man the River"

1995: Kathryn Woodward for "Of Marranos and Gilded Angels"

1996: Elyse Gasco for "Can You Wave Bye Bye, Baby?"

1997 (shared): Gabriella Goliger for "Maladies of the Inner Ear"
        Anne Simpson for "Dreaming Snow"

1998: John Brooke for "The Finer Points of Apples"

1999: Alissa York for "The Back of the Bear's Mouth"

2000: Timothy Taylor for "Doves of Townsend"

2001: Kevin Armstrong for "The Cane Field"

2002: Jocelyn Brown for "Miss Canada"

2003: Jessica Grant for "My Husband's Jump"

2004: Devin Krukoff for "The Last Spark"

2005: Matt Shaw for "Matchbook for a Mother's Hair"

2006: Heather Birrell for "BriannaSusannaAlana"

2007: Craig Boyko for "OZY"

2008: Saleema Nawaz for "My Three Girls"

2009: Yasuko Thanh for "Floating Like the Dead"

2010: Devon Code for "Uncle Oscar"

2011: Miranda Hill for "Petitions to Saint Chronic"

2012: Alex Pugsley for "Crisis on Earth-X"

2013: Naben Ruthnum for "Cinema Rex"

THE BEST OF CANADA'S NEW WRITERS

THE JOURNEY PRIZE

STORIES

SELECTED BY
STEVEN W. BEATTIE
CRAIG DAVIDSON
SALEEMA NAWAZ

McCLELLAND & STEWART

Library and Archives of Canada Cataloguing in Publication is available
upon request

ISBN 978-0-7710-5050-3
eISBN 978-0-7710-5051-0

Published simultaneously in the United States of America by
McClelland & Stewart, a division of Random House of Canada Limited

Library of Congress Control Number available upon request

Cover art: © iStock.com/Dutch Scenery
Cover design: Leah Springate

Printed and bound in the USA

McClelland & Stewart,
a division of Random House of Canada Limited,
a Penguin Random House Company
www.randomhouse.ca

1 2 3 4 5   18 17 16 15 14

ABOUT THE JOURNEY PRIZE STORIES

The $10,000 Journey Prize is awarded annually to an emerging writer of distinction. This award, now in its twenty-sixth year, and given for the fourteenth time in association with the Writers' Trust of Canada as the Writers' Trust of Canada/McClelland & Stewart Journey Prize, is made possible by James A. Michener's generous donation of his Canadian royalty earnings from his novel *Journey*, published by McClelland & Stewart in 1988. The Journey Prize itself is the most significant monetary award given in Canada to a developing writer for a short story or excerpt from a fiction work in progress. The winner of this year's Journey Prize will be selected from among the thirteen stories in this book.

The Journey Prize Stories has established itself as the most prestigious annual fiction anthology in the country, introducing readers to the finest new literary writers from coast to coast for more than two decades. It has become a who's who of up-and-coming writers, and many of the authors who have appeared in the anthology's pages have gone on to distinguish themselves with short story collections, novels, and literary awards. The anthology comprises a selection from submissions made by the editors of literary journals from across the country, who have chosen what, in their view, is the most exciting writing in English that they have published in the previous year. In recognition of the vital role journals play in fostering literary voices, McClelland & Stewart makes its own award of

$2,000 to the journal that originally published and submitted the winning entry.

This year the selection jury comprised three writers:

Steven W. Beattie is the review editor of *Quill & Quire* magazine. His writing has been published in the *Globe and Mail*, the *National Post*, *The Walrus*, *Canadian Notes & Queries*, and elsewhere. Please visit www.shakespeareanrag.com.

Craig Davidson is the author of four books of fiction: the short story collection *Rust and Bone*, which was made into an Oscar-nominated feature film of the same name, and the novels *The Fighter*, *Sarah Court*, and *Cataract City*, a finalist for the Scotiabank Giller Prize and the Trillium Book Award. Davidson is a graduate of the Iowa Writers' Workshop, and his articles and journalism have been published in the *National Post*, *Esquire*, *GQ*, *The Walrus*, and *The Washington Post*, among other places. He lives in Toronto, with his partner and their child. Please visit www.craigdavidson.net.

Saleema Nawaz's fiction has appeared in literary journals such as *Prairie Fire*, *PRISM international*, *Grain*, and *The New Quarterly*. Her debut collection, *Mother Superior*, was a finalist for the Quebec Writers' Federation's McAuslan First Book Prize, and her first novel, *Bone and Bread*, was the winner of the QWF Paragraphe Hugh MacLennan Prize for Fiction. Her short story "My Three Girls" was the winner of the 2008 Writers' Trust of Canada / McClelland & Stewart Journey Prize. She lives in Montreal and blogs at metaphysical-conceit.blogspot.com.

The jury read a total of eighty-seven submissions without knowing the names of the authors or those of the journals in which the stories originally appeared. McClelland & Stewart would like to thank the jury for their efforts in selecting this year's anthology and, ultimately, the winner of this year's Journey Prize.

McClelland & Stewart would also like to acknowledge the continuing enthusiastic support of writers, literary journal editors, and the public in the common celebration of new voices in Canadian fiction.

For more information about *The Journey Prize Stories*, please visit www.facebook.com/TheJourneyPrize.

CONTENTS

INTRODUCTION

One of the joyous aspects of reading for the Journey Prize is the feeling of discovery: the jury process allows for exposure to a new generation of writers who are extending the tradition of Canadian short fiction well into the twenty-first century. Additionally, it was a pleasure to discover writers with such a wide range and diversity of approaches to the short story form. Much of the appeal short fiction holds – for writers and readers alike – is its potential for experimentation, for stretching and expanding both form and content.

As jury members, we went in without checklists or agendas, but with passion kindled to fight for our favourites. We tried our best to acknowledge our blind spots and biases, and we were pleased to discover that it was not difficult to reread, discuss, and *agree* – without needing to compromise. All of the stories in this volume made an impression. Chief in importance was the quality of the writing, though skilful writing alone was not enough to keep a story afloat. We valued insight, surprise, and humour where we found it.

Julie Roorda's "How to Tell if Your Frog Is Dead" is a perfect example. Plotless and characterless (assuming a conventional definition of what defines a "character" in fiction), the piece requires readers to radically reconsider their concept of what qualifies as a fully formed story. Yet Roorda's vignette is tightly calibrated, possessed of internal unity, and – not for nothing – is also gut-bustingly funny. Does it qualify as a "story"? Why ever not?

Not quite as radical, but nonetheless challenging in its presentation of contemporary themes and concerns is Nancy Jo Cullen's "Hashtag Maggie Vandermeer," a story that will resonate (uncomfortably, one hesitates to admit) with readers of a certain age, but also possesses a sharp sense of humour and a sensitivity to the demands and drawbacks of trying to keep pace with a wired world. The protagonist's commingled confusion and discomfort with modern methods of communication is sharp in its satire; her resultant inability to connect with her daughter lends the story an emotional poignancy that is unexpected and quite moving.

And on a more traditional note, Jeremy Lanaway's "Downturn" channels Cheever and Updike, but does so in a highly sophisticated, surprising way. The story is traditional in the best possible sense: it is aware of what came before and is not afraid to exist in homage, while also breaking new ground in its specific details.

In an art form based on invention, textured description lends authority and authenticity. Kevin Hardcastle's "Old Man Marchuk" has a gritty, grease-under-the-fingernails power to its writing. Hardcastle gets his rural setting and characterizations just right, infusing the story with both a lived-in sense of realism and quieter moments of grace.

Tyler Keevil's "Sealskin" was a stunner. The writing is straightforward and not flashy, but it hums with subsurface power; Keevil builds scenes that reverberate with insightful detail and keen characterizations, all of which funnel toward a scene of shocking power and pathos.

Andrew MacDonald's "Four Minutes" is a risky piece: a high-wire act that, if told in the wrong way, could edge perilously close to melodrama or movie-of-the-week bathos. It's a tribute to MacDonald's skill as a writer that he manages to take a risky premise and offer up a touching story about a boy's love for his sister.

But the protagonists of these stories are no angels. They shoplift, drive getaway cars, and flirt with infidelity. In Clea Young's "Juvenile," a B.C. ferry crossing is the setting for an original and unflinching look at ordinary human cruelty and compulsions. Featuring a deft shift of perspectives, Young's story shows both points of view as a former couple, estranged since high school, come together in a chance encounter. Old grievances and obsessions reverberate through the characters' psyches and come to the fore, creating a vivid world of memory and meaning for the protagonists, and by extension, the reader.

If there is one shared trait among the writers we have selected, it is their discernment of the human condition. Rosaria Campbell's "Probabilities" accepts the writer's challenge of putting the ineffable into words: in this case, intuition, mental anguish, and the inescapability of home. Relentless in its empathy, "Probabilities" outlines the protagonist's struggle to understand her brother's experience as a gay teen in rural Newfoundland and his state of mind following a serious diagnosis and, later, a lapse in personal judgment. This attempt to build a bridge of understanding between one individual and another is no less than the shared undertaking of all fiction, as well as its noblest effect.

Another is to make the familiar unfamiliar. From food courts and french fries to crimped hair and goatees, the world somehow seems different than it was before we spent time with the narrator of Amy Jones' "Wolves, Cigarettes, Gum." The perfect mix of tender and funny, Jones' story brings romance and a light touch to a tale of petty crime.

In the end, the work will speak for itself. Take a good look at the table of contents, as there are many more excellent stories than the ones we have outlined here. And remember the authors' names – you could be hearing them a lot more over the coming years.

We believe any reader would be hard pressed not to find something to like within these pages. And such evident diversity of sensibility and subject matter seems to ensure that the short story, Canada's most vibrant literary form, is in good hands for some time to come.

Steven W. Beattie
Craig Davidson
Saleema Nawaz
June 2014

LORI McNULTY

MONSOON SEASON

Monsoon rains will flood the main roads by fall but it's early June when Jess lies bloated and raw on bed six in a shared ward of Phuket International Hospital.

Morning rounds, four days after surgery, her doctor arrives bending from the waist, palms open, the way a magician reveals he has nothing to hide.

"Any pain today, Jess?"

She feels like a tortured prisoner in one of those exotic European thrillers, a brooding smile pinned to her mouth. "Like someone just shoved a pickaxe up my pelvis."

"Let's have a look," Dr. Jemjai says.

Gently, he probes her abdomen, a two-fingered touch as if patting down a row of garden seeds.

"Stop." His hands too close to her hipbone. "Please."

When he lifts her gown to peel away the dressing, her stitches are bloodied. She feels wetness spreading beneath her bottom, imagines copper-coloured stains seeping through to the crisp cotton sheets below.

Finally, he nods to her, she breathes deep. Deep inhale, again, while she slides two tight fists beneath the sheets, and he checks the stent in her swollen vagina.

She is a fucking French crêpe, folded in two. Pain radiates from her bowels, her stomach, oozes out between her teeth.

He orders the nurse to push morphine.

"Any bowel movements?"

The nurse replies *suai*, shaking her head.

Jess knows *suai* means either bad luck or beautiful, depending on the rising or falling tone. Her bowels were fabulous from the sphincter up but never beautiful.

A rip? Necrosis? Slow tissue death, choking off blood supply. She thumbs through the outcomes in her head. No. No. An infection crawling in, eight days before her scheduled flight back to Toronto.

She thinks about her life before the doctor. Girl on the verge in a prison march. Then, the collapse. Has he just split her body apart, or sewn her back together?

"When will you know?" Jess asks, pressing his hand.

"Tomorrow," Dr. Jemjai replies, patting her wrist. "We'll see tomorrow."

On her first night at the Thai guesthouse, Jess awakened, cotton-mouthed, dry heaving into a wicker basket. A knock forced her to her feet.

"You feeling o-kay, Miss?"

It was the pretty Thai hostess who had checked her in. No, she was not okay. Definitely not. Head dunked in the basket, she felt like . . . what was the Thai word? *Kee ok*: bird shit.

She accepted the bamboo tray carrying a bowl of clear

soup, little slivers of ginger floating on top. The tingling warmth settled her roiling stomach, gave her courage to join the others downstairs.

At the end of a long teak table, a tall woman rose, introducing herself as Fran Günter.

"I'm from Stuttgart, it's in the south," Fran said, her square face sitting on her neck like the rubber tip of a pencil – hard, pink, firm. But there was an unexpected stillness in her smile.

Jess pressed her right eyelid to stop its nervous jitter then. A third guest arrived behind her, introducing herself as Betty, whose long vowels curled and stretched from her tongue like a woman who'd tipped back a few martinis.

"So, when do you all go under?" she asked, not waiting for an answer. "I'm taking a Phang Nga Bay cruise with my lover, then we'll tour the temples. Ten days, then everything changes."

A young hostess arrived in the room, laying out tea and coconut cake on four oval-shaped, gold-rimmed plates. Jess pushed the plate away.

Despite years of vitamins, hormones, lipo-, hippo-, and laser therapy, Jess had never held a lover. A crude, midnight circle of one-night stands, sure. Men who'd fuck anything in a short skirt, yes. She was their shape-shifting Queen Street tranny. Fuckable. Transgressive. Freak. Subject, object, verb. No agreement.

"I'm Lydia. Welcome to Dr. Jemjai's Guesthouse."

Jess turned to see a Thai woman in a tight-fitting turquoise dress do a twirl so a river of cinnamon hair plunged to the small of her back. Her long legs draped to the floor. Between them, not a bump or bulge.

"I know you're excited. Maybe a little scared of all you've heard about the operation. Oh, the dilations, diarrhea . . ."

"Having a shunt up our cunts." Betty added, whooping.

Jess snorted, muffling her face with the cloth napkin. She leaned forward, in love with Lydia's heart-shaped mouth. Jess was proud most of her pewter eyes – the fathomless deep of a wishing well – and long eyelashes. The pills had softened her face – all-woman from padded bra to silicone-stuffed bottom – next to Lydia's beatific beauty, she was a gorilla in the mist.

Fran asked Lydia about functionality after the healing. Lydia wagged a telling finger. "What you really want to know is . . . yes, my coochie makes me come."

Fran slammed her tiny cup down. "We're not Thai lady-boys. I don't want a coochie. I want a vagina, like any woman."

Lydia folded her napkin twice and laid it across her lap. "Go to the Nana Plaza, or Patpong any night. See go-go girls and cowboys. Some go with the *farang* for money but how else do you think they can afford to look and talk like women?"

"Well, I say if every fuck is closer to losing the prick, lose the prick at any price," Betty chimed in.

Jess felt as if her soul were being trimmed by a long knife. She was all concealer and three-layer cover-up, pencilling her lips, to erase the rough outer edges of her life. Still, she bled. While they chatted, she mentally extracted her organs and laid them out on the long teak table. Heart, lungs, spleen, liver, plopped down and seeping. She counted each one then tucked them beneath her skin. Okay. There. She was all there.

Lydia explained she came to Bangkok when the family rice crops in her home province of Thai Binh were ruined by swarms of planthoppers.

"My father ran coal mines in the Ruhr Valley," Fran said, making a gesture of wiping her hands clean. Hating the bleak mines, she pursued a career in journalism, working as Arnt Werden. When she was exposed as Fran in a German tabloid a few years later, her disgraced family tried to chase her off with hush money.

"My father told me an heir could run the family empire; an heiress would ruin it."

"Did you run?" Jess asked.

"In these heels?" Fran joked, pointing to her leather pumps. "I took an assignment covering exploited Thai migrant workers arriving from Burma and Cambodia, and ended up wandering into a field of orchids in Doi Saket. They grow Cattleya hybrids. Lavender-blue orchids with frilly petals and dark, slate-blue lips. Vivid blue lips, can you imagine?"

Jess took a slate-blue bite of her coconut cake, felt the frills and lace drifting to the ground.

"I didn't have anywhere else to go," she said quietly and Fran squeezed her knee beneath the table.

Lydia stood, apologizing that she had to leave early, urging them not to be shy about exploring their vagina coastlines – where it curves, conceals, contracts.

That night Jess dreamt she was swimming in sheltered Kata Noi Bay beach. Dark bellied clouds rolled in as she drifted further from shore, the wind whipping up, battering the palm trees, bent and shivering toward the sea. The tide flooded her ears, she swallowed waves, slapped at them, then the scene went black.

When her body surfaced, it wore her mother Margaret's face.

—

Nine days after surgery, there are forms to sign. Prescriptions packed in a neat white sack. Dr. Jemjai slips a rubber doughnut beneath her and wheels her to the hospital ambulance bay. Outside, they pass a billboard featuring two Thai nurses in tuck-waist dresses with white winged caps. *Phuket. Let your baby be born in paradise.*

"Paradise Lost," Jess muses, shaking her head. "Satan wore a red satin teddy. All hell broke loose."

He smiles and wheels her to the waiting ambulance.

It will be a short hop from Phuket International to Bangkok, where she'll stay overnight, before boarding again for the long-haul flight back to Toronto. The attendants lift Jess into the back of the ambulance. Climbing in behind them, Dr. Jemjai tucks a note inside her carry-on.

"What's that?"

"For your physician in Toronto."

Jess tilts her head toward him. When he holds his hand out, her chin falls into his fleshy palm.

"Drink more water than you want to. Use the creams. If your legs ever become tender or swollen, seek medical help. Immediately."

Jess tries to take hold of his sleeve, but he pulls away. "I can't feel anything below the waist."

"Good," he says with a smile, shutting the double doors behind him.

Margaret picks up the old red kitchen phone with the annoying buzz. The line is crackly, but she doesn't dare hang up. Wisps of cigarette smoke twine through her nest of curly grey hair.

"Terry?" She hears a crowd murmuring at the end of the line.

"Yeah, it's me. I'm at Bangkok airport."

Margaret presses the phone harder against her ear. She has lived through his teen turmoil, his tough-on-the-outside talk, but the voice. Two years since they've talked. Her son's low tenor is now soprano smooth. Not soft on the vowels, not a slight lilt, but a young woman's voice. It's a gun flash. The moment her son goes missing.

"Did you get my postcard?"

Player's Light dangling from her hand, Margaret walks over to the refrigerator.

"Mom?"

Greetings from Phuket. She turns the card over.

Hi. I'm in Thailand. There are stray dogs everywhere. Yesterday, a lady went out to rescue a lab from a flooded water buffalo field. She got sick so they had to cut her legs off. Not the dog, the lady.
   P.S. Sorry for the long silence.

Margaret reads and remembers this: Terry at age seven, the night Margaret got the emergency call. A six-year-old German shepherd hit by a tow truck. Could she come? Harold was away on business, wouldn't be home for a few days. Margaret tucked her son in the backseat of her Datsun with a juice box, and off they sped to the clinic.

A young couple was cradling their battered dog in a sleeping bag when she arrived. He was cut straight through the underbelly, a ragged slice from gullet to mid-stomach. Her hands were shaking as she placed the dog on the gurney to examine him.

She led the owners back to her surgery to break the news. The shepherd's head was tilted sideways on the table, a draped sheet across his lacerated gut. The bereft couple retreated to their car while Margaret shaved the dog's leg and filled the syringe. Her sleepy son ambled in, pawing his eyes, and refusing to leave. With the dog still partially tucked inside the fleece-lined sleeping bag, Margaret laid him sideways across their laps. Terry found one of the dog's paws and held it in his small hands. He stroked the fur tufts above the collar.

Margaret cooed, "You're a good boy, you will always be loved."

Even after needle pierced skin, even when the shepherd's breath grew faint, Terry held on. Through the last muscle twitch. Wouldn't let go.

"The postcard? Did you get it?" The high voice, a stranger on the line, asks.

"Yes," she says, folding the card in half.

Margaret expels a sharp plume of smoke through her nose. "Are you in trouble?"

"Had plastic surgery in Phuket. Some complications."

"Oh my God, Terry. Are you . . . ?"

Silence.

She remembers when Terry stopped talking altogether. He was thin and twelve and boot-wedged into school lockers. Margaret temporarily exchanged her vet's licence for a recipe box, sent him to school with fresh-baked banana bread. At home, her life became sensible, Saran-sealed. Terry seemed happier, Harold more rooted, staying at home for longer stretches between work trips.

They found crack in Terry's room at sixteen. He was selling, not smoking, he swore, but they didn't believe it. By then he was wearing off-the-shoulder shimmery black T-shirts, a David Bowie glitter phase that left him bloodied at school.

One night Harold returned on the red eye for an early start on the weekend. He found Terry making out with another boy on the shoddy basement couch, their freckled backs covered in bites and scratches.

Harold ordered his dealing, punk rock glitter girl out.

"Go find yourself another fairy castle," he said. Terry pitched his clothes in a duffel bag and left. Margaret had no more energy to stop them.

Margaret taps the spoon hard against the rim of her coffee cup. "What happened?" she demands, drawing smoke up through her lungs, holding the burn.

"Will you come?"

"I'm still your mother."

"Yes, you gave me life and intermittent asthma. What I need now is a pick up at Pearson."

Margaret pitches a saucer into the sink. "I'll have to borrow Emma's car. Mine's kaput."

"What about Harold's Lincoln?"

"It's easier this way, Terry, believe me," she says, walking over to the front door. She pulls back the sheers to watch Harold pull up in the driveway. She glares when he slams the car door, balancing a load of empty moving boxes he'll use to haul out the remains of their twenty-eight-year marriage.

"Thai Airways, flight 783. Two p.m. tomorrow."

Harold rings the bell.

"Hang on, hang on, Terry. Mable's at the door."

Margaret muffles the phone in her hand, mouthing *you're late* at her soon-to-be ex-husband through the side window. She watches Harold jiggle the doorknob furiously.

"Shouldn't you be writing this down?" Jess asks.

"No, got it. Thai Airways, 783. See you at the airport, Terry." Margaret hangs up. She stands, watching Harold struggle with the knob, then slowly slides the front door bolt back, leaving the chain.

The next day, Margaret circles the luggage carrier clockwise, then reverses her orbit.

What version of Terry will she see? Her tight-lipped, punk rock drop-out with the long lashes? Her tall, baby-faced boy with the beautiful hands?

The passengers stream by. Terry is nowhere. A flight attendant taps Margaret on the shoulder, delivering Jess in her wheelchair.

Terry's eyes are sunken back, his face pallid. Margaret looks down. Beneath his stretchy, apple green sweater, her son has breasts.

Terry reaches, pushes up from the chair, trying to stand. Margaret hooks her arm around his waist, before he goes limp in her arms.

The last thing Jess recalls before blacking out at the airport is a German shepherd riding the escalator.

She awakens on a futon in Harold's office, minus the desk,

filing cabinets, and Harold. Margaret stands over her holding a tray of hot black coffee.

"What have you done?" she asks, dropping the tray beside Jess.

Jess tries to sit up. She can't begin to say. In her mother's hand, she sees the note Dr. Jemjai left in her tote bag.

Margaret drops it next to the coffee. With that, she does an about-face, banging her way back down to the kitchen.

Jess rises, taking short, careful steps down the stairs to the kitchen. Margaret is pouring the dregs of the coffee pot into a chipped ceramic cup. She takes one sip and dumps the rest down the drain.

Jess pulls out a chair, about to sit, then thinks better of it, afraid to rest without her rubber doughnut.

"You know, I get it. My son is gay. But this is . . . this is . . ." Margaret gestures wildly in Jess' direction.

"Sick?" Jess asks.

"Extreme. Even for you."

A wave of nausea hits. Jess feels her eyes tilt back, the room pitch forward. She steadies herself on the chair back.

"Good thing Harold's gone," Margaret says, pitching her toast crusts into the garbage. "He wouldn't survive it."

Jess feels liquid trickling down her left leg. Blood? Urine? She's afraid she might have to heave into the sink.

"Harold leaves, you come back as Cher. Think this makes you a woman?" Margaret gestures vaguely below Jess' waist.

"I'm sorry."

"That all you have to say?"

"What else is there? I saw *Martyr Mother* from the front row. A one-woman show. You play all the parts."

—

Jess manages to avoid Margaret for almost two weeks. They are magnetic North poles; she in Harold's office, her mother in the garden, she upstairs, her mother out for groceries, repelled by her son's embrace.

Now with the house to herself, Jess closes the bathroom door behind her. Sitting on the toilet, she remembers how her hands shook the first time she dialled Dr. Jemjai in Phuket. He told her he could make her Neo-Vagina look any way she wanted. He could emphasize the lips, so her Neo-Vagina would resemble a pouting face. Did he really say pouting face? His assistant sent her links to his work. She clicked and cried, moist under her arms, seeing the before and after.

The great burden of her body rushed through her like metastatic tissue. One organ, spreading to the rest of her parts. She was the penis in a one-act play. Had a penis personality. A penis future. Hostage to an abnormal cell, her body cut and cut again, splitting her in two. Female or male? What if you were a morphologic mistake? What if you were more?

She was in a dream, star-struck, when she spoke to Dr. Jemjai the second time. Vaginoplasty, clitoroplasty, and labiaplasty had come a long way, he explained. Moist, elastic, hairless – these were the benchmarks of his profession now. He spoke about flaps and grafts and good vascularity. A hot blush washed over her cheeks when he told her she would have orgasmic capabilities when a penis entered her. The diagrams he sent looked like the tampon instructions she read as a boy with delighted horror in her mother's bathroom.

During their third call, Dr. Jemjai went through each step.

He would take grafts from her scrotal sack, remove the testes, and invert skin from her penis, saving the nerve bundles for sensation. A penile inversion with flap technique. Her Neo-Vagina would be totally normal. Stop, she told him, no more technical specs. She wanted to hold onto the word, Neo-Vagina. Turn it over on her tongue. An ache spread in her chest. Her head and heart couldn't catch up to each other. Neo-Vagina, a glamorous new entrance after a lifetime of exits.

Legs splayed like a Russian gymnast, Jess takes a deep breath on the toilet. She's happy to be alone. Knees spread, fingers slick, she works her way inside. Holding her dilator like a pen, she lubes the tip, holding it at a downward angle. She double-checks the angle in the pocket mirror. Deep breath, then, spreading her labia, she pushes the dilator gently along the gummy pink wall, every quarter inch a miracle. Don't force it, she thinks, relax. Probing depth and diameter, the dilator disappears deeper, filling her with elation and fear. Will she close up? Will she bleed out if she pushes too hard? She checks the depth mark on the dilator. Not bad. In a few months, she'll work her way up to the six-inch dilator. Inches give her meaning now. It's been four weeks since her surgery – a lifetime since she shared Dr. Jemjai's guesthouse with Fran.

Her pants bunched around her ankles, she gently removes the dilator. Pressing her knees together, she thinks about Fran. They had spoken twice a week since the surgery, always with Margaret out of earshot.

They asked, but each one knew.

"No. Do you miss a lung tumour?"

"No. Do you miss acid wash jeans?"

Neo-Vaginas were about to take-off, Jess said, cheering Fran up after a bad patch of spotting. She made up commercials in an announcer's deep-throated voice that always made Fran laugh.

Now available in Europe: the racy new Neo-Vagina. German engineering with sleek Thai styling. Neo-Vagina: Engineering perfection under the hooded flap.

Need a flawless look to lift your spirits? Neo-Vagina. It's like lipstick between your legs!

Back in their Thai guesthouse, they'd planned a giddy reunion in Paris: a one-year-after celebration to parade their post-op, post-modern chic. Then Fran decided to get a tracheal shave. Soon after the procedure, the calls from Fran stopped. Jess consoled herself by thinking that even with a local anesthetic, Fran would be raspy and hoarse for a while.

Standing up again, Jess feels a sudden fullness below her waist. Her legs are weak. She looks down. Are they swollen? Oh God. No. Her breath accelerates. Not. Enough. Air. In.

Pulling up her pants, she heads for Harold's office and picks up the phone to dial 9-1-1, hyperventilating.

Margaret enters, taking the receiver from her hand.

"False alarm," she says calmly into the phone before hanging up.

"It's a clot!" Jess bursts.

"Not likely," Margaret says. She settles Jess back onto the bed. "Breathe in through the nose for two, out through the mouth for two."

Jess tries to speak. Her mother shakes her head, making a

show of filling her own lungs. Jess extends her arms out, beginning to cry.

"It's anxiety. Terriers are terrible for it. A Jack Russell once bit off my finger tip when I snapped my clipboard."

Margaret rubs her son's shoulders. "Your father had them, too. Anxiety attacks. Used to get him to snap a rubber band on his wrist." Margaret points to a spot on Jess's wrist. "Nasty email. SNAP. Insurance claimant sues. SNAP."

Jess wants nothing more than to curl up in her mother's arms.

"You're all right," Margaret repeats, pulling away sharply. "Girls are coming over for bridge tonight," she says, moving to the doorway. "Make yourself scarce. We wrap up at eleven."

Jess crosses her arms over her chest.

"It's better. You'll be on your own soon enough anyway." Margaret adds.

Disappearances. Jess is used to them. Especially in five-floor mazes like this one, where salespeople make brisk, efficient escapes whenever she comes near. Like the time a security guard chased her from the restroom in ladies lingerie after an older woman shrieked, throwing her purse at Jess. *Attention shoppers: Grotesque mistake in women's privates, plus two-for-one on ladies low-rise thongs.*

Teenage boys pounded each other on the escalator, or shoppers with quick, forward strides pretended not to see her. Sudden. Ruthless. Monsoon. A boy on a white sandy beach stands next to his dog, who is snapping at waves. Cool air rushes inland, the wind shifts, heavy rains begin pounding the shore. A boy is there, suddenly, he's gone.

Now, in her best dress, a sunflower-coloured trim cotton polo with stand-up collar, she is real. Two weeks without setbacks, runway-ready smile. Cinderella lost her balls, now she needs a gown.

Jess sifts through an end-of-season-sale rack. She pulls off a white scooped-neck DNKY blouse from the rack. "DINKY is right," she grimaces. At the end of the sale row, she spots a perfect sleeveless wrap dress and heads for the changeroom.

"Take any one," a saleswomen gestures, not bothering to look up. Jess hooks her clothes up, then draws the curtain over, coming face to face with the masque of death.

"Jess?"

"Ursuline?"

Fuck. Ursuline from her Queer West days. Pity-filled, Viking-faced Ursuline, still sporting her Hurricane Katrina bangs.

"Wow. I haven't seen you in forever." Ursuline examines Jess as if inspecting a sweater, a cheap poly blend, looking for flaws, pulling at loose stitches. "Since Robbie's."

Robbie's Play Palace had been an underground drag bar off Church Street, where trannies and hipsters paraded their chains and puckering PVC, gathered to watch Miss Demeanor play two shows nightly. Robbie stood behind the polished brass bar sporting electric blue Alice Cooper hair and a pet boa named Seymour. She pushed signature cocktails and, tucked inside her blue napkins, pushed a little E.

Dressed in soft chiffon, Terry came into Robbie's three nights a week, stood alone by the bar, watching the crowd throw shade against the burning light. Robbie noticed and took Terry under her wing. Terry began doing Robbie's makeup. Robbie turned Terry loose on her wardrobe. Within two years, Terry was calling herself Jess, ordering estrogen and anti-androgen pills through Robbie's U.S. connections. Jess began to distribute candy bags of E for Robbie, pocketing a healthy profit. Soon, she could afford to make herself over. First, her pimples disappeared, then the facial hair. Her chest, once covered in chestnut wisps, grew smooth and soft. Jess became fattier around the hips and calves, prone to barfing in public. Suited up in chenille skirts, she was no longer the terrible mistake her parents had made.

"You took off in a hurry after Melody."

No after, Jess thought, willing the world to open up now and swallow time with it.

Melody was Robbie's dream girl, a lanky blonde with a delicious pumpkin mouth. One morning long after close, the cops found Melody's pantyhose in a bloody puddle off Bloor Street. Just like that, Robbie had boarded up the bar and left. Jess made her way to the Annex, crowding in among the hot and hungry U of T students. Too lurid for their pansexual play, she was their ticket to little green pills. Jess swallowed some of the profits. She made out with a man in a hotel room. They had popped four pills before kissing, the sensation of travel, sheer astral beauty. She remembered moans coming from the room, her heart pounding before the comedown; later, she opened her eyes, saw facial hair reflected back in the mirror.

"So, I have to ask," Urs tilts her head coyly. "Did you ever go through with it?"

Shove your scenes, your BS, your elliptical sentences, Jess wants to say, but manages only, "I've got to get back."

"Well, I hope *this* works out," Ursuline says, tossing Jess back onto the pile of polyester.

"And I really hope you find a stylist," Jess strokes Ursula's dirty blonde hair. "Because this shag is animal cruelty."

Jess steps inside the change room. In the mirror, tries to gather her refracted self: face, chest, legs, eyes, a blue tide retracting, leaving bodies strewn across the beach.

At the end of her mother's block, Jess lurks like a prowler, watching the bridge brigade file back in their cars to hurry back to their North York townhouses. Entering the front door, she hears her mother crash-landing coffee mugs in the dishwasher. Quietly, she slips upstairs into her mother's walk-in closet to try on her new dress before the full-length mirror. Pressing the tight-fitting dress to her hips, she frowns. Too much scoop, not enough shimmer. Thumbing through her mother's dreary line of polyester, she spots a long, elegant black A-line wrapped in plastic. Faint Lily of the Valley scent when she tears away the cover.

Slipping the dress from the hanger, Jess inches it over her shoulders where it falls easily over her hips. Admiring herself in the mirror, Jess doesn't hear Margaret arrive at the doorway.

Margaret walks over to her dressing table, plops herself down. Jess reaches for a cover-up housecoat. She emerges from the closet, drawing the belt tight around her waist.

"Sorry, I was just looking for a sweatshirt. It's cold in Harold's office," she says, arms crossing her chest before heading for the door without another word.

"Harold's a cold bastard," Margaret muses, smoothing a tangle of hair. She reaches for her brush, the bristles swarming with grey strands, and runs it awkwardly through her unruly nest. Jess notices her mother's puckered elbows, the soft wattle beneath her chin. Overnight, her mother has become an old woman.

"The girls are telling me to get out there." Margaret drops the hairbrush on her table with a loud clatter. She tugs on one eyelid. Reaching for her wine, she almost slips off her seat.

"Maybe you should lie down," Jess urges.

"Not sleepy," Margaret grunts. Her eyes float over to Jess, like a soft cloud over a translucent moon.

"Am I not enough woman?" She rises, moving unsteadily toward Jess, who steps out of reach. Margaret grabs her own breasts then lets her arms drop to her side.

"Harold's found himself a young lady underwriter," she says, then reaches across the dressing table, takes a long swig of tobacco-stained Merlot. "Fucking whore."

Jess braces when her mother takes a tentative step toward her. Without a word, Margaret buries her face in the shoulder of Jess' thick, white housecoat. Margaret's head pitches back then forward so their cheeks touch. Together, they sway in grief's slow, steady rhythm.

"My son is prettier than me," she whispers but her voice breaks. Jess draws her closer, feels her mother's life tightening around her, her own future opening out.

Jess eases her mother onto the bed, where Margaret falls asleep immediately, snoring deeply.

When Margaret awakens, Jess is gone.

Two floors above the traffic stream, in her sublet on Queen Street, Jess dials Fran in Stuttgart. The voice at the end of the line is thin, vaguely hoarse.

"I had some trouble with the Percocet," Fran admits.

Fran's voice is an electric current in her fingertips. Jess thinks she hears a sob but it could be the connection. She knows a tracheal shave is risky. Stretching the vocal cords forward, then clipping off the excess. It could raise or lower her pitch. Not as extreme as going from Johnny Cash to Julie Andrews, but you never knew.

Jess hears the clipped drawl, knows Fran is far too tired for English at this hour. Fran suggests a call the following week but her voice trails off without a promise. Jess will try Fran six more times in the next month, knowing the return call will probably never come.

Two months in her new place, Jess slips into her first hot bath since before the surgery. Spreading her legs in the clawfoot tub, she probes with wet fingertips, the raw nerve endings, electric. Her body soft and sudden and soon. Her face flushes.

She pats herself down with a fluffy towel, pulls on a camel-coloured sweater dress. Around her neck she knots a bright green paisley scarf, letting her hair curl carefully around her neck. Feeling warm but awake, she brushes her cheeks with pale cream blush before heading out.

Rain, rain, blue and yawning. On Queen Street young faces stare out absently behind foggy, candlelit hideouts. Jess swings her black bead-and-sequin clutch, satin-lined with a kiss clasp – an unwitting gift from her mother, rescued from a locked box in her walk-in closet. She crosses Bathurst Street where pretty crowds snake around the hot clubs on Queen, shouting out names she no longer knows.

Margaret can keep the gorgeous A-line, the gloomy overcast

from her thick-bodied Merlot. Every season demands its bold accessory.

Jess turns up her collar, braces for the southwest rains to come.

SHANA MYARA

REMAINDERS

t was three a.m. when the missile fell into our backyard. If it hadn't been so hot, I might have missed its long, clear whistle and dead thud against the lawn.

That summer, sleep was a game of trickery – reinterpreting the warm air, coaxing stiff muscles to give against the heat. The flannel sheets I'd brought from Canada took up space in the closet and both of us, Ben and I, sweated onto a thin bed cover. I ran my arm under the cool side of the pillow. Breathed in. Breathed out.

Beside me, Ben lay heavy in sleep. A child of this weather, he dreamed in Hebrew and his lips twitched to words I didn't yet know. We were a mismatched pair, but love was love, and we could say it in both languages. When we'd first met in Eilat, he'd pointed to the sky to describe where he lived. In the north.

A change in the stagnant air. Any breeze was a salve – in a moment it could send me to sleep on the cool grass, on the tiled poolside. But this breeze, on this night, came from the air being parted. I pulled the curtain back and saw a shadow penetrating the yard. Its peal gave it the sheen it was missing – a metallic dirge, glinting before it hit. It tanked onto the pomegranate bushes.

I waited too long, I think. I choked back excited laughter, almost pointing and clapping. *Look at that!*

Ben stood on the porch calling out orders. Naomi! *Hatelpon!* Tel-eph-one.

I picked up the receiver and held it up so he could see. I dragged the dial each time he shouted a number. The phone felt cool against my ear. The living room was just as we left it. My hands began to tremble as I imagined what might have happened to the cupboards, so neatly stacked with plates and bowls. A vase made of Jerusalem glass.

Ben had gone into action immediately. From sleep, he stepped back into war. He'd been on both sides of it long before I'd pulled my finger along a map of the Mediterranean to Eretez Israel. I was a Jew from Canada. Mount Royal. Bagels. Old altecackers who spoke Yiddish, French, and English. When they so seldom spoke about the war, it was about something unthinkable, machinated in another time.

Here, the possibility of war seeped into the everyday – Fridays, the streets brightened with soldiers carrying bouquets of flowers home for Shabbat; virgins with rifles smoked cigarettes at bus stops. They flirted with the Canadian girls. I'll teach you Hebrew, the boys offered. But until something happened, the mind could make it all look like decoration – this is how they do things here, in this strange country. There are palm trees at the side of the road. Desert.

My gentle Ben, like every man in this country, was a soldier. He told me it's a rite of passage here; everyone goes through three years of service and comes back changed. Then, for twenty more years, they must go back one month a year as reservists. For Ben's service he'd trained parachutists. When the war broke out, he'd almost gone with them, but his captain saw that his eyes had started to blink too rapidly. The vibration of the M-16s, their noise, the smoke, it'd ruined his eyes. He blinked in double-time now, squinted into the dim or bright light. It gave him the appearance of a questioning suitor. Tell me, he'd command, like all the Israelis. Naomi, tell me – eyes stuttering.

This night, he blinked against the dark, trying in vain, I knew, to see past the border.

From the other end of the line the army man told me to stay in the house. We're coming, he said.

Ben and I waited.

Adrenaline courses through the body and then it stops. I curled up on the cold floor with the soldier's calm, confident voice at my ear, and I slept.

A Russian Katyusha. The army arrived at sunrise and young men in uniforms knocked on doors and called into open windows. Clear the area. Katyusha.

Five hours later they were gone. They took the defect away.

By noon, the house held the worst of the summer's heat. The wood floors relented underfoot. Ben and I slipped in and out of the cool bath. We made love on the tiles – languorous and disbelieving on the wet floor.

So – two unexpected things happened that day.

The rocket.

And my body, like our yard, became host to a polite invader. She took over my insides and I said aloud that she was a gift from the gods. From God, Ben corrected, winking. I thanked the shoddy Russian machinery. Hot nights I spent sleepless, plotting a child's fantasy of making weapons impotent. In my mind I was Lucille Ball, sabotaging missiles instead of chocolates on the assembly line. I swallowed fuses, swapped gunpowder for cocoa. Each morning I woke up sick.

Me: I never planned to stay this long.

Ben: I never asked you to take me away to Canada.

Weeks turned into months and I never made a decision to stay. I acquired more things for our home. Picture frames and glass jugs for water. A white crib.

We ate fresh figs from wild trees. Ben took me to the Red Sea and we opened our eyes underwater at schools of neon fish. At Pesach, we read the questions from the Haggadah with Ben's old mother and father in Jerusalem – "why is this night different from all other nights" – and we reminded ourselves that we had been passed over. My stomach grew as if in testament; red lines stretched from my navel and radiated outward.

At forty-one weeks, the doctors sliced a line into my belly and pulled her out. She came to be. The benign gift.

Ben divined the future of our little *tinoqet*. Our baby girl would be a ballerina with those toes. A head of state with that head. Her tiny fingers pushed against my breast, making sense of home.

A Russian nurse at the hospital told me Katyusha was a nickname. They name the bombs and the hurricanes after women, she said. You're not a little Katyusha, she cooed, you're a Sarah-sha. *Kikiriki* goes the rooster, Ben read in a singsong that matched the thrum of his lashes. I learned along with my daughter. *Kikiriki* goes the *tarnegol*.

She has my eyes.

But my mouth, *nakhon*?

Ben and I claimed her parts right then, as if we planned to carve her up one day and take just pieces of her with us.

Days before, the radio had crackled with news of giving up land for peace. The opposition had compared it to cleaving a child in two, like the Bible story. No one on either side could agree: What land? What divisions? Then new bombings killed two vendors in Netanya, and the television cameras followed Hasidic men as they picked up pieces of flesh so the dead could be buried whole. The army retaliated. And many on the other side died – only miles away but unreal, unspoken here. On the streets, men in black hats shouted into megaphones that Israel was indivisible. So it is written!

Threat seeped into the everyday here. Into the chill of a breeze. What we had built was impossible. In the home, table corners like sharp stakes. Outside, fences delicate as pomegranate bushes. Our Jerusalem glass vase from Ben's parents cast light like a kaleidoscope but shattered at the baby's reach. I looked to the bald patch in the backyard and I thought about how glass could make so much noise when something so big came so quietly, so gently in the night.

When the borders opened in months of ceasefire, the trucks with green licence plates repopulated the highway. The same trucks as anyone else, carrying T-shirts embroidered by mothers and daughters over there for cheap; or fruit, or livestock. When I had been here only a few months, living on a kibbutz, I accepted a ride down the long dirt road that led to the main hall like I saw so many others do in that small community. The man was vibrantly handsome, a little older than me. He smiled at me each time I said something in my halting Hebrew, and he punctuated each of his polite questions with the same sparkling smile. It wasn't until we arrived at the hall and a man from the kibbutz came to shout at me that I realized I'd accepted a ride from a driver with green plates.

The kibbutznik admonished me. I was a silly, stupid girl. I shouldn't travel by myself if I had no sense.

Surely, I wouldn't have stepped into this man's cab if I had known. Surely, I wouldn't have let him drive me somewhere else to act on our instant chemistry; I wouldn't have consented to his finger drawing a line down my chest, to my navel, opening me in two. I remember I would have. I would. We had no problems between us, this handsome man and I.

In my small, tidy house with Ben and Sarah-sha, I wondered about that smiling man. Each day, waiting in line at the border, perhaps, his truck loaded with product, trying to get home or leave home. Idling the engine, perhaps, tapping his finger on the steering wheel at the nagging thought that something bad would happen today. Maybe the pimple-faced Israeli guard would usher him through. Maybe not. Whole days spent that way.

I said to Ben's friends once and they tsked me: open the borders and let hormones fuel the peace.

First they will rape you, they said. And then they will bomb you.

But – they didn't know about the smiling Palestinian man. I said: in Canada, I knew Palestinians. In Canada! they said. Then Ben had leaned close. You have a big heart, he whispered, but you don't know. He slid two fingernails together until they clicked. You don't know *this much* about it yet.

After Sarah was born, I tried to picture our future here. I heard a falling whistle each time, as I saw us among the fresh fruit in the *shuk*, or still in our beds. And when I tried to imagine otherwise, I remembered how the others laughed at what the Canadian thought she knew.

Over on the sofa, Ben rubbed kisses over Sarah's face. *Apchee*, he said in amazement. *Apchee*.

He blew air loudly in a mock sneeze, and then did it again on her belly. A small blast, a rabbit's sneeze – the *arnevet* goes *apchee*.

Ben's month had arrived again. May. He packed his army boots. Along with all the other men, he would return for a month to his command. The joke was that they returned with one extra inch around their bellies for each year that passed. Their gaits slower, their children inches taller or now conscripts themselves.

Ben was still young, under thirty, still in his prime except for his eyes.

I read the newspaper as I tried to do every day, puzzling over every other word. *Un-ee-ver-si-ta*. A student uprising at a university. More rockets in the north. Predictions that we would soon invade.

He smoothed the flat of his palm against my brow. It'll be okay, he said.

That night in bed I whispered secrets into the small of his back. I prayed to the rocket god or to Elohim – I just closed my eyes and willed it to still be true: we had been passed over, we would be safe.

Promise?

I'll be okay.

Promise.

I promise.

Sarah fussed in the other room. Ben went to check on her and then carried her back to our bed.

Just for tonight, he said. And we slept with her in the middle of us, as if we afforded some protection, and our promises were any kind of covenant but superstition.

In the morning, Ben left for his service. He lied to me and said he'd blow kisses from way up in the sky.

The heat turned the dirt on the side of the road to dust. Each afternoon I carried Sarah past our front lawn to the street and we walked the neighborhood to the pool. I stopped to taste the tart fruit from lemon trees and shook hard green olives from their branches – a novelty for me still, even though I'd become an *olah-chadesha*, a new immigrant, the month before. The heat warmed the lemons on the trees. I picked them and my fingers shone with fragrant oil.

The days passed like this. One week. Two weeks.

Sometimes the school bus would pass us on our way home. It pulled its heavy weight up the slope, trailing dust like ghost stories behind it. Small hands poked out of windows and young voices formed pitch-perfect words – half of it squeals of nonsense to my ears. I watched the yellow of it proceed. A target in yellow, I thought.

The borders were closed again. No green licence plates to watch for. Would I accept a ride again? I thought of that handsome man's kind eyes. I imagined his truck door closing, us coasting away from the city. But, no. I wouldn't chance it now. Not with Sarah-sha. Not with any driver, I told myself.

I held her tight and we walked up the hill from the pool. Sarah's hair dried in the heat after only moments out of the water; mine too, until it became wet again with sweat.

This evening, instead of running cool water in the tub, I laid Sarah out in a blanket in the backyard and tugged the hose close. I let the water run free like my parents did in Canada. Here, it was an unthinkable extravagance. In English, I would plead ignorance if the neighbour came to yell at me.

This was the first time I'd lingered in that space since the rocket. Now, small pomegranates hung from the bush's spindly branches.

The sun dipped, but heat still clogged the air. I dabbed water to Sarah's face and then doused myself, directing the stream to my brow, my armpits, my lap.

Dripping, I picked one of the pomegranates. I banged it on the ground like Ben had taught me, then pried it in half to pluck the little gems. Piercing their thin membranes, small bursts of juice bloodied my tongue. I pressed a seed to Sarah's mouth and coloured her lips red. We were two vampires together, undead, feasting in the last light of day.

To the eyes, nothing had changed – although maybe it's true that he was darker, maybe a bit leaner – but when Ben returned after that month away he looked so much like himself I wondered if I had been remembering him out of focus. He noted that the silvery leaves of the pomegranate bush had filled out. A few dozen pieces of red fruit had sprouted. Sarah gained fourteen ounces, I told him.

Something happened, he said. And when I started, he added, I didn't want you to worry.

He asked if I remembered Aviam, Natasha's boyfriend.

He grimaced meaningfully. Then, a solemn nod.

I flushed with cold adrenaline. Awful relief first, that it had been Aviam and not Ben. Then I felt it so clearly, how they felt here. How emotion outpaces reason. A rush of energy like a man was chasing me; like I might turn and fight.

At the end of the world – *be sof ha'olam* – in Canada, people did not admit these feelings. By the smell of a person's food, the brownness of their skin, that's how bigots in Canada shortcut to hate. Here. Here it is different. The thing that matters is real estate; the languages are cousins. If they weren't on the mount by now, arm in arm, Mohammed and Moses were frauds. Where were they now if not convincing the land to open up, fatten for us all?

I hadn't meant to stay.

I cupped my hands to Ben's jaw and kissed him. His lips were parched and he smelled like cigarettes, just like all the soldiers.

It's enough, I said. I walked to the crib and lifted Sarah.

You can come with me or you can stay. *It's happening.*

Why? Sarah would ask when she was older. She would grow into a force of nature, obsessed with the smiles and grimaces of other children. Latching onto empathy first, knowing, perhaps, that this would be the ultimate thing her birthright would test. Why is that child crying? she would ask, crying. And once her mind blossomed so big and empathic and hopeful, she would realize that, by birth, she had taken sides, and it would take an exceptional person not to. Why? I told my daughter that I was not exceptional.

I *shockeled* Sarah and sucked kisses on her forehead. The two of us would fly early the next week to my mother's in Montreal.

When he could stand it no longer, Ben would come to be with us. In Canada, something in his face would change, his blinking would slow, even though he assured me such a thing wasn't possible. His face would grow smooth and enigmatic like a statue, and I'd spend our years together looking for clues in the small muscle movements in his face. You could see it when he looked at me. He hated me in that small potent way just under the surface – the way hatred should be held, complicated, and close. Sarah left for school each morning, and each afternoon she came home with benign stories to tell. We listened, Ben and I, and grew fat with relief – and I said to him, When our time comes to die, we'll go by cancer or a car crash, something like that.

NANCY JO CULLEN

HASHTAG MAGGIE VANDERMEER

At 1:27 a.m. Maggie's phone blinked and whistled on her bedside table. Startled out of sleep, she knocked the cat off the bed. The grey beast yowled and sashayed out of the room. (To register his ill will the cat peed on the bath mat, but Maggie wouldn't take note of that for another six hours.) Maggie grabbed the phone, Lacey Vandermeer Text Message, it read. What on earth? She ran her finger across the glass screen and Lacey's message popped up: Ty for the great fuck, baby I needed that. Right above Lacey's message was Maggie's earlier message, highlighted in green and sent at 8:37 p.m.: Don't forget you're coming to show me how to make tapenade tomorrow. 2 p.m. sharp. ;-)

Maggie blushed and sweat sprang from her pores. She kicked the blankets off her legs. I think u meant to send this elsewhere she typed quickly and hit send. Maggie pulled off her nightie, wiped her brow and armpits then lay spread-eagle on the bed waiting for the flash to dissipate. Again, her phone whistled: MOM! LOL!! Ooops!

It's bloody scary to get a text in the middle of the night. Maggie hit send.

Srsly mom, I'm sorry, came the reply.

And now she was awake, thank you very much. Maggie turned off the sound on her phone and tossed it across the bed. The streetlights glowed from behind her white curtains. Bloody light pollution. She flipped onto her stomach but it was no good either. She grabbed her phone and opened Twitter. Sure enough at the top of her feed was a post from Lacey: That moment when u send ur mom a text meant for your lover. #awkward #atleastimgettingsome. The tweet had been favourited by Dane Davis. (Good God, who named their child Dane Davis?) Maggie opened up Dane's profile: short, dark hair, thick black glasses, buttoned-up shirt, and brownish complexion. Boy or girl? Hard to say and, with Lacey, impossible to predict.

Maggie switched on the lamp and typed another message: I have a job interview tomorrow FFS!

You'll do great!

NOT my point!

An honest mistake!

Maggie switched off the lamp and, again, tucked her phone under the pillow. She was going to feel like hell in the morning.

By 2 p.m. Maggie had finished a 10K run, forty push-ups, forty chair dips, and one hundred crunches. Her left hip was giving her trouble, but twenty bucks for a yoga class was out of the question at this point in time. Maggie faced herself in the dining room mirror (hung just so to make her apartment look larger than it was) and lifted her arms above her shoulders; so far she was staving off scrotarms. Her face was another matter, her complexion was smooth but the lines around her eyes were deepening and the skin on her upper chest was starting to pucker. On the upside, no double chin and her hair colour looked totally natural.

Of course Lacey was late. Maggie flopped onto the couch. Her stomach was killing her, the side effect of another job interview. The interview was conducted by a toxic little snot named Jasmine; Maggie guessed her chances for the job were nil as soon as she walked through the door and spied Jasmine's Bettie Page hair cut and gold stud in the left bottom corner of her mouth.

"Maggie?"

Maggie thrust her right hand forward. "Maggie Vander-meer."

Jasmine passed Maggie a limp hand then quickly withdrew it. She ran her finger down Maggie's resume. "So, you've been working in PR for –" she stopped her finger back at the top of the page and looked up – "six years?" Her voice rose with the question.

"Closer to twenty-three," Maggie said. "Since my daughter was almost four. That's my selected resume." She pulled a four-page document out of her bag. "I have the complete resume here."

"That won't be necessary. Are you conversant in social media?"

"I use Facebook and Twitter. I'm Linked In."

"My mom doesn't get Facebook at all," Jasmine said. "You know, she posts weird things on my wall. Unnecessary things. That touchy, feely stuff with sunsets and oceans."

Maggie gave Jasmine an understanding nod.

"We're trying to build a brand here so our staff have to be adept at social media. You know, we want to trend because people like us, not because we look like sentimental throwbacks. Not because people are laughing at us."

Maggie nodded again.

"So it's important that our people can leverage a strong social media presence."

"I have twenty-plus years of public relations experience to leverage."

"Mmm hmm," Jasmine said. "What would you say your greatest weakness is?"

The interview didn't improve. As her chances faded Maggie made a last-ditch attempt to get Jasmine to look at her resume by mentioning that her daughter was Pushyboots, which definitely excited Jasmine's attention, just not in the way Maggie had hoped that her close relationship to the famous sex-advice blogger would do.

Jasmine slapped her desk and exclaimed, "So, *you're* the Former Drinker?"

Maggie nodded. "Ten years this September."

"I can't believe I just interviewed the FD!" Jasmine stood up.

"I guess you'll have something to talk about over lunch."

Jasmine opened her office door. "Well, thank you very much, Maggie Vandermeer. Say hi to Pushy. We totally love her."

Lacey arrived at 2:24 p.m. "I said 2 p.m. sharp," Maggie said.

"Artichokes, olives, capers," Lacey raised the cloth bag in her hand, "besides you could do this yourself. It's totally easy."

"The point was to have a visit with you."

"I'll make us a coffee." Lacey walked into the kitchen.

It wasn't the afternoon Maggie planned for. Although she arrived in a happy mood Lacey was gone at 4:13 p.m. At 2:31, Lacey bubbled with excitement over a pending book deal based on her blog. She was thinking about quitting her bartending job.

"Trust me, you might regret that," Maggie said.

"My book contract?"

"No, quitting the bar."

"I've been doing it a long time," Lacey said. "I can always find another gig."

That was true enough. By the time Lacey was seven, Maggie had trained her in the art of the perfect vodka martini. A fearless inventory had caused her to recognize that. Lacey should be allowed to say so.

The tapenade took all of three minutes in the food processor. Maggie lifted a spoonful of the mixture to Lacey's mouth.

"No." Lacey held her hand up. "It's best to let it steep for a couple of hours."

"Well, I can't eat it all by myself!" Maggie said.

"Don't be crazy. It's great with a chicken breast, or on pasta."

"I don't eat pasta." Maggie patted her stomach.

"Jesus, Mom," Lacey said, "You have to stop obsessing on your weight."

"Caring about how you look is different from obsessing." Maggie licked the tapenade off her fingers to prove her point then changed the subject. "I met a Pushyboots fan at my interview today."

"How did Pushyboots come up?" Lacey asked.

"Well, you know, she didn't think I could trend. Or whatever."

"What?"

"*Trend* as a verb. You know, make something trend. So I told her you were my daughter. It's tough out there," Maggie said. "At my age."

"It's hard everywhere these days. That's why people strike out on their own, make their own work."

Maggie lifted her eyebrows but said nothing. Of course, Lacey was right. And, also, grossly oversimplifying the situation. As if she hadn't thought of going out on her own. Of course she'd thought of it, but she preferred the structure of a job. At a job, work starts at 9 a.m., work ends at 5 p.m., overtime is banked and paid days off are taken in lieu. It was efficient.

"It's kind of weird though, you bringing up Pushyboots."

Maggie never should have said mentioned it. "I was losing the interview."

Lacey shrugged. "You shouldn't do it."

"I can't say you're my daughter?"

"Not in that context."

"I don't complain about you writing about me."

"I don't write about you."

"What about the FD?"

"I'm writing about myself, even if I mention you. Plus, it's in code, nobody knows who you are."

"Jasmine knows who I am."

"Who's Jasmine?"

"The little twot who interviewed me."

"That's harsh."

"Who's Dane?"

"Jesus, Mom, stop creeping me or I'll block you."

"I didn't thank you for the great fuck."

"Oh. My. God. Let it rest!"

"Let's just try a little bit of that dip now. These lentil chips are yummy."

"You go ahead."

"Look at me. Don't I look like someone who could trend?"

Lacey nodded. Barely.

"I'm not stupid."

"They probably want someone young enough to train. You know, in their way of doing things and such."

"I'd be obliging."

Lacey raised her eyebrows.

Maggie pointed a finger at Lacey. "You have no idea."

Lacey looked at her phone. "I've got to go, Mom."

"Say hi to Dane for me."

"Very funny." She kissed her mom on the cheek and closed the door behind her.

And then, the long evening stretched in front of Maggie.

It is a commonly held belief among those abstaining from alcohol that sobriety maintenance cannot be managed by enjoying any sort of relationship with other stimulants, aside from coffee and cigarettes, neither of which Maggie could tolerate. However, a little weed could go a long way toward mitigating the effects of life. Most certainly she wasn't smoking all day long, and it certainly wasn't as if she was getting her kid to roll her a spliff, but weed created for Maggie a soft focus lens view of the day. In fact, it helped a great deal. Of course, she didn't announce it at meetings, and she was careful to only attend a meeting if she was straight. For sure, the meetings helped too, but some days Maggie just needed a little more. It was hardly a crime.

It was hot and close, a perfect summer evening. The sidewalk was crowded with pedestrians, and lovers, and drunks, and on the roads helmetless bicyclists in shorts and tank tops pedalled around traffic, slowed by the din and sparkle of nightfall. In summer everything was young.

Maggie turned into the gates of the park. The white stone and wrought iron of the arches were, Maggie believed, resplendent. She liked to amble through the gates as though she was walking onto her own estate, and that further up the park stood her own Pemberley, or some such place. She tilted her head slightly and smiled, then took her place on a bench and crossed her legs carefully, one flat gold flip-flop dangling from her toes. She held her iced latte in front of her turquoise painted toes and snapped a photo. She typed #lactosefree #summernights #turquoisetoes #maggieVandermeer, then she posted it to her Instagram account. She knew how to bloody trend.

A burst of laughter rang from behind the bench. Maggie turned. Two university-aged girls in light cotton dresses lay on their stomachs reading a small newspaper. Their long hair fell over their shoulders and grazed the top of the blanket. One of them rolled onto her back, holding her stomach, still giggling. They were as beautiful as they ever would be. From Maggie's perspective, they were near perfect.

She stood up and walked casually in their direction. She smiled at the girl on her back. The girl on her back smiled at Maggie.

"Beautiful night," Maggie said.

The girl flipped back onto her stomach. "It is," she said. She turned toward her friend and flipped to the next page of the paper.

Maggie could take a hint. "Have a nice night," she said. "Don't talk to strangers." She walked up the path toward the north end of the park, peals of the girls' laughter chiming. "Being alone is not the same as being lonely," Maggie reminded herself. She held her phone against her ear so as not to look crazy. "Being alone is not the same as being lonely," she said.

It wasn't for want of trying. Maggie had taken photos of: a cupcake piled with maple icing and topped with a slice of bacon, #reward, #runninglife, #maggieVandermeer (of course, she'd only had two bites and thrown the rest away); herself in new white-framed sunglasses, #summer, #instacute, #maggieVandermeer; the cat wasted on catnip, #wasted, #catnipped, #maggie Vandermeer; and a photo of her with a dashing Mexican actor who played in some spy show Maggie hadn't seen, but there was a crowd of women encircling him so it seemed like a good idea to get a snap, #hotstuff, #javierdiaz, #swoon, #maggieVandermeer. In addition, she'd been tweeting weather reports, news of the day, photos of cute animals, and whimsical observations such as, *As much as it is reality we will not live trouble-free lives, so we will worry when they come*, all followed by the hashtag Maggie Vandermeer. Still, she failed to trend.

"What's up with the hashtag?" Lacey asked.

"I'm trying to trend."

The phone was silent, then Lacey sighed heavily. "Maybe you need to see someone," she said.

"Being alone is not the same as being lonely," Maggie said.

"I meant a doctor, not a date. I think you're depressed."

"I'm being proactive."

"It's ridiculous, Mom."

"It's ridiculous to take action?" Maggie was indignant.

"It's ridiculous to think you're going to trend."

"You're a fine one to talk," Maggie said and hung up.

When Lacey called back, Maggie put her phone on Do Not Disturb.

And so Maggie found herself at the job fair sitting in a hard chair in a banquet room crowded with college graduates and the LocaFolk! logo projected on a screen at the front of the room. Flanking the screen sat a row of festival workers there to explain the month-long food and cultural festival that the girl with the microphone, Kayla, kept referring to as a harvest festival as though no one in the audience had ever eaten a Thanksgiving meal in their lives.

I want to poke myself in the eye #punishing #jobunfair #ihatedpeprallies #maggieVandermeer, she tweeted.

She returned her attention to Kayla just in time to catch the warning that under no circumstances could anyone selected as LocaFolk try to engage the attention of the celebrity chefs that attended the event. Apparently, that was the last thing a celebrity chef was interested in, and if you even tried to talk to a Jamie Kennedy or some other such person you would be promptly fired. Capiche?

The crowd nodded its head in agreement. Maggie suppressed an urge to bleat like a sheep. Desperate times.

After waiting for an hour (she was number fifty-eight), Maggie was led to a room where six tables were set at a discreet distance apart from one another; each table was occupied by two interviewers and one interviewee. A bearded boy with a waxed moustache and a sallow-faced girl with large framed glasses interviewed Maggie.

Her first mistake: Maggie shook their hands vigorously. Did no one care about the importance of having a firm handshake? As soon as her butt hit the chair Maggie felt the energy drain from her body. Deflated, she could barely muster the force to open her mouth.

The girl, Maggie thought her name was Jenna but in the span of thirty seconds could no longer be sure, held a pen poised in front of a pad of paper where she'd neatly printed "Maggie Vandermeer" across the top. The boy, Dustin, clasped his hands and asked her gravely, "Have you been to any of our events at LocaFolk?"

Maggie nodded and smiled. "No. Not really. I don't eat out much."

Probably Jenna scribbled a note.

"Food intolerances," Maggie added.

"What brought you to LocaFolk?"

"Yeah," Maggie nodded again. "You know, I'm not sure." She drew a deep breath. "Okay, I need a job."

Dustin blinked, Jenna wrote another note. Her letters were neat and round.

Maggie tried again. "I'm forty-eight years old. I've been in the workforce nearly as long as you've been alive. I don't even know what I know, but I know a lot. Trust me, I'd be an asset. I'm not just saying that."

Dustin nodded. Jenna tapped her tooth with the end of her pen.

"And I'm very fit. I can run 10K in forty-five to forty-eight minutes."

Jenna started to scribble again.

"So, you know, I can stand for long periods."

Dustin and Jenna exchanged a glance. Dustin pushed his chair back.

"Would you like to know what I'd do if a customer was displeased?"

"No, no, that's good," Dustin said. "Thank you, Maggie. It's been great."

"Thank you, Maggie," Jenna said airily.

Maggie graced the pair with a full-toothed, sparkly smile. "The pleasure has been all mine," she said. She stood up and pulled her bag onto her shoulder. She wasn't going to try to shake their limp hands again.

I could start an etiquette school. . . ? Maggie sent the text to Lacey.

Lacey's reply rang back in less than a minute. It's 4 a.m.!

Well what do you think? Maggie hit send.

No!! Jesus. Turning phone off. Now.

Maggie flicked the burning ash off her joint and dropped it in the ashtray. She opened Twitter. Well, that was a stupid idea, she typed, #maggieVandermeer.

It's not like she really believed she was going to trend.

She set herself up on the floor and executed ten push-ups, careful to keep her shoulders away from her neck and her spine straight. She flipped onto her back. She tightened her core (keeping her spine in a neutral position), then she lifted her legs six inches off the floor and held the position. She should apply for a job at Lululemon, or be a fitness instructor. The baby boomers would relate to her. She let her legs drop. She'd like to see pasty little Jenna pull that off. Or that Dustin; she saw the tobacco stains on his fingers.

She could teach all those fat chefs how to eat properly.

She pushed herself into a back bend. How many thirty-year-olds could do that?

Her kitchen was shining. From this angle she could see the freshly polished, black fridge door. She could start a cleaning business. She let herself back down into a resting position. Except, ew. There was something about other people's pubic hair that just made the bile rise in her throat.

Maybe Lacey could get her a bartending job. It would be nice to talk to the people and to help them. Except not really, unless she wanted to kiss her sobriety goodbye.

When the stores opened she would buy a lottery ticket. Why the hell not?

Lacey was awfully quick to judge for someone who, herself, sent unwanted texts in the middle of the night. Maggie sat up, grabbed her phone and texted Lacey: Judge not lest ye be judged. She wondered if Lacey, who had never even set foot inside a church, would know even what she was talking about.

If you know what I mean. Maggie hit send.

Really, Lacey had some nerve. I mean, SRSLY?? Maggie hit send.

You're turning off your phone??? Maggie was on a tear. She hit send.

Do unto others. Maggie hit send.

If you know what I mean again. Maggie hit send.

A better person would stop texting. Maggie stood up and brushed her hands on her thighs. She was hungry so she poured herself a glass of water. She was exhausted and completely wide awake. Her blood was ringing in her veins. She really shouldn't have sent those messages.

Mommy loves you sweetie. Maggie hit send.

Don't ever forget it! Maggie hit send.

But show a little gratitude maybe. Maggie hit send.

I'm not drinking if that's what you think. Maggie hit send.

When you reach mid-life you can't sleep any more. Maggie hit send.

A little something to look forward to! :-D Maggie hit send.

Maggie took a photo of her fridge door, her outline reflected in the image. At least my kitchen is clean! She typed under the photo and hit send.

Because she didn't want Lacey to worry, Maggie texted: Rocking out to Fleetwood Mac!

I guess I'm second hand news too ;-/ Maggie hit send. Hopefully that wasn't too glum.

Don't stop thinking about tomorrow! ;^* That was better, Maggie hit send.

Say hi to Dane. Maggie hit send.

Unless Dane was a 1-nighter. Maggie hit send. Jesus, she was tired. And hungry. She grabbed six almonds from the fridge then wiped it free of fingerprints. She lay down on the couch.

Is a 1-night stand even safe? Maggie hit send.

Trust me it's not. Maggie hit send.

I'm going to try to sleep now. Maggie hit send.

Sometimes I get the feeling you don't even like me. Maggie hit send.

What if someone breaks in and your phone is turned off?? Maggie hit send.

You shouldn't just assume everything is fine. Maggie hit send.

I'm talking about you, not me. Maggie hit send.

But your book thing is great! Maggie hit send.

If you need my help with anything just call. Maggie hit send.

But not as soon as you wake up. Maggie hit send.

Because I'm going to go to sleep now. :D For real. Maggie hit send.

So don't call when you wake up. Maggie hit send.

She turned her face toward the back of the couch. The cat sprang from his chair and curled himself at the end of Maggie's feet.

She sent her final text of the night: Have a sweet day :-p

Then: @>--- >---

And then: I mean it. Don't call.

And just in case Lacey would worry she was crazy, Maggie typed her final, final message on her phone's small screen: It's all good.

She hit send.

M.A. FOX

PIANO BOY

That year, his senior year in high school, Addison Ormsby was Mr. Stone's favourite pupil. Addison did not understand that there might be any complicated reasons for his position. He was not burdened by modesty. He was, far and away, he thought, Mr. Stone's best pupil. He was preparing for his audition for Julliard: Bach, *The Goldberg Variations*; Beethoven, *The Hammerklavier*; Liszt, *Sposalizio*; Debussy, *L'Isle joyeuse*; Prokofiev, *The Stalingrad* Sonata. Addison did not doubt that he would be admitted. If he was auditioning for Peabody, Curtis, and the Montreal Conservatoire, it was only because his mother insisted.

From the perspective of Reginald Stone, the reasons Addison was his favourite were not so simple. All of Reginald Stone's pupils were remarkably gifted. He had retired from an exalted position in the Faculty of Music some five years ago, and if he now coached a select handful of pupils – more than the Graces, less than the Muses, he liked to say – it was for his own satisfaction, to pass along the mysteries of a sterling technique, to foster deep musicality in a new generation. He did not need the income. He owned a beautiful penthouse apartment with a south view over the playing fields of Victoria College, the towers of Bay Street, the gleaming grey of the lake. His living room could accommodate twenty-five auditors facing the nine-foot Bechstein, perched on rows of white folding chairs set up on the expanse of hand-knotted off-white carpet. Reginald Stone did not need pupils either for occupation or for self-assurance. He had had a Career, not perhaps a career of the first water, playing concerti with the world's major orchestras, but a fine career nonetheless. He had accompanied some famous singers; he had been the long-time pianist in the Jubilate Trio; and he had, after all, played his share of concerti, with the Winnipeg, the Buffalo, the Orchestre de Lille. He had studied composition with Stravinsky, and piano with Nadia Boulanger. If the view of Toronto from his living room window did not compare with the view of Paris from his studio in Montmartre, he was not discontented with his life. He was still invited to give master classes, wooed for juries. He was working, somewhat desultorily, with a very handsome young graduate student, on his book, part memoir, part technical manual.

What Reginald Stone felt for his favourite students was love. It began with the whiff of promise, not just technical brilliance, but something in the personality, some susceptibility to the magic of music, an emotionality that poured out of them when they played, a capacity for ecstasy. To be enthused, to be filled with the Divine. When he met such a capacity in young girls, he was fatherly, kind, generous with his time, his support. But in a boy, this promise made his heart drum in his ears, raised the hairs on his forearms, and with them he was motherly, tender, demanding. Reginald Stone was extremely careful that nothing improper in thought, glance, or act should occur. It had been different in his day, of course. Poulenc had listened dutifully to his playing, made some highly technical suggestions while caressing the back of his neck, and led him from the living room with its crowd of Louis Quinze pieces to his bedroom, where an enormous four-poster dominated. And he had gone to rehearse with Ned Rorem, whose songs were on the program he was planning with a wonderful young lyric soprano. He remembered those rehearsals with a frisson even now, half a century later, Rorem then still youthful, vigorous, impossibly handsome, kneeling worshipfully on the floor before him, gently undoing his fly.

No, for that he had a collection of old and sometime lovers, the occasional young rent boy. With his favourites, he allowed himself only the feeling of love, the delicious sensation that rose from the pit of his stomach, made his throat ache, his eyes fill. This was not a sensation that Addison Ormsby had at first aroused in him. Reginald himself was meticulously clean, elegantly clothed, dapper. The boy looked as if he lived on the streets. To the despair of his mother, who had laid out a presentable outfit on his messy bed, Addison had slouched in for his audition with Reginald dressed in torn jeans, a worn T-shirt that shouted "Rage Against The Machine," and a very wrinkled and ill-fitting plaid shirt. His hair, of a blond his mother now paid extravagant sums to a hairdresser to restore, was tortured into dreadlocks that fell in his face and over his shoulders. When asked to leave his filthy workboots on the mat at the door, he revealed grimy socks, the big toe of his right foot with its dirty nail poking through a hole. His mother made all the small talk, looking nervously at Addison's feet. After a particularly awkward silence, Reginald invited the boy to sit at the piano. Addison slouched and scowled, held his wrists awkwardly high, and played the *Polonaise Héroïque* at breakneck speed, with far too much pedal. But he also played with astonishing strength and passion. At the end of the piece, while Addison was picking at his nails, and his mother was actually wringing her hands, Reginald said, "Please describe your practice routine to me."

"I just kind of play until I'm finished," Addison said.

"If you wish to study with me," Reginald told him, "I shall put you on a technical regimen, with which you must begin a daily practice of at least two and a half hours, more if I require it. I shall select the pieces for you to work on. Anything of your choosing may be played outside the appointed hours of practice. I have time for you on Tuesdays at two p.m. I shall be pleased to write a note to the relevant authorities at your school, excusing your absence. And, Mrs. Ormsby, I would ask that you send the fee for each lesson with Addison in an envelope, in cash."

They began the following Tuesday. For the first few months, there was no tenderness, only technique. Reginald sat beside Addison on the piano bench, and cruelly parodied his hand position. He explained, in metaphor, in detailed description, in demonstration, how the keys must not be hammered, but caressed, pulling from the fingertip to the centre of the palm, reaching the key bed. He pressed his palm against Addison's sweaty lower back, poked a rigid forefinger between his shoulder blades, intolerant of slouch. "The piano is your partner in the dance," Reginald told him. "You must approach it with confidence and grace. You will lead, the piano will follow. Like a good dancer, you want to hold your frame. Otherwise you will be clumsy, uncontrolled, a boy with sweaty palms who treads on his partner's toes."

Unlike most piano students, Addison never apologized, not for wrong notes, or mistaken tempi, or forgetting to sit up straight. He responded to corrections with a grunt, if at all. In the beginning, Reginald doubted very much that Addison was practising as he had been instructed, suspected he was sight-reading the Scarlatti, and probably slouched over the keyboard at home just as he pleased. He did not possess any of the physical traits Reginald found beautiful. He was stocky and compact, like a wrestler, his nose a snub snout, his mouth curiously small and fleshy, an incongruous rosebud. It would not hurt him to bathe more frequently, and as Reginald leaned over his shoulder, writing in a more sensible fingering, he sometimes picked up a strong smell of marijuana.

But Addison kept coming to his lessons, on time, and at some point, things began to change. The quality of the sound he produced grew richer, more controlled. He acquired a true pianissimo, no longer failing to draw sound on every note. He was weaned from overdependence on the sustaining pedal. He responded to correction with interest. He demonstrated that he had been working on the assigned exercises from Philipp's *Exercises for Independence of the Fingers*, though he persisted in calling M. Philipp, "Fill-eep" with an exaggerated squawk. He began to talk with Reginald, about technique, when the lessons were over, asking intelligent questions, even expressing appreciation. One kind of talk led to another. Not yet in love, but pleased with the boy, Reginald offered cups of delicately perfumed lapsang souchong, served in his beautiful Limoges porcelain, and gold-tipped Sobranie cigarettes.

Reginald had an interest in psychoanalysis. He himself had, for a time, seen the illustrious, irritating, and mysterious Jacques Lacan, and later undergone a Jungian analysis. These experiences had not only handed him the key to his own behaviours, but illuminated his pupils'. The peculiar intimacy of teaching music, alone in the studio side by side on a narrow padded bench, the way music touched and drew forth emotions, had led his pupils to treat him very much as one treats one's analyst, bringing him their hidden thoughts, their fears, their dreams, describing the most intimate details of their lives. Like an analyst, Reginald nodded and answered questions with questions. "What do you think that means, then?" "How does that make you feel?" The combination of a ready sympathy and a detached manner was helpful, he thought. He was not surprised they talked to him in this way. He was receptive, intuitive.

Once Addison began to talk, all the unattractive elements of his behaviour and his presentation made sense. Reginald pitied him, understood him, was touched by his trust and his confusion, began to find him lovable, and ended by being in love with him. Addison's troubles began, inevitably, with his mother. Reginald knew her a little, from long before, when as Edith Buford, and then Edith Buford-Ormsby, she had been the second violinist in the Spadina Quartet. This was long before they were renowned, a celebration achieved only after she and the violist had been bumped in favour of a brilliant brother and sister, Chinese students the first violinist had discovered in a master class, and somewhat indiscriminately fucked. Their tone and technique raised the quartet to a whole new level of artistry. Dropped from the Quartet, she lost her confidence, was possessed by a crippling stagefright, muffed auditions. She languished, took on a number of elementary pupils, and began to have her own children. There were three young Ormsbys. Macauley, the eldest, was a perfect product. He was nice-looking, well-mannered, academically high-achieving; he played the violin with care and style, and was now doing a master's of music performance in Berlin. Edith had hoped for a girl the second time out, although her relations with her own mother and sister were rather fraught. She swallowed her disappointment and tried once more, after Addison. The youngest boy, Steele, was also quite perfect, more gregarious and charming than Macauley, and already, at the age of fourteen, the lead cello in the Toronto Symphony Youth Orchestra, and a straight-A student. Both her eldest and her youngest had reaped the benefits of a Steiner education. But Addison, who picked up and dropped a number of different instruments before settling on the piano, had been rebellious and difficult even in elementary school, and was finally expelled from the Steiner high school for smoking dope on the playing field.

Clifford Ormsby, the father, contributed his own ingredients to Addison's psychic mix. An enormously successful entrepreneur, an engineer who had made some brilliant advances in biomedical technology, he was utterly absorbed in his work, putting in long hours, travelling frequently, and emotionally absent even on family holidays. Reginald had glimpsed him, his face illuminated by the light of his smartphone, dealing with messages during a recital. Clifford saw his role in the family as that of provider, and he provided very well indeed. He left everything else to Edith. She structured and guided the children's lives, judged and dealt out consequences, positive or negative. He paid the bills. He clearly approved of Macauley, and was charmed by Steele's high spirits. Addison baffled and irritated him. He engaged with his middle son as little as possible, and when he spoke to him, his tone was ironically critical. He hoped, for Edith's sake, that the boy would get into some conservatory. If not, he would have to leave home, get himself whatever kind of job waited for those who did not apply themselves, flipping hamburgers, standing behind a cash register in a supermarket.

And while Macauley sailed effortlessly from success to success, never intoxicated, Addison thought, with anything, drugs, drink, girls, music, and Steele was endlessly winning, it was he, Addison, who was the one with real talent. How was he supposed to behave? He could not imitate his brothers. They had taken up both possible versions of the good child, excelled at them. He was the flawed impression. He felt like a ghost, a shadow, in his parents' house. Nothing he did could make them really see him, even when he took up the role of the restless, confrontational bad boy.

Reginald tried to suggest to him that the role of rebel might not be a constructive choice for Addison himself, that if he felt slighted by his parents and his brothers and his teachers, he might be better served by pursuing his authentic self, doing what was good for him. Then Addison revealed what lay beneath the rather banal costume and the display of attitude. He had the heart of a true romantic. Like Goethe and Byron, he was filled with yearning, for beauty and meaning, reverent before the mystery of life. That was the moment that Reginald felt the first stirrings of love for this unlikely object, decided to give him Liszt and Rachmaninov. Reginald was very strict about how he must learn the pieces, playing them with agonizing slowness, *sans pédale*, hands separately, each piece broken by Reginald's markings into small sections to be practised one at a time, in order. He did not allow Addison to move on to the next section until the one assigned was perfect, played with the utmost accuracy, memorized. "You must know the music by heart," he said. "Think about what that means." He drew lines where Addison must take a breath. "The music must be sung," he said. "You cannot produce a decent line if you do not breathe, if you run out of breath before the line has been fully extended." Addison embraced these instructions, even expressed gratitude. He was in love with this music, he honoured it.

Reginald felt that Addison was ready for the next step. It would be good for him to take on the role of accompanist, to learn to modulate his playing in support of someone else. Given Addison's vexed relationship with his string-playing brothers and mother, Reginald thought it might be better to pair him with a singer. He thought it would be good for him to be paired with someone gentle and modest, so that he would have to rein himself in, listen attentively. That was when he introduced Addison to Jade Jong.

Jade was the daughter of his piano tuner, himself a person of great interest to Reginald. Jade's father had once been a musician of great promise, a clarinetist who got on the wrong side of the authorities in the Cultural Revolution, just at the moment when his career was blossoming. Suddenly his hard-won mastery of the Western Classical tradition was regarded with suspicion. Pulled from his home by a gang of exuberant youths in the uniform of the Red Guard, he was forced to kneel in a public square. A placard was hung around his neck, labelling him a capitalist running dog. His beautiful Rampone instrument was taken from him and broken into pieces while the self-proclaimed "worker-peasant-soldiers" droned on about the evils of studying anything that hindered socialist transformation. In order to understand the struggles of the peasants and the dignity of labour, he was transported to a remote rural backwater. His delicate hands were damaged by the brutal work they set him to do, the cold and damp of rice-planting knotted his fingers with arthritis. He was separated from his beloved wife, a pediatrician who had trained in Guy's Hospital in London, for almost three years. She too was sent for re-education through heavy manual labour. With the ascension of Deng Xiaoping, they were able to return to Shanghai, to find each other. After the birth of their son, they managed somehow to get to Canada, where Jade was born.

Newly arrived, penniless, without connections, there was neither time nor money for Lan to re-qualify as a pediatrician, so she had ended up as a pediatric nurse who often knew more than the specialists. Because he had absolute pitch, Wing took a course on line as a piano technician, then found work with the Remenyi House of Music, who held the contract for the pianos at the Faculty, which is how he met Reginald. Jade's older brother, as dutiful as Macauley Ormsby, was now in medical school at Western. But Jade had early demonstrated remarkable musicality. In exchange for tuning the Bechstein (a very unequal exchange, for lessons required an hour or more per week, while the piano needed work only once every season), Reginald started the child, his only beginning pupil, on piano lessons. One fall day, she had grown over the summer, her little breasts were starting to sprout, Reginald was trying to get her to bring out the melody in a Chopin waltz, and he asked her to sing it for him. Her voice astonished him. It was high, clear, and pure as spring water, her pitch as accurate as her father's. "Who taught you to sing like that?" he said.

She lowered her eyes, as if the answer were written on the tops of her shoes. "No one. I just like to sing, that's all. I sing along with the radio."

"And you've never joined a choir?"

"At school, I sing in the choir, in the alto section."

"But you're not an alto."

"No, I think I am a soprano, but they don't have enough altos, and I can hit the low notes, so Miss Carrington . . ."

"And Miss Carrington has never suggested you should have singing lessons?"

"My father does not tune sopranos," she said.

Reginald had pulled his own strings, brought her to sing for the head of Voice at the Faculty, who was now grooming her for her own conservatory auditions. She would have to win a scholarship to go anywhere outside of Toronto. He worried about her. Her voice had a rare beauty, but it was not big. The prestigious schools were looking for future opera stars. Neither Reginald nor her voice teacher could figure out why her sound remained so small. She was herself tiny, it is true, but it was a myth that you had to be the size of Jessye Norman to produce a big sound. She was young, and shy. The moment would come, he felt sure, when the walls came down, when her voice would soar, piercingly sweet, over a full orchestra. Just as he thought it would be good for Addison to temper his big personality to hers, she might expand under his influence.

Reginald was not matchmaking in any baser sense. He introduced them at one of his soirées, the gatherings he organized for his pupils to perform their best pieces to a select audience of friends and other students. Jade of course was diffident, Addison swaggering, but they agreed to work on some pieces together, Hugo Wolf songs from the *Italienisches Liederbuch*, a nice complement to Addison's work on the Liszt, a good practice for Jade's diction. But if he had been looking at the young people instead of the score, he would have seen the golden arrow flash from Addison's blue eyes to her black ones, seen them gaze upon each other with wonder and reverence.

Jade was very beautiful, though she did not think so, magically exotic for Addison, her creamy skin, her almond eyes, her shining fall of silken black hair, the delicacy of her bones. And she saw past the dreadlocks and the dreadful clothes to a body as perfect as a Greek statue, muscled and compact. The music did the rest, highly coloured, expressive. Poetry spoke words of love beyond their own adolescent eloquence. They discovered that they both had been going to the same high school for four years. They had not met because Addison disdained the music program, and because Jade was in the gifted stream, a model student, while he pulled a mediocre performance in the regular college preparatory classes, when he could be bothered to attend. They began to meet every day after school, rehearsing in the empty music classroom. The piano was not very good, an old Heintzman apartment grand that had taken a lot of abuse, but it was kept in tune, and Jade, wisely refraining from revealing the name of her accompanist, had begged the use of it from Miss Carrington.

By November, they were practising in the demi-twilight. Alone in the dim room, pouring out their hearts in the music and in tender glances and almost accidental brushings and touches, they created an enchanted world. Inhaling the perfume of her, shampoo and soap and fruit-scented lotions, Addison became aware of his own smell. He threw out his disgusting socks, he put his clothes in the laundry hamper every night, he showered every morning, and shaved carefully so she would touch his cheek. He nicked his father's bottle of Habit Rouge. They arranged their transits through the labyrinthine halls of the school so they could pass each other between classes, slip each other notes. Late at night, her parents safely in bed, Jade took the hall phone, which had a very long cord, into her bedroom closet. Turning on the bare bulb that hung from the closet ceiling, having carefully closed both her bedroom and the closet doors, Jade crouched under the ranks of her dresses, whispering to Addison. He of course did not have to crouch in the closet. He had his own cellphone, and had the entirety of his parents' spacious Rosedale basement to himself. His own piano, a Steinway, was there, the rest of the house insulated from his practising by soundproof ceiling tiles. He liked to say they'd banished him to the dungeon, but in fact it was not even really underground. The backyard sloped away from a wall of plate glass windows. It ran on a separate HVAC system from the rest of the house, so that he could roll himself a joint or light up his hash pipe while he talked at a normal volume.

In the snug safety of her closet, insulated from Addison's breathtaking physicality, Jade could talk easily and amusingly, sharing anecdotes about her teachers and classmates, asserting her own opinions about music and movies, and regaling him with the plots of the nineteenth-century novels she favoured. Addison's English grades improved, though he was not consciously stealing her insights. Sometimes he helped her, over the phone, to study for tests, and she helped him with his homework. Since he was on a cellphone, he could sit in front of his computer or his notebooks. It was annoying that his mid-term report card gave his parents so much pleasure, but they increased his allowance, and he spent it on Jade, taking her on the sort of dates that would not alarm her parents, to concerts and recitals, to the Opera, to serious, literary plays, grabbing a bite beforehand. She taught him to read the program notes, to use chopsticks; he taught her to lie to her parents, to kiss.

Because no one ever came down into the basement, even the cleaning lady, and because he could sneak in through the sliding doors, Addison had long been used to coming and going as he pleased. Before Jade, he had smuggled his dope-smoking friends, and other girls, in and out in the middle of the night without his parents being the wiser. For Christmas, he gave her a ring, a circle of heavy gold with a carved jade seal. He told her jade was the stone of wisdom and prosperity. The signet was carved with a rather Egyptian-looking boat, its sails wide, and the letters A J, backwards. Her fingers were thin, so she wore it on her thumb. If her parents noticed, they said nothing. When Addison gave it to her, he told her that he loved her, would love her forever. He recited a carefully memorized sonnet.

After that, she felt as if they had been secretly married in the cell of some kindly friar. As she grew accustomed to visiting his basement, and became confident that no one would ever interrupt them, she gave him more and more of herself. Without his clothes, Addison was marble white, white as the ivory keys of the piano, his skin was soft and smooth over the bulk of his muscles. The hairs on his legs and arms were golden in the candlelight. She seemed to him a sylph, not really a fleshly creature, but made of moonlight and water. They made love with the same intensity with which they made music, silent though their heads were full of melodies. After, they dressed quickly, and he took her home, kissed her goodnight in the elevator because they did not want to risk being surprised by her parents. Addison knew he must never make her late for her curfew. As they walked down the corridor toward the apartment door, he saw her put on the mask of the good daughter, compliant and self-contained.

March was the month of auditions, Montreal, New York, Philadelphia, Baltimore. Addison went everywhere with his mother, first-class plane tickets, hotels with plenty of stars. He refused to cut his hair, but submitted to wearing his new suit, and let his father teach him how to tie a Windsor knot. Jade went to her auditions alone. Reginald felt she should certainly try for Curtis, Peabody, Julliard, hope for a scholarship. He transferred the points on his credit card to obtain her tickets, he phoned old friends in every city to arrange a place for her to stay. Her auditions went well, sometimes there was even a scattering of applause from the jurors, but she despaired when she heard the others, their voices already huge, mature, swelling with confidence and rich, bright sound. Addison's auditions were uneven. He played too fast and too loudly for Curtis, he had an unaccountable memory lapse at Peabody, and became rattled, and consequently rather bumptious in interview. But at Julliard, he played as well as he had ever played in his life. As the last note of the Shostakovich died away, he turned on the bench and looked down to see the jurors nodding at each other.

He got in, Jade did not. Though she was shortlisted everywhere, the consensus was that her voice, while lovely, and very promising, was not yet mature. The consolation was that she had been offered not only a place but a full scholarship at Toronto, where she had always expected to go in any case. She would continue her studies with her own beloved teacher, she could continue going to Reginald for coaching. She truly rejoiced in Addison's good fortune, though her heart ached at the thought of their separation. She tried not to say anything pathetic. She did not beg him not to forget her, extracted no promises of faithfulness.

His response confounded not only Jade but everyone around him, including Reginald. She was not coming to New York? Well then, he would not go. His refusal was loud, angry, and absolute. He had a place at Toronto, too, of course, though he had not particularly exerted himself for the audition. By now, everyone knew that he and Jade were romantically involved, though her parents' imaginings did not extend to the basement. Reginald felt dismay, and not a little guilt. He knew perfectly well that they were lovers – he was certainly no puritan – but was not convinced of Jade's wisdom in bestowing her pure and ardent heart on such an unreliable recipient. He suspected that, like a swan, she would mate for life. Addison was not a constant star, he was an emotional trainwreck, playing for the moment at Romeo and Juliet. He needed to go to Julliard, needed the humbling and challenge of serious competition if he were to make anything of himself, heal his psyche. As a big fish in a relatively small pond, already reaching the limits, if not of what Reginald had to teach him, then certainly of what he was prepared to learn from Reginald, Addison would surely soon regret his choice, blame poor Jade for it. Like everyone else, he tried to reason with the boy, but found him adamant.

Clifford Ormsby was not accustomed to defeat. He knew better than to think he could persuade his recalcitrant son of anything, but he was adept and inventive in solving problems. Patient, orderly, he assessed the point of weakness, gathered the necessary information, prepared his brief. It was not difficult to figure out that the best time to catch Jade on her own, with the advantage of surprise and unencumbered by the presence of anyone who might interfere, was after her voice lesson. He cleared his schedule, and settled himself in a chair outside the studio, calmly reading the most recent issue of *The Economist.* When the studio door opened, he rose, nodding affably to her teacher, and possessed himself of her elbow. Would she allow him to bend her ear a tick, buy her a cup of coffee? Numbly, unable to think of an excuse, she allowed him to pilot her to the café bar in the newly refurbished Royal Conservatory. The coffee was excellent, which was important to Clifford, who did not have room in his life for the mediocre. He wanted to have privacy and quiet. The café tables were set at a discreet distance from each other, the space was open to the roof several storeys overhead, and conversation drifted up into its heights, muffled and indistinct. And yet it was a familiar space, filled with music students and professors, not intimidating and alien as a hotel bar might have been. He wanted her full attention for what he was about to say. She held her cup tightly between both hands, and would not meet his eyes. "My dear," he said, placing his hands gently, briefly, over her own, "you will wonder why I have waylaid you in this fashion. But I need to ask your help. With Addison."

She nodded, but said nothing.

"Now, I am perfectly well aware that you agree with us, with everyone really, that he must and should accept the place Julliard has offered him. And that this mad scheme of giving it up to stay in Toronto is not your wish, but his fantasy, that he believes he must stay here to be with you, that he cannot bear to be parted from you. You may have given some thought to what he is giving up, but you may not be aware how the plans and hopes of so many others are contingent on his. I have a golden opportunity to take up a rather, shall we say, exalted position for an international firm with its head offices in New York. It was my plan to relocate my family there. We have already secured a place for his little brother in perhaps the premier Steiner school on the continent, where in fact there's a job for Edith, teaching music, and you know she's had rather a slow time of it, trying to get back into the workforce here. We've got an offer in on a really terrific apartment on the East Side, the piano will be no problem, and we've actually already sold our place here, with a closing date in July." She was looking alarmed, and he suspected she was holding back tears.

Still clutching her mug of coffee, looking down into it and addressing her answers to its depths, she spoke carefully, in a pleading tone, as if she had somehow, without willing it, unconsciously, behaved wrongly. "I hope you understand, Mr. Ormsby, that I totally agree that Addison should accept the offer from Julliard? I always knew he would get in, and I never thought I would. I mean, it was clear to me that he would be going to New York and I would be staying here, right from the start. I've told him and told him he's crazy not to go. It's not as if I'm going to forget all about him the minute his plane takes off. And it's only for eight months, right, and then we can see each other in the summer. Maybe I could even come down at Christmas?" She looked up at him, as if for reassurance. Clifford waited out her silence, smiling just a little, giving nothing away. "But it's hopeless. You know how he is, he gets mad, he rages around, he won't listen. I mean, if you and Mrs. Ormsby can't convince him, I don't really see how I can . . ." She trailed off.

Clifford leaned forward toward her, his forearms resting on the table, palms up. "So much hinges on his going, not only the opportunities for my wife, for his brother, but the very harmony of our family. It is too late, now, for the rest of us to stay in Toronto, but how can we leave him behind? His mother will fret, any mother would. She will be torn in two. And Addison? He's never managed on his own, and he doesn't have the habits, the frame of mind to adjust to the demands of being someone's roommate. He's pampered, spoiled even, but I can hardly set him up in a luxury apartment with maid service and meals, where he can bang on the piano any time of day or night and not elicit a peep of protest. And what of his development as a pianist, his career? He has made great strides over the past year or so, but without further challenges, he will lose focus, backslide. You don't want to ruin things for so many people, do you, my dear? Surely you can see it's best all around, if he goes?"

She took a sip of her coffee, almost recoiling from the cup, and put it down hastily. It was evidently too hot. "It's not up to me," she said. "I've really tried, Mr. Ormsby, I have, but what can I do?"

"I believe you," he said, injecting his words with just the right amount of sympathy and warmth. He smiled at her, a gentle, sad smile, practised over the years on employees whose work was unsatisfactory. Then he leaned back, turned his hands over, pushing against the edge of the table, so that her coffee sloshed a little over the rim of the mug. "But you are wrong when you say there is nothing you can do. What keeps Addison here, what makes him dig in his heels and refuse to leave? Only you, you tie him to Toronto, that is all."

She was bewildered, and hurt. "But he . . ." she could not finish the sentence, say that he loved her. "That is, it's not me, not exactly. It's his feelings, and I can't change those."

"Can't you now? Let us be logical. Addison will not leave you, granted. But if you were to break off your relationship? If you made it clear you no longer wished to be . . . involved with him? Hmm?"

Now her eyes were bright with tears. "I couldn't do that," she swallowed, tried to keep her voice from rising into a wail. "And even if I told him it was over between us, he would know it wasn't honest, he would see what I was doing."

Clifford frowned impatiently, tapped his finger, just twice, against the table top. "Not if you just mouthed the words, no. You would have to put in a little effort, write him a chilly note, perhaps flirt with some other boy, rub his nose in it a little."

She shook her head. A tear made its way down her cheek, and she did nothing to erase it.

Clifford leaned forward once more, made her look into his eyes. "He has a hot temper, does my son, he is jealous and possessive. It wouldn't take much to make him believe he has a rival, that someone else has risen over him in your affections. Oh you think he's deeply sensitive, that he will read your true feelings. But I know better, trust me. He may seem terribly deep, with sheet music in front of him, but when it comes to reading people, he's not so perceptive or clever."

Jade gave up trying to argue, and began to cry in earnest, soundlessly, her shoulders shaking, the tears pouring out. Clifford extracted the expertly folded, immaculately clean white handkerchief from his breast pocket, and extended it to her with a sympathetic expression. "I feel dreadful demanding this of you," he said, "but I'm afraid I have no choice. And it really is a demand." She looked up at him fearfully. He held her gaze for a long moment, then looked at his watch. "I've kept you long enough," he said. "Promise me you'll give it some thought?" She nodded. "Good girl. It's for the best, all around. I'm sure your parents would agree. No, no, keep the handkerchief." He pushed back his chair, stood, gave a quick squeeze to her shoulder, and walked off. She watched him till he had passed through the doors to the outside world. He never looked back.

Addison grew moody and distracted. All he could talk about was the steadily worsening situation at home. He was fighting with everyone, not just his parents, but his brothers too. Macauley called him from Berlin, and when he hung up on him, began persecuting him with messages on Facebook, diatribes on his ingratitude and stupidity. It was when Jade learned that he had fought with Mr. Stone, actually yelled at him and smashed one of the porcelain teacups by throwing it against the wall, stalked out of his lesson declaring he was never coming back, that she knew she had no choice.

The Senior Prom was announced. Addison of course declared he would not go, pouring scorn on the whole enterprise. This would have been fine with Jade, who was not very comfortable dancing, and did not enjoy being crowded in a hot room, bombarded with the kind of music she hated blasting at full volume. They were in the lunchroom, Addison holding forth about the stupidity of the thing, everyone getting all hyped up about participating in such a cliché of teenage life, when Sandy Brickline turned toward Jade. "What about you, gorgeous, don't you want to have a prom dress and pin on a corsage? Or won't you go unless Addy does?"

Jade had disdained to flirt, it was a point of feminist pride to her, but she knew how it was done. She favoured Sandy with a Mona Lisa smile, opened her eyes wide, and looked into his. "Oh, if the right person asked me . . ." She gave a little shrug, actually tossed her hair.

"I'd take you, baby, in a heartbeat, so would half the guys at this table."

"Is that an invitation?" she turned her head a little, looked at him sideways.

"You bet," he said. "It's a date?" He sprang up, pulling his wallet from his back pocket, dislodging a condom, which fluttered to the floor. He laughed, stooped to pocket it, "Always be prepared, that's the Boy Scout motto," he said. He made his way over to the table where the prom committee was selling tickets, plunked down two twenty-dollar bills, turning to make sure she was watching him, grinning at her over his shoulder like an eager dog.

Addison mimed gagging, but he was watching her closely, through narrowed eyes.

"Why not?" she said to him in a challenging voice he had never heard before. "It's not as if you're going to ask me." She tossed her hair again, hoped she wasn't overusing the gesture.

He tried repeatedly to provoke a fight over it, he demanded, then he wheedled, but she stuck to her guns, cool and determined. Sandy Brickline was a perfect choice. He was contemptible, a show-off, a would-be player. Addison despised him, she despised him herself. He would also, she knew, try to put his hands all over her. After the prom, after the after-party, he tried to get something happening in the back seat of his parents' car. She submitted just enough to get his hopes up, drawing a firm line when she couldn't stand it anymore. She didn't let him get very far – his tongue in her mouth and his hand down her bodice and up her skirt, pressing himself and his hopeful erection against her thigh. Hardly a conquest, but she knew Sandy would broadcast it all over the school, and make up for her failure to put out by exaggeration and outright lies. Addison would hear about it, and what he heard would make her sound like a nymphomaniac.

The Monday after the prom, Addison yanked open the door to her French class, yelled "you fucking whore!" and was sent to the office. After that, he avoided her in the halls, perhaps was skipping school, she never saw him.

Reginald guessed most of this, the falling in love, becoming lovers. He could read it in the way they looked, some change of posture, voice, movements, some special grace that illuminated their smiles. He was worried at first, not for Addison, but for Jade, afraid that once he'd uncovered her mysteries, he would lose interest in her, drop her, hard, and without warning. So he spied on them, took the pulse of their happiness, guilty, apologetic. Then, when Addison was digging in his heels over leaving her, Reginald knew Jade would find a way to make him let go. His anxiety extended itself to the boy. He repented having introduced them to each other, thought himself meddlesome and lacking in foresight. He did not guess Clifford's role.

Reginald left Tuesdays at two open, and stayed at home, listening, for the intercom, for the telephone, for the doorbell, waiting for Addison to come around, to sulk and backtrack his way through some approximation of an apology. In the last week of June, right on the hour, he was rewarded by the crackling of the intercom. He could not make out what was being said, simply let the visitor in. So sure was he that it was Addison, that he was startled to open the door to Edith, bringing flowers and a replacement for the broken teacup. "Addy is so sorry for his bad . . . for failing to control his temper," she said. "He would have come himself" – this Reginald doubted – "but you know, the end of term and all that, exams, final papers. The movers come on Friday." And, then, leaning toward him, across the coffee table, for he had invited her in, seated her on the white leather of the couch, made her tea, she half-whispered, dropping her voice as if someone might overhear, "And he's completely broken up over that girl," meaning Jade. "He just can't make sense of her behaviour, dumping him like that. Not that I'm surprised, really. The Chinese, I have found, are fearfully ambitious. They do not feel things as we do. A very cold race, I'm sorry to say." She did not sound sorry at all. "I'm just glad that we are going to New York. Friday can't come soon enough. I think once we're settled there, and he's got the routine of the school to bolster him up, he'll pull himself together. Find a new girl. He's not even eighteen yet, you know."

The replacement teacup, though of a similar pattern, was new and not old. Reginald put it beside one from his own set, and tried to figure out the difference. The writing on the bottom of the cup said "*Fait à la main*," but he thought the flowers looked too uniform, stenciled, not free-hand. He put it in the cupboard alongside the other cups, then kept taking it out by mistake. Whether he used it or replaced it with one of his own cups, it disturbed him with thoughts of Addison, and his own mistakes. One day in August, instead of putting the cup back on the shelf, he threw it against the wall, then threw the saucer after it.

He did not see Jade all summer. She went, as she always did, to a number of music camps, Domaine Fourget, Inglenook, and then, on a fellowship, to Banff. The Canadians appreciated her voice at least, he thought, heard the promise in it. When it was time for the Bechstein's fall tuning, Reginald asked Wing about his daughter. Jade was doing very well at school, working away, but he could see she was heartbroken over that idiot boy. He had known it could never come to much good, but who could school the young in the ways of the heart? "Perhaps next time," Wing said, "she will find a boy who will treat her with respect, who will make her feel beautiful and worthy of love. A boy with decent values."

"A nice Chinese boy?" Reginald teased. "I know, my friend, it is hard to see the girl suffer so. The first heartbreak is the most terrible." He placed his hand on Wing's smooth forearm. He permitted himself such little flutterings.

In time Jade came back to him. He thought she was thinner, but she was brave, said nothing of her secret sorrow. She brought him her pieces, for help with the German or the Italian, to note the breathings, to correct the tempi. Bit by bit, ever sympathetic and discreet, he teased it from her, Clifford's cruel demand, her caving in, the crude mechanism of Sandy. He did not push her to admit her resentment. He waited, it was a kind of penance for his ill-conceived interference.

A snowy February day, shedding her schoolgirl hat, scarf, unbecoming down-filled jacket, her clunky boots, he saw she was agitated. He drew her into the kitchen, made her tea, waited for her to come out with it. "Why does everyone think I have to everlastingly sing these same baroque pieces?" she wailed. "I'm going to enter the Norcop, if I win I get to go for the summer to Vienna, everyone's saying I should. But you know what he wants me to prep?" He being her voice teacher. "'Exsultate, Jubilate'! I was singing that when I was in grade nine!"

"Is there something you would rather sing instead then, dear?" He was thinking of Cherubino, "Voi che sapete."

"A real aria," she said, "a stretch, a challenge. The cabaletta, from *La Traviata*."

He thought about the high notes, whether she could reach them. Why not? She would not win by merely showing off her range, offering her promise yet again. He had noticed the slow coming of change into her production, a new dynamic breadth, something rich and moving under the flawless exactitude of her pitch.

"Please, Mr. Stone, could you work with me on it? If I get it really ready, so I can sing it for him, maybe he'll let me."

"He doesn't have to sign off on your application, you know," Reginald said. "And of course I'm delighted to help you with whatever you wish."

"I'm just sick to death of it, everybody in the whole world telling me what to do!"

"You can't stop people from having their little opinions," he said. Gently. The corollary, that they could not stop her from having hers, from doing what she wanted, hung in the air between them. He did not say it, not so baldly. He said, "Why do you rely on them?"

She moved impatiently, rattled her teacup. "I don't know, I just always have. People tell me what to do, and I do it."

"And how does that feel?"

"I hate it!" Passionately. "I hate the way it makes me feel, like a sheep, like I don't have any will of my own. Half the time I think they're totally out to lunch. And then I'm so angry. At them, at myself. It makes me feel so ugly."

"Compliance, or being dominated? Or the feeling of anger?"

"Both! All three. Anger is such a useless emotion."

"Is it?" He thought of the lines from *The Iliad*, quoted them. "'Anger, like a plume of smoke, coiled in his belly.' There are gifts to be drawn from our emotions, my dear, from rage, from suffering. They can be a source of authenticity, and of strength. I have always thought there was more in you. An operatic voice. Not Wagnerian," he laughed at the thought of her in a helmet with horns, "bel canto, of course, but there are great roles,

Handel is very much in vogue now, and you could certainly sing Rossini, Bellini, Donizetti." He smiled at her, a mild and encouraging smile, but with a challenge lying under it. Her voice had always been limited. Perfect in its way, but an instrument suited for a living room, hardly big enough to fill a concert hall, lost on an operatic stage. A small, still voice, Reginald thought. But if it were a small voice, it was because she was holding herself back, confining herself within walls of her own construction, timidity, crippling modesty, shame, fear. "You need boldness," he said to her. "To step across the threshold without waiting for someone else to tell you it's time. Life belongs to the courageous," Schnabel had said this once, in a master class. He'd stored it away, waiting for the right moment and the right student. "You have brought the score? Come, let's go to the piano."

In the audience, Reginald wiped tears from his eyes. She sang about love as a cross and a delight to the heart, about her own folly, and ended on a ringing high note, forever free, *sempre libre*. In that moment what he felt for her could only be described as love. It beat in his ears with the dying note, until his heart corrected him: she was not a boy, however beautiful. But he had felt it, acknowledged it. When she was called forward to the stage to accept the award, he took her hand and lifted it to his lips. The judges praised her purity of tone, the perfection of her legato, the elegant portamento which supported her phrasing, the exquisite way she turned her ornaments. Accepting the award, her eyes searched him out. He was the first she thanked, before her voice teacher, her parents. My favourite teacher, she called him. There was a little scattering of applause, he was urged to stand. "My favourite pupil," he said. And in that moment, it was true.

JEREMY LANAWAY

DOWNTURN

He appears at the corner of the house, a pool skimmer teetering on his shoulder and a bucket of shock treatment swinging in his fist. He's dressed for the part: board shorts, T-shirt, thongs, Oakleys, backwards ball cap. His forearms are flaked with the remains of sunburned skin. I wasn't expecting to see him, not in our backyard, not anywhere, and I consider drawing the blind. He's put on weight. He hasn't returned to his regular size, but he's added fifteen or twenty pounds that he was lacking at his housewarming barbecue a year ago. I've heard that he lost even more weight after the divorce, six months later, but I can't corroborate the rumour. I wasn't around to witness his diminishment.

He shuffles past the floor-to-ceiling window in his flip-flops, and I lift my arm in the initial stage of a wave, but I change my mind mid-movement and lower my hand. He walks by without noticing me. I start to let down the blind, stop, and then raise it again. I keep watching him. I murmur a greeting, *Hey, Dan*, testing the words with the tip of my tongue, as if gauging the potency of a spice to ascertain the safety of its consumption. He sets down the bucket and pole. He stands up and surveys the backyard, taking in the sequined surface of the pool, the ceramic planters, the outdoor fireplace, the gas bar-becue, the pedestal umbrella, the brickwork patio, the designer deckchairs.

He accentuates his regard with a rattly belch.

Backhanding a dribble of sweat from his forehead, he reaches into the nylon fannypack strapped to his waist and retrieves a cylindrical package of chemically-treated dipsticks. He bends down, drags a dipstick through the water, and holds it up next to the cylinder, which has colour-coded levels dis-played on its side, to assess the chemical content of the pool. If he notices anything in need of adjustment, he doesn't show it. His attention has already been displaced by the pressing matter of tapping a cigarette out of a pack of Player's Light and lighting it with a fluorescent green Bic.

He sucks on the cigarette, gazing past the landscaping toward the apple-budded trees tiered along the valley's slant, eleven acres of greenery separating our backyard from the prop-erty line of our nearest neighbours, Mr. and Mrs. Zimmerman, pleasant enough people, although the number of words that we've exchanged during our time as neighbours could easily be transcribed within the 160-character limit of a text message. His back inflates with one last puff, which he emphasizes with a weary skyward glance. He expels the smoke into the mid-July air, scratches at his unkempt goatee, and then proceeds to flick the still-sizzling butt into Erica's favourite rosebush.

I blink his image out of my head, questioning the reasons that could've led to his replacing our usual pool cleaner, what's-his-name, the kid with the headphones and the one-grunt replies. I'm reaching for the chain to lower the blind again, already turning away from the window with thoughts of a morning coffee settling into the forefront of my focus, when his stance shifts at the rim of my vision. My gaze swivels. I find him staring at me – or maybe he's just staring at glared glass; I can't be certain either way – and once again the notion of waving enters my mind. I don't move, and he mirrors my inertia. I stare at him for a few more seconds, then raise my hand to shoulder-height and mime a smile.

"Hey, Dan," I say, teetering at the edge of the pool.

Dan stops pouring shock treatment into the water, which is swirled with the green reach of chlorine. His sunglasses wink at me across the burbling pool, hinting at a shared joke that I've long since forgotten. Finally the familiarity returns, and he addresses me across the span of foaming water, shaking his head and chuckling in disbelief.

"Get the fuck out of here."

"How's it going?"

"Are you fucking kidding me? Is this your house?"

"We just moved in."

"I heard you and Erica were building a house. I didn't know it was in orchard country, though." He stares at the orchard. He wags his head and whistles. "Not bad, Pete. Not bad at all."

"We like it," I say.

Dan nods to indicate that he also likes the house – or maybe just to show that he's heard me say that we like it. It's impossible to tell. Five, ten, fifteen seconds of silence pass before we both ask a question at the same time; we blurt them out, loudly and awkwardly, as if the rift in dialogue has made us feel self-conscious, embarrassed, maybe even slightly ashamed of the roles that we're performing in the scene unfolding around us.

"How long have you worked for Blue Haven?" I ask.

"How's Erica?" he asks at the same time.

I wait for Dan to go first, but he just grins at me in silence, so I say, "She's training for a marathon right now. She spends all her free time running." I don't know why I tell him about Erica's running. Her running has nothing to do with anything. I decide to repeat my question: "How long have you worked for Blue Haven?"

"I don't really work for them," Dan says. "I'm just helping them out for a bit, you know, temporarily, until they hire a couple of new guys. One of their cleaners broke his leg, and another one quit, so they've got nobody else to help them right now." He dumps the rest of the shock treatment into the pool, rinsing the bucket out afterwards with a scoop of water. "I like it – being outside all day, working on my tan, not having some douche boss looking over my shoulder all the time. I should've gotten out of the real estate game a long time ago. Being a pool guy – that's where it's at."

I smile because I know that he's joking – even though I can't see it on his face.

"Nobody's buying houses anyway. Not in this fucking market."

I ask Dan about his apartment, but even before I get all the words out of my mouth, I recognize that I've made a mistake. I can't help it. I'm working with four-month-old intelligence – that's how long it's been since Erica has filled me in on Dan's situation. Erica's close friend is Dan's ex-wife. Her name is

Heather. She used to tell Erica about Dan – about his cocaine addiction, his weight loss, his getting fired from the real estate agency that he'd worked at for fifteen years, his real estate and driver's licences being revoked, his custom-built, million-dollar, lakefront house being repossessed by the bank, his losing custody of his kids, his failure to pay child support – and Erica used to relay the information to me. Then Heather met a city councilman named Tony, and the information about Dan stopped coming down the pipe.

"I'm staying at Jeff's place for a while. Breaking in his new couch."

I nod my head, understanding that anything I say will be wrong.

"What about Amy?" Dan says. "She's got to be – what – three by now?"

"Not quite. Her birthday's on Saturday."

"Make sure you wish her happy birthday from me."

"Okay."

He shakes his head: "Isn't it fucked up, man?"

I look at him.

"How fast they grow up. One minute you're changing their diapers, the next minute you're letting go of their bike and watching them ride off on their own." He turns away from me to look for the skimmer lying on the deck behind him. He takes a long time to reach for it.

I don't ask about his children.

"So how's the banking business going? Pretty good by the looks of things."

"I can't complain," I say, and actually mean it.

—

"You look good," I tell him, kneeling down and dipping my hand into the swirled water. I make a mental note to turn up the heater a few degrees for Amy's birthday party. I immediately regret bringing up his appearance – although I'm being sincere about his looking good – because the implication is that he didn't look good a year ago. He knows that he didn't look good a year ago – that the missing parts of himself outweighed the parts that remained – but I don't want to say anything to connect him to his past.

"Everyone keeps telling me I look good." He does a few reps of arm curls with the skimmer, his face a mask of exertion. He flips the skimmer onto his shoulders and executes a clumsy lunge. "It must be this new health program I've started. It's really easy to follow. I just drink a few beers whenever I get the urge to snort a line, maybe treat myself to a Crown and Coke or two, and voila – I gain weight, I stay clean. Easy, breezy, cheap, and sleazy."

"Whatever you're doing, it's working," I tell him.

"I saw you driving along Pleasant Valley Road the other day," Dan says, removing a clutch of leaves from the edge of the pool with a scoop of the skimmer. "I mean, Erica was driving, and you were in the passenger's seat. I was hitching. You didn't pick me up."

"We didn't pick you up?" I say, and feel my face flare from the idiocy of my question.

"You didn't pick me up."

"I didn't see you."

"We made eye contact."

"Where were you – ?"

"Pleasant Valley Road, a few blocks past Hunter's Store, last Tuesday, a little after five."

"I didn't see you."

"You said that already."

"I must've been daydreaming."

Dan ladles another leaf from the water's rumpled surface, then another one, then another one, depositing each one in turn into the cavity of a nearby shrub. He doesn't say a word. He swings the skimmer back over the pool, already targeting another leaf, but he halts it in mid-descent. He looks at me across the pool, and then starts to laugh.

"I'm just fucking with you, man," he says, flicking water at me. I smile and say, "Okay."

"I'll leave you to it," I say, and glance at my watch without registering the time. "I have to get to the office." I lift my chin in a clumsy gesture of farewell. I listen to the sprinkler's watery arc in the distance, *chook-chook-chook-chook*, lulled momentarily by the unflawed cadence of its enterprise, and it occurs to me that some things can never be found after they've been lost. They exist, and then they don't exist, and no amount of apologizing or pleading or dealmaking or promising will ever bring them back.

"The money's not going to count itself," Dan says through a half-smile.

"See you around."

"Yup."

I'm rolling through the stop sign at the end of the street when I notice that I've forgotten my briefcase. I spit a half-hearted *fuck* into the interior of the car, yank on the steering wheel to negotiate a U-turn, and head back to the house. I pull up on a man driving a scooter a few blocks later, braking to thirty klicks in his wobbly wake, discharging more *fucks* at the windshield. Knuckling the steering wheel, I swerve left into the oncoming lane and accelerate with a stamp of my shoe. I glance in the rear-view mirror and see the man teetering along the edge of the road, all elbows and knees, his teeth bared in rage. He finally regains control of the scooter and flips me the finger, three exaggerated prods at the sky, and I realize that it's Mr. Zimmerman, my neighbour, hurling curses at my rear window. I start to tell him to go fuck himself, but the imperative quickly devolves into an extended, shuddering grunt. I watch Mr. Zimmerman signal – with the scooter's turning light and his left arm – and turn onto his street. I wring the steering wheel and allow my thoughts to return to Dan. I consider parking the car on the street and walking down the driveway, to avoid another exchange with him, another goodbye, but I reject the idea with a self-reproving head-shake.

"It's your house, asshole," I remind myself.

I coast down the driveway, park, and hurry into the house, leaving the engine idling and the door ajar. I open the front door and retrieve my briefcase from the bench-seat in the foyer, and as I'm turning to go, I catch a glimpse of white through the family room window – the same window that I was standing at when Dan walked back into my life thirty-odd minutes earlier. I squint, blink, squint again, but the image doesn't disappear or right itself – it just gets clearer and clearer. I follow my feet toward the patio door, and every step I take to get closer to the whiteness in the backyard leads me farther away from understanding it. I unlock the door, push it open, and step onto the patio.

Dan stands at the edge of the pool, his shorts bunched around his knees, one hand on his uncovered hip, the other holding his penis at a forty-five-degree angle to maximize the arc and distance of his piss. The whiteness that caught my eye from inside the house is his ass – a stark stripe dividing the deep browns of his lower back and the backs of his legs. He leans backwards slightly, and the yellow curve climbs higher into the sky, impossibly high, spiralling upward and outward until its momentum ultimately exhausts itself, allowing gravity to finalize its trajectory into the middle of the pool, where it lands with a lathery splash. Ripples expand from the yellowy epicentre.

"What the hell, Dan?"

He slowly turns his head to face me, and I see nothing in his expression – no surprise, no embarrassment, no apology, no regret whatsoever – nothing to corroborate the fact that he's urinating in my pool. He stares at me, absently kneading the final drops of piss from his cock, before raising his shorts with a series of unhurried tugs.

"Heather told me our house couldn't be a home," he says, "not as long as I was living in it." I watch him.

"Isn't it amazing," he continues, "how everything can change because of a few simple words?" He stoops down to pick up the skimmer and the bucket of shock treatment. Balancing the pole on his shoulder, he lifts his sunglasses and perches them on top of his ball cap. He looks at me for the first time, and who knows – maybe for the last time as well. "What do you do when the things you want don't exist anymore?"

"I don't know."

He waits for me to give him the answer.

"I did see you hitchhiking last week," I say.

"It's okay," he says, knocking his sunglasses back into position on the bridge of his nose with a flick of his wrist. He starts shuffling toward the breezeway and the rectangle of front yard that it reveals. "See you around, Peter," he tells me, making his exit, and this time it sounds like he actually means the farewell – or at least like he wants to mean it.

Or maybe it's just me.

"Okay," I say.

I say *okay* instead of telling him that I'm experiencing my own downturn in life. Instead of telling him that sex with Erica has become a bodily function, a task of tedious utility, like brushing my teeth or shaving. Instead of telling him that we often sit through entire dinners conversing tangentially through Amy's ceaseless chatter, not silent but silent, cleaning up the kitchen afterwards in non-intersecting lanes, leaning outward to avoid contact as we pass each other en route to our next domestic duty, our eyes set to prevent meeting. Instead of telling him that I've become jealous of a marathon. I say *okay* instead of telling him all these things – and many more things that I haven't even said to myself – things that have brought me to the edge of a measureless descent, and I understand that I have my reasons for saying *okay*, but I don't have any more time to think about them. I'm late for work.

JULIE ROORDA

HOW TO TELL IF YOUR FROG IS DEAD

The African clawed frog is native to sub-Saharan Africa where it resides in stagnant pools and backwaters. Provided you construct a vivarium with conditions simulating this natural environment, these frogs can thrive in captivity and make excellent pets. The word *vivarium* is derived from the Latin *vivus*, meaning "to live." Cared for properly, a pet frog may live for up to fifteen years, and your child will enjoy the benefits of interacting with an exotic species while learning valuable lessons about commitment and responsibility. But if you fail to maintain the delicate balance of conditions required for life inside the vivarium, your frog may die.

Although African clawed frogs breathe air, they spend most of their time underwater. The water must be kept between twenty and twenty-four degrees Celsius. If a hurricane or other extreme weather cuts off your source of electrical power and the water temperature drops below twenty degrees, your frog may die, but your child will learn an important lesson about the effects of climate change.

Be sure the top of the vivarium is covered. If it is not properly sealed and your frog hops out, it could starve, or become dried out before you are able to locate and return it to safety. The bottom of the vivarium must be lined with medium-sized pebbles and stones to create nooks and crannies where your frog can hide. If the stones are too small, your frog may accidentally ingest them; if they are too big, your frog could be crushed or pinned, and may die. Your child will learn attention to detail and the value of moderation.

For optimal health, feed your frog a balanced diet that includes live guppies and crickets. If your child is distressed by the fate of these creatures, take the opportunity to discuss the basic dynamics of the food chain. You may wish to explain that the chicken, fish, or hamburgers you had for dinner all similarly died to become food. Your child may choose to become a vegetarian, in which case nuts and legumes are good alternative sources of protein.

Approximately every two weeks, your frog will shed its skin, which it will usually proceed to eat. This is perfectly normal and not a sign of emotional instability. Sometimes the frog will leave the skin behind, providing your child with a fascinating natural artifact to present at Show and Tell.

The vivarium can be lit by either fluorescent or incandescent bulbs; just remember to turn these off at night. Your child may be tempted to use the vivarium as a nightlight, but if the light remains on, your frog's circadian rhythm will be disrupted and it may die. Either way, your child will learn to distinguish imaginary monsters from the real terrors of living and dying.

If you go away on holiday, you will have to ask a friend to feed your frog and monitor conditions inside the vivarium. The friend should be paid a reasonable, but not exorbitant, fee for performing these tasks. Demonstrate and review all procedures until you are sure your friend has learned how to properly care for the frog. Still, friends can be lazy and forgetful; your frog may die, and your child will learn a valuable lesson about loyalty and trust. If the frog dies, the friend need not be paid.

Do not allow cats to approach within a metre's circumference of the vivarium. Cats do not generally prey on frogs for food, but they may wish to engage in the type of play your frog will not enjoy. Your frog may die. If your frog dies, do not blame the cat. Cats are cruel and haughty by nature. Moreover, they do not respond to punishment. Attempting to punish your cat will only increase its disdain.

You may wish to introduce your frog to a suitable companion. Male frogs, unlike humans, are usually smaller than their female counterparts, and when they are ready to breed, they sing. Frogs may breed up to four times a year. If you allow them to over-breed, your frogs may die. *Amplexus* is the Latin word used to describe the mating position of frogs. It means embrace. Sometimes a female frog will *amplex* another female, or a male another male. This is nothing to be alarmed about. It is perfectly natural, and your child will learn a valuable lesson about tolerance and diversity.

If your frog dies, do not attempt to flush it down the toilet. Your frog is not a goldfish. It has rather the shape of a rubber plug closely approximating the diameter of the pipe connecting your toilet to the municipal sewer system. Should your toilet become plugged, you will have to call a plumber. The plumber will use a snake to dislodge the clog caused by your frog. You may wish to reassure your child that the plumber will not be sending a real snake into the pipes, such as those seen on YouTube swallowing frogs whole. A plumber's snake is a tool so-named metaphorically, because of its long, sinuous shape and flexibility. Even if it were a real snake, it would only prey on live frogs, not dead ones.

It is best to dispose of your frog by burial in a biodegradable container or wrap. A Q-tip box is ideal, as it allows an open-casket option for mourners to pay their respects. You may wish to conduct a modest ceremony commemorating the life of your frog. A few simple songs would be appropriate, particularly if the dead frog is male. Popular choices include "Let's Go to the Hop" and "It's Not Easy Being Green."

You may wish to mark the frog's grave with a small stone. Be sure the stone is not too small to spot, and avoid, when you are cutting the grass, or it might shoot out the back of the lawnmower, at bullet speed, and your child could lose an eye.

It is inadvisable to disguise or gloss over the fact of your frog's death when you discuss it with your child. If you say the frog has gone to live on a farm, your child will eventually learn the truth and may require expensive therapy. Couching the tragedy in spiritual terms is also unwise. Although some deities have been known to employ a plague of frogs as an agent of wrath, religion is generally silent on the subject of their afterlife.

Before you make any firm plans to bury or memorialize your frog, remember that frogs hibernate for several months of each year. In this state, a frog practically ceases to breathe and its pulse becomes undetectable. Do not attempt to wake your frog.

Contemplating this condition of deathlike stillness can be beneficial, particularly if your child is prone to hyperactivity. But even the most careful observation may fail to distinguish between life and death. The only way to know for sure whether your frog is dead is to be patient and wait for spring. If you suspect you have erroneously buried your frog alive, you will have learned a valuable lesson.

TYLER KEEVIL

SEALSKIN

A t the foot of Gore Avenue, Alex pulled up in the parking lot that overlooked the Western Fishing Company Plant. He turned off his car but did not get out and instead sat listening to the engine, which tinked intermittently like slow-cracking glass. The plant was a barn-like structure, at least a hundred yards long, with a peaked, shingled roof and red siding; it sat on a concrete wharf jutting out from shore. Above it a column of seagulls turned around and around in a sluggish tornado. They were attracted by the fetid reek of herring roe, which permeated the air all along the waterfront. It was a terrible smell and Alex thought that if there was such a thing as hell it probably smelled a little like that. He waited and watched the clock on his dash: it was quarter to seven and their shift didn't start until seven. The other guys would already be inside having coffee, but Alex had stopped partaking in that ritual.

As he sat there a black Ford truck wheeled into the lot. It was Bill, their boss. He parked a few spots over and climbed out, dressed in the blue, one-piece coveralls that all the union guys wore. Some of them came and left like that and skipped the change room, as if they lived in their coveralls even when not at work. Bill noticed Alex and waved at him and asked if he was coming in for coffee.

"Nah. I'm good."

"You avoiding Rick?"

Alex shrugged. He still had both hands on the steering wheel, as if ready to drive away.

"Don't pay any attention to that asshole."

"I'll be there in a bit."

"Suit yourself."

Bill locked his truck and headed off toward the plant.

Alex waited until 6:55 before he got out and from the back-seat took his own coveralls and workboots, which he carried with him across the lot. That morning the tide was low and around the perimeter of the harbour you could see the high-water mark: the rocks above it were sun-bleached white, the ones below were slick with seaweed. At this end of the plant was the shipwrights' warehouse and gear locker, which could be seen through a garage door. Next to it was a regular door-way that led to the lunchroom and office. Alex could hear the others in there and avoided them by going through the ware-house to get to the change room. All the lockers had names and union numbers on them except one, which was his. He kicked off his shoes and took off his clothes and stuffed these articles into the locker.

He'd left his coveralls sprawled on the floor like a deflated person. He had an old set that Bill had dug out of the gear locker for him; they were thin and threadbare and dull grey instead of blue, and that colour difference served to set Alex apart from the union guys. Alex picked them up and stepped into the legs one foot at a time and slipped into the sleeves one arm at a time before zipping the front up from his crotch to his chin. Doing this always made him think of those sea creatures that could change from people to seals and back again; each morning he put on this grey skin and became somebody else, somebody owned, and after work he peeled it off and became himself again, or at least somebody closer to himself. Next he tied up his boots, which he'd found in the dumpster behind the plant and which were a size too big for him. After that he checked his watch, waited another minute or so, and went to face the men in the lunchroom.

He had timed it right and the guys were all standing around the table, having just finished their morning coffees. Aside from Bill there were five others: Diego, Steve, Jimmy, Elmore, and Rick. Rick was big and pushing fifty, with a shaved head and saggy skin and the hefty, muscular build of an old bull walrus. As soon as he saw Alex he started in on him, calling him a scab and a lazy Newfie in a way that sounded like a joke but wasn't and they all knew it.

"Must be nice not punching the union clock," Rick said. He was gnawing on a chunk of chew, his mouth full of black juices. "Being able to wander in whenever you please."

"It's seven by my watch," Alex said.

"Seven, my ass. What happened? Your mom forget to wake you?"

The only one who laughed was Elmore; he always laughed at Rick's jokes.

"Nah," Alex said. "But your mom did. I stayed over at her place last night."

That got a laugh and Rick spat into his empty coffee cup, using it as a spittoon.

"You lippy little shit."

Bill chuckled. "Admit it, Rick. He got you good."

"Like hell he got me. He couldn't get his own cock out to piss."

There was some more snickering and Bill waited for it to settle down before handing out the worksheets for the day. The other guys accepted the sheets without looking at them and shuffled out, stretching and yawning. They all knew what jobs they were doing but Alex didn't. Bill used him as a utility man and his duties changed from day to day. He was given his sheet last. Bill passed it over with a small smile of apology and when Alex saw the task at the top of his list he knew why: it said he would be working on the Western Kraken today.

"Rick needs some help," Bill explained.

"Doing what?"

"His precious decking."

Rick had stayed behind the others; when Alex looked at him, the seam of his mouth split open – the lips peeling back to reveal teeth stained brown like rotten kernels of corn.

"Hear that, scab?" he said. "You're fucking mine today."

———

They walked down the wharf together, with Rick a few steps ahead and Alex trudging behind like a one-man chain gang. The walkway was as wide as a road and ran the full length of the wharf, with a long drop to the water on the left, and the packing plant and cannery on the right. When they passed the open doors of the processing area Alex glanced inside at the rows of workers; they all wore lab coats and rubber gloves and face masks, and they were already at work sorting the slabs of yellow roe that looked like elongated banana slugs, rushing past on the conveyor belts. Even outside the stench was sweet and fetid, nearly overwhelming. Most of the workers were Asian immigrants: Chinese, Japanese, or Korean.

"Know why them Chinks wear those masks?" Rick asked.

"So they don't have to smell the roe."

"No – so they don't have to smell each other."

From the wharf they descended a gangplank that led to the docks and marina where the fishing boats were moored. Beneath the gangplank, near the crane, was the spot where his seal usually appeared. Alex checked but couldn't see it in the water at the base of the wharf.

Rick caught him looking and asked, "You still feeding that fucking thing?"

"No."

"Better not be."

Near the northwest corner of the marina they came to the Kraken, a seventy-five foot seiner. Like all the vessels in the Westco fleet the hull was painted black and the bridge was painted red and white. It was Rick's boat. He wasn't the skipper, but when the Kraken was in dock he worked on it, and when it went out during the salmon and herring seasons he was its engineer. Rick hopped onto a bollard, using it as a step-ladder as he hauled himself over the gunwale, and after him Alex did the same. Rick waited for him amidships; he had his can of chewing tobacco resting open in his palm.

"Finally finished the forward deck," he said.

Alex came to stand beside him, being careful not to step on the deck, and studied it in the way Rick wanted him to: with appreciation. About half the planks had been replaced and the new ones looked odd and incongruous set next to the older wood that was more worn. The seams between the planking had been caulked and paid with tar.

"Took me damn near a month to get it done."

Alex nodded. "Looks good."

"Course it looks good."

He pinched a fingerful of chew; the clump of tobacco looked like a large hairy spider, which he stuffed in his mouth and chewed on hungrily, an errant strand dangling from his lips like one of the spider's leg. Rick nodded toward the bow, where he had piled all the excess scrap from his repair job: torn-up planking and rusty nails and carriage bolts and sawdust and woodchips and dried bits of tar that resembled deer turds.

"First job is to get all that off of here. Then we're gonna sand down this decking and varnish it."

"I'll go get my tug."

"It ain't your tug."

"I'll go get the tug, then."

"Be quick about it."

The tug was not a real tug but a ten-foot aluminum skiff with a deep hull and powerful engine and fenders made from old tires lining the gunwales. It was tied up in the same place that the seal usually appeared: near the gangplank that led from the wharf to the docks. The docks rose and fell with the tide; since it was low tide, the wharf stood twenty feet overhead on wooden pilings, many of them leaning at angles, all of them pockmarked with barnacles and draped in seaweed.

In the shadows of the wharf the tug sat nestled like a sleeping duck.

Two tie-lines held the tug in place, and Alex undid these before hopping aboard. The tug had a small wheelhouse with room for only the wheel and the dashboard and the driver. When he turned the key in the ignition and pressed the starter button the engine fired up with a low, hoarse rumble, coughing several times in the process; the tug began to shake and diesel smoke belched out of the exhaust pipe above the wheelhouse. Alex let the engine idle for a minute before easing forward the lever that controlled the throttle. To steer he stood behind the large wheel and held it with both hands, feeling through them the rumble of the motor.

The marina was separated from Burrard Inlet by a jumble of rock and concrete that acted as a breakwater, and it was between the breakwater and docks that Alex piloted the tug toward the Kraken. The larger boat was moored with its bow toward shore and portside facing the water. Alex could see Rick standing on deck, waiting for him, and he made his approach carefully; he dropped the throttle into reverse, countering his momentum, and turned hard to port so that the tug drifted in at an angle. As the two vessels came together he stepped out of the wheelhouse to brace against the Kraken's hull with his palms, softening the impact to a kiss. Rick didn't offer to take his tie-lines so Alex went to the bow to gather the first one himself, draping it over his shoulder like a lasso and climbing aboard the Kraken.

Before he was able to tie off, a series of waves entered the marina from the inlet and rolled beneath the docks, and because the tug was still loose it pivoted to port and ground its prow into the side of the Kraken. Alex yanked on the rope and held it taut, trying to steady the tug as it bucked up and down like a startled horse on the swells.

"Jesus Christ!" Rick shouted. "Watch what the fuck you're doing!"

"It was an accident."

"You scraped the shit out of my hull."

The waves had settled. Alex tied the rope off as fast as he could, looping it in quick figure eights around the nearest cleat and then finishing with a half-hitch.

"It was those waves," he said. "You could have helped me tie her up."

"I could help you wipe your ass, too. But I figured even a Newfie scab like you would be capable of doing something that fucking simple."

Alex leapt down onto the tug, picked up the aft tie-line, and threw it on deck. Then he climbed back up and tied it off, too. Rick was leaning over the side with both hands on the gunwale, peering down to inspect the damage; there was a clear scrape in the paint of the hull where the orange primer now showed through.

"You better touch that up."

"You want me to do that now?"

"Don't be an ass. Get rid of that goddamn scrap first."

Rick continued to swear and curse about the damage as Alex pulled on his work gloves. Trudging to the bow, he seized one of the splintered planks with both hands and carried it to starboard. On the forward deck of his tug was a steel container they used as a garbage skip, and into it he tossed the plank before heading back for another. He had to step around Rick who was kneeling on the deck, using a rag dipped in turpentine to wipe away excess tar, which in places had bled from the seams into the edges of the planks. For a time they worked like this with neither of them talking to the other and the only sound that of waves slapping against the metal hull of the tug and the wooden hull of the seiner.

Then, without preamble, Rick began talking about the Kraken. He said it was a hundred years old and had been used to carry supplies across the Atlantic in the Allied convoys during the Second World War. He also said that it had survived three attacks by the Krauts when a lot of other boats didn't. Alex continued working and only half-listened and every so often made an affirmative or noncommittal sound in the back of his throat.

"What do you think of that?" Rick asked.

"That's really something."

"Damn straight it's something."

Alex hefted another piece of plank, this one riddled with nails, and lifted it carefully over Rick, telling him to watch his back, and Rick told him to watch his own. As Alex stepped up to starboard, he saw in the water a bulbous head that shone wetly and had the same blue-grey sheen as the waves, as if part of the sea had simply taken shape. It was his seal and she was looking at him curiously. Alex set down the plank and made a shooing motion with his hands, and when that didn't work he picked up a crooked nail and tossed it in the water – not directly at the seal but near enough to startle her. The nail made a plopping sound and the animal dropped beneath the surface, leaving concentric ripples radiating in its absence.

Alex looked back at Rick; he hadn't noticed anything and was still rambling on about the boat. He was saying that the company didn't build wooden boats anymore because they were too cheap, but everybody knew wooden boats were better quality and lasted longer and handled more easily in the water. Rick sat back on his knees and waved his rag at the boat moored opposite, which was a modern packer with an aluminium hull, bridge, and cabin.

"Think that no-account tin can is gonna be around in a hundred years?"

"No," Alex said.

"Fucking rights it won't."

After that Rick stopped telling him about the boat and they worked in silence again. Alex cleared the remaining pieces of planking, some of which had to be sawed in half or quartered to fit in the skip; then he gathered up the smaller chunks of wood and metal in a bucket, which he lowered down to the deck of the tug; lastly he got out a broom and swept the slivers and splinters and woodchips and sawdust into piles, and with a dustpan shovelled these piles into black garbage bags. When he said he was finished Rick stood up to check over the work and muttered about Alex's uselessness without being able to find any faults.

"Get rid of that shit and come right back."

"Bill might have some other jobs for me."

"I said you come right back – and I better not catch you feeding no fucking seal."

Alex undid his tie-lines and tossed them onto the tug and then jumped down after them, his workboots ringing off the metal deck. The engine was warm now and in starting up did not cough or choke like it had earlier that morning but rumbled smoothly to a full-throated roar. Alex put the throttle in reverse and spun the wheel as he glided away, turning the tug one hundred and eighty degrees before heading back toward the plant.

Halfway there the seal appeared again. She surfaced off to starboard and kept pace, floating alongside him and following him all the way to the wharf. She hovered about ten feet away as he docked and tied up and turned off the engine. He looked around to make sure he was alone, and then leaned over the side of the tug and spoke softly to the seal, as you might to a dog. He chastised her for turning up when Rick was around. He asked if she was hungry again, and also if she was lonely, and if that was why she acted so friendly toward him. The seal gave no indication that it understood any of these questions, but simply stared at him. There were no whites to her eyes, or irises or pupils – just twin orbs that were the colour of water in a well and almost as fathomless.

"I'll be right back, girl," Alex said. "Just sit tight for a sec."

He walked up the gangplank to the wharf. In the corner of the wharf, above where he moored the tug, was the hydraulic crane they used to load supplies onto the boats. At the base of the crane was its control box and he used this to manipulate the arm and the cable, which had a steel hook on the end, like a giant fishhook. He lowered the hook to within a foot of his tug, then trotted down there to attach the hook to the carry-ropes on either side of the garbage skip. The seal was still waiting patiently and he spoke assurances to her again before trotting back up and raising the crane until the cable tightened and the ropes went taut and the skip left the ground, swinging in the air with a pendulous motion. Beside the crane was a wheeled cart onto which he lowered the skip. He then detached the hook and left it hanging there as he pushed the cart toward the dumpster at the far end of the plant.

In passing the warehouse door he spotted Bill, who was taking inventory: studying the shelves lining the walls and jotting tallies down on a clipboard. Alex let his cart roll to a halt and went in. When Bill heard him coming he looked up, pen poised over his inventory sheet.

"Problem, Alex?"

"Just thought I'd check to see if you had any other jobs need doing."

"You and Rick done already?"

"Not really."

Alex didn't explain but stood with his hands on his hips, hoping.

"Hmm." Bill tucked the pen behind his ear and scratched his jaw. "Tell you what – Frank left some scrap on the Seattle. After lunch I'll send you over there to clean it up, eh?"

"Sounds good."

"Give you a break from Rick, at least."

Alex was already walking off. He called back: "What I need is a clean break."

"You got to have thick skin around that guy."

"I know it."

Behind the gear locker and their lunch room were the garbage dumpsters. That was where Alex emptied the skip, tossing the larger pieces of wood in one at a time and dumping the smaller scraps out using the plastic bucket. When it was done he left the cart and skip there and carried the bucket with him as he walked back along the wharf.

En route he stopped at the processing area. The stench was getting worse in the midday heat, and now had a physical, oppressive presence that made Alex retch, but the workers seemed oblivious: they continued to sort the passing roe with precise, repetitive motions, as if performing some important ritual or rite. Just inside the entrance was a plastic tub filled with herring. After the roe was extricated, the gutted fish were sent to another part of the plant to be turned into feed and fertilizer, but the workers always kept a few here; on their breaks they liked to toss them to the seagulls and watch the ensuing fights and place bets on which bird would end up with the fish. He had never asked if it was okay for him to take a few fish, but they had never challenged him about it, either. He grabbed half a dozen herring, all sleek and shimmering and slippery, and dropped them in his bucket. When he walked out with his load several gulls descended on him, squawking and flapping, and he made fake kicking motions to keep them at bay as he carried the bucket away, back toward the crane and docks.

At the bottom of the gangplank the seal was still waiting for him; she knew what gift he was bringing her and she rolled over once, slow and lazy as a log, to show her pleasure.

"Over here, girl," he said. "I got you a feast, today."

He stepped between the tug and the pilings, into the shadows of the wharf, where he would be shielded from the rest of the marina. Crouching down, he reached into the bucket and scooped out one of the herring, which he tossed in the water. It landed with a slap and hung there suspended, trailing smoke-like streaks of blood across the surface. The seal moved in to take it, snapping it up and tilting her head back to let the herring slip down her gullet. She had teeth like a dog's and used her jaw the same way, but her snub nose and watery whiskers reminded him more of a cat. When she finished he tossed her the next fish, and the next. She was bold but not stupid and would only come within five or six feet, so he had to throw each one that far and then wait for her to finish it before giving her another.

"Good girl," Alex said. "Tasty, eh?"

Between portions she would weave back and forth in the water, and by studying the torpedo shape of her body he developed an understanding of the way she controlled it – using gentle movements of her fins, tilting and twisting them, elegant as the fan of a geisha. When she rotated, the water rolled off her skin; it had a rubbery texture that looked thick and tough and impervious, and he wished he could touch it just to see what it felt like. It was dappled with shades of black and grey, and glistened like the sea on a cloudy day.

As he tossed her the last fish he heard footsteps coming down the gangplank; he stood up abruptly, hurried to the tug, and hid the bucket behind the gunwale. Then he began to undo his tie-lines, moving casually and with what he hoped looked like nonchalance. He did not check to see who it was right away but waited until the person reached the dock; then he saw that it was Elmore, lumbering along with his arms dangling at his sides like a Neanderthal. But he wasn't looking in Alex's direction and didn't seem to have noticed Alex or the seal. She was still floating in the sheltered waters beneath the wharf and after Elmore had passed out of sight, Alex told her that he had to get back to work now. She twisted and rolled as if she understood, and continued performing as he rinsed the blood from his gloves and fired up the tug and pushed off. Thinking she might follow him he watched the water in his wake as he chugged over to the Kraken, but she seemed to have figured it out and did not reappear.

Before he'd had the chance to tie up, Rick stuck his head over the gunwale and shouted down, "Thought I told you to come right back."

"I'm here, aren't I?"

He heaved himself aboard and brushed by Rick and began tying off.

"Where the fuck you been?"

"I stopped in to see Bill."

"If you been feeding that fucking seal . . ."

"I ain't been feeding it, all right?"

"Told you what I'd do if I caught you feeding that pest again."

"Yeah, yeah."

"I'll catch it and kill it, like we do when we're at sea. Skin the fucking thing." Rick chuckled, as if imagining it. "That's right. Skin it and make me a pair of sealskin boots."

Alex had finished with the tie-lines. He tugged on his gloves one at a time, twisting his wrists back and forth and flexing his fingers to fit them into the fingers of the gloves.

"What do you want me to do?" he asked.

"I want you to get to work instead of slacking off, scab."

"I'm not a scab, okay?"

"What are you, then?"

"Just a worker."

Rick bent to the toolbox he kept on deck, and began rooting through it. "If you work here and you're not union you're a scab."

"I tried to join the union and they wouldn't let me. I told you."

"They probably thought you were too dumb."

"They said I'm only temporary so that's why."

"I don't give a shit what they said." Rick stood up. He had a sanding block in one hand and a sheaf of sandpaper in the other. He tossed these at Alex's feet. "Now would you quit yapping about it and get to work? I want this deck sanded by lunch so I can oil it after."

"Yes sir, Captain."

Alex sat cross-legged on deck and fiddled with the sanding block and thought of all the other things he could have said and wanted to say but hadn't. He was sweating from heat and frustration and the sweat made his coveralls itch so he unzipped the top to his sternum, baring his chest. Taking a sheet of sandpaper he folded it in thirds and tore off a strip along the first fold and fitted the strip into the sanding block. Rick watched him do this and also watched him as he knelt and began to sand, using both hands to pull the block up and down the first plank along the wood grain. The paper made a whispering sound and gave off small puffs of sawdust. Soon his gloves and forearms were sprinkled with it, like yellow powder.

He could feel the sun on his back through the coveralls like the weight of a hot iron, and he could feel Rick's eyes on him as he worked. Rick was drinking coffee and observing from beside the galley door, and as far as Alex could tell that was all he was doing. At one point he asked Rick if they could turn on the radio in the galley and Rick told him no because all they played these days was rap and nigger music and there was no point listening to that.

"It's not all rap."

"Don't worry about the goddamn radio – worry about the goddamn decking. I want it smooth as a baby's ass before I oil it up later."

Alex finished one plank and crawled on his knees up to the next. As he scrubbed at it Rick came to stand beside him and scrutinize what he was doing; every so often Rick would criticize some aspect of his sanding, telling him to go faster or slower or to go back and redo a particular patch. Eventually Alex straightened and sat on his knees and looked up at him. Rick loomed blimp-like above him and his shape was just a shadow with the sun behind it.

"Don't you have something to do?"

"Yeah – I got to make sure you don't fuck up my decking."

"I won't fuck up your deck, all right? But I won't get much done with you standing there looking at my ass."

"I ain't looking at your ass, you little queer."

"Sure – I'm the queer."

The shadow stood motionless for a few seconds. Then Alex felt something wet sprinkle in his hair and he smelled the bitterness of coffee beans.

"What the hell was that?"

"An accident – like you."

Rick walked away snickering; Alex bent to the deck and sanded as if he were trying to erase something or scrub out a stain, and as he knelt and worked like that, lathered in his own sweat, he could see the long summer of slavery that stretched before him, and it seemed to be endless and indefinite and eternal, each day melting into the next and Rick the only constant.

———

At noon the union men gathered in the lunchroom next to the gear locker. They sat together around a rectangular table and undid the top halves of their coveralls, which they allowed to hang down from the backs of the chairs so that the sleeves just brushed the floor. To Alex it looked as if they had sloughed off part of the skin that they worked in, making them more human, but he knew this was deceptive since below the table they still wore their uniforms.

As the men ate their sandwiches and drank their coffee they talked about Elmore's new Harley and the strip club up the street and the best way to repair a broken compressor on a fridge. Alex listened to all this and said nothing. Originally he had tried to take part in these conversations, but anything he said had left him open to some barb or rebuttal from Rick, and he'd learned instead to sit and eat and wait for lunch to end. He'd grown so accustomed to doing this and tuning out their talk that it startled him when he heard his name mentioned; he looked up, still chewing a mouthful of macaroni. Elmore was telling them all how he'd seen Alex feeding the seal.

Alex swallowed his food and said, "No, I weren't."

"What do you mean you weren't?" Elmore said. "I saw you."

Then he looked over at Rick, as if anticipating how he'd react.

"You little liar," Rick said. "You little fucking liar."

"It was only a couple of herring."

"Those things are a goddamn pest. If you'd ever been on a real fishing boat you'd know that. Tear holes in nets and eat the catch. Just giant rats is all they are." He sat back and crossed his arms and chuckled. "Looks like I'm gonna go a-seal-hunting this afternoon, boys. Catch me a seal and do it in like them Eskimos – bash in its little head."

Alex put down his fork, then picked it up again. "Yeah, right," he said.

"Don't think I would?"

"You better not."

"Or what?" Rick said. "What you gonna do, scab?"

There was a long silence and Alex didn't answer and they stared at each other in silence. Then Bill burped, long and low, distracting them and making all the guys laugh.

"Take it easy, Rick," Bill said.

"You on his side, boss?"

"I'm not on anybody's side – I'm just saying take it easy."

"I'll take it easy when this scab starts doing his job, not feeding no fucking seal."

"That reminds me," Bill said, scratching his jaw, "there's a bit of a mess on the Seattle, from Frank's rebuild. It needs clearing and I figured Alex could tackle it this afternoon."

"No problem," Alex said.

"Like hell," Rick said. "You're oiling up my deck this afternoon."

Bill shook his head. "Sorry, Rick – the Seattle's skipper is coming down tomorrow to check her out, so I want her looking slick. You might have to finish the deck on your own."

Rick looked from Bill to Alex as if he suspected the plot they'd concocted. Without saying anything, he stood up and went over to the sink and flicked his coffee into the basin. He rinsed the cup thoroughly and deliberately, using his fingers to wipe out the dregs, and placed it upside down on the counter next to the taps. The men all watched him do this. Then, still without saying anything, he went out, and Elmore went out after him.

Later Alex would remember all that, and the way it had happened.

———

To reach the Seattle Alex had to pilot his tug by the gap in the breakwater that gave access to Burrard Inlet, and through which the fishing boats passed during the herring and salmon seasons. Out there the water was choppy and surging with whitecaps; he could see sailboats skimming the surface and cargo freighters lying flat like toppled skyscrapers, and beyond them he could see the North Shore, where he lived, with its beaches and condos and wooded slopes, and its mountains that rose up in grey swells still topped by snow, like larger versions of the white-capped waves. The sense of space was vast and captivating and as always when heading that way he imagined momentously turning the wheel, hand over hand, and steering out through the gap into the uncharted waters beyond, and as always he didn't do this or even seriously consider it but instead stayed on course and continued toward his destination.

The Seattle was as old as the Kraken and just as imposing. Frank was the contractor who had been hired to rebuild the cabin, on behalf of the Native owners, after the end of last herring season back in March. Frank was younger than the union guys and had treated Alex differently from them. For long stretches, especially when Frank had been replacing the strakes in the hull, Alex had worked alongside him, but the job was done now and so was Frank.

In the galley Frank had left the old cupboards that he'd removed, as well as a series of rusty two-inch pipes that looked like they'd been part of the boat's freshwater supply system. Sprinkled on the surrounding linoleum were wood chips, sawdust, and flakes of rust, and all that mess needed cleaning. With a crowbar Alex broke the cupboards into individual panels; beneath the fake oak laminate they were made of cheap plyboard that cracked easily. The counter was thicker and stronger and had to be cut down with a handsaw. He carried the pieces out one at a time, followed by the piping, and laid it all down on deck near the bow. Next he set to work on the debris, which he swept slowly into piles, then re-swept for no real reason except to waste time. With a dustpan he transferred the rust, wood, and sawdust into a black garbage bag that had turned hot and tacky in the heat. Then he walked around deck, carrying the bag and hoping he looked busy and trying to think of something else to do.

The new counters in the galley were still dusty so he wiped those down, smearing the dust into grey streaks and then wiping the surface a second time. He did the same to the table and when he finished he sat at it, twisting the damp cloth back and forth in his palms and feeling the easy, listing rhythm of the ship beneath him. He checked his watch and knew it was time to go but found it difficult to make himself move. As he sat there he glanced out the galley porthole; across the marina he noticed two blue-clad figures, tiny as toys, standing by his tug in the shadow of the wharf. It was the same spot that he usually fed the seal.

He went outside and clambered onto the starboard gunwale and perched there, bracing one hand against the cabin roof for balance. He shielded his eyes from the sun to peer at the two men and tried to make them out. It looked like Rick and Elmore. He couldn't tell what they were doing but they were hunched over something on the dock. He felt it then: a sense of anticipation and foreboding, a kind of sickness, blossoming in his stomach.

"Son of a bitch."

From the gunwale he jumped down to the dock and landed hard, tumbling forward onto his hands and knees. Then he was scrambling upright, sprinting full-tilt through the marina; his boots pounded on the wooden docks, which swayed and rocked underfoot like the floor in a funhouse. At one of the gaps between sections of dock he tripped and stumbled and caught himself and kept running. As he drew near the gangplank he slowed down. The men were there, in the shadows of the wharf. It was Rick and Elmore like he'd thought and they were hoisting something off the dock, using a rope they'd looped over one of the crossbeams that supported the underside of the wharf. He could tell by the tubular shape that it was a seal, his seal, but at first he didn't know what they had done to her; she was no longer grey and speckled like the sea but bright crimson as if they'd dipped her in red paint and made a piñata out of her. Then he saw the blood drizzling from her tail, and he saw the bare muscles and tendons, and he saw the way she hung there all skinless and garish and shining like some nightmarish vision of hell. He saw all that and the men saw him at the same time. Rick was squatting down and tying off the rope they'd used to string up the seal and Elmore was standing at his side. They turned to face Alex and for a brief moment seemed uncertain how to behave. Spread at their feet were the tools they'd used to catch and kill her: a bucket of herring, a fishing gaff, some netting, a claw hammer, a serrated six-inch knife. There was also something grey and reddish and rubbery that looked like a large jellyfish. Rick bent down to pick it up, clenching it in his fists and lifting it so it unfolded to reveal itself. It was the seal's skin. The side Rick displayed was red as a matador's cape, and like a matador Rick shook it to taunt him.

"I warned you, didn't I? I told you what I'd do."

Alex said nothing but only stood there. He had started to cry and when they saw that they made sad and sympathetic and mocking faces; they joked about killing his little pet and snickered at the jokes for each other's benefit. Standing there laughing, with their tools strewn about them and the skinned body hung behind them and their coveralls spattered in red, they looked less like men and more like demons or some malevolent imitation of men.

Alex made an outraged, animal sound that wasn't a word and wasn't a scream but something in between, and then ran at Rick and grabbed him and started hitting him. They wrestled and clawed and punched at each other until Alex felt something connect with the side of his head and then he was on the dock. He pushed himself up and rushed at Rick again and got hit again and went down again, and this time he stayed down as they stood over him and kicked him a few times – quick and vicious toe-punts – in the ribs, the back, the kidneys.

He had closed his eyes and when the blows stopped he opened them and saw the two men standing over him. They told him that he was crazy and that he had brought this on himself and that he had got what he deserved. Then they were gone and he was alone on the dock staring up at a blue sky. The seagulls were circling up there; they'd already caught the scent of fresh blood and meat and flesh. A few swooped down and settled on the dock; they eyed Alex and eyed the hanging seal as if trying to decide which one was dead. When he moved they fluttered back out of reach and began to squawk indignantly as he rolled over and pushed up onto his hands and knees and eased himself to his feet. He felt as if he had been in a car accident: not quite sure how it had happened but knowing that it was bad and knowing also that it was partly his fault. He was still crying but not sobbing, just weeping steadily from the pain, the tears blending with the blood on his cheeks as if his eyes were bleeding.

He shuffled over to the rope that was lashed to a cleat on the dock. He untied the rope and held it, struggling with the weight of the seal, which was surprisingly heavy – probably a hundred pounds or more. He allowed the rope to slither through his hands, the nylon threads scouring his palms, and in this way lowered the seal down to the dock. She landed wetly and heavily in the puddle of blood that had pooled beneath her, and as she did her body bent and slumped over to the side.

She looked as if she had been turned inside out and he didn't understand how her innards could hold together like that without spilling everywhere. She did not resemble his seal anymore, but he recognized her by the eyes: they were still dark and doe-like and gazed up from the depths of death as if she recognized him and understood the part he had played in her fate. There were cracks in her bare skull where they had hit her, and they'd used the end of the gaff as a makeshift meat hook, shoved up underneath her shoulder blades to hoist her.

He gripped the hook and yanked it down and it came out with a soft sucking sound, like a spade shearing turf. Laying it aside he knelt with her and petted her muscled back, so tender and vulnerable without the tough hide, and spoke to her in the friendly tones he had used while feeding her. The seagulls created a circle around him like the attendants at a funeral, waiting for him to finish his mourning so they could enjoy the after-service feast.

To prevent that, he slid his hands beneath the seal and rolled her toward the edge of the dock and off into the sea. She landed with a splash and bobbed back up, before the head dipped under and dragged the rest of the body down, dropping as still and silent as a scuttled ship. As he stood the gulls cawed indignantly and hopped forward to inspect the place where the seal had lain. Others approached the skin Rick had left on the dock and began to peck at it. Alex swatted them away and picked up the skin, clutching it protectively. He stroked it. One side felt just like he expected it to feel: sleek and smooth as human skin, but thicker and stronger and more resilient. The other side, the inside, was tender and had a wet, gelatinous quality, softened by fat and blubber. He held it draped over one arm and carried it with him up the gangplank. He was limping badly; one of their kicks had given him a charley horse in his thigh and the muscle spasmed at each step.

Outside the processing area two workers stood with their face masks pulled down around their throats like the breathing sacs on frogs. The workers were smoking and they stopped smoking to watch Alex as he walked by carrying the sealskin. He knew he was bleeding because he could feel the warmth of the blood on his chin and taste it in his mouth, and because red drops splashed onto the concrete every few steps, but he didn't know how bad it was until he got to their warehouse and went into the washrooms and turned on the lights and looked in the mirror.

His lip was split wide and his nose was bleeding and swollen and probably broken; one of his molars felt loose and he could wriggle it like a kid about to lose one of his primary teeth. He draped the sealskin over the nearest sink and then ran the tap in the sink next to it and splashed water on his face. The water was cold but each handful seemed to burn. As he washed the blood away more continued to drizzle from his nose. It hurt too much to pinch the bridge so from one of the stalls he tore off pieces of toilet paper, which he twisted into plugs that he stuffed up his nostrils to stem the flow of blood. He had just finished doing this when Bill appeared in the doorway. When he saw Alex, Bill stopped in mid-stride, and then came another few steps forward. Alex didn't turn around but gazed at Bill in the mirror and waited for him to speak. Without quite meeting his eyes Bill told him that he had heard what they'd done and that it was a shitty thing and that he was sorry. He didn't say exactly what he'd heard, but the sealskin was right there in the sink and Bill glanced at it uneasily without commenting on it so it seemed as if he knew everything.

"They worked you over good, eh?"

Alex acknowledged that they had.

"I'll make sure they get written up for it. It's almost impossible to fire these union guys but they'll get a warning, at least." Bill scratched at his beard in that nervous way of his and twisted his left boot back and forth on the linoleum floor, making it squeak. The tap was still running and Alex stood over it with his hands braced on either side of the sink.

"Tell you what," Bill said. "Why don't you take the rest of the day off? Take a couple days off if you want. Don't come back until you're ready."

Alex said that he'd do that and thanked him and waited some more. Bill said he was sorry again and eventually, finally, he left. The twisted tissues that Alex had jammed in his nostrils had bled through. He plucked them out and discarded them and replaced them with fresh ones. Afterwards he looked at himself in the mirror for several minutes as he thought about what had happened and then thought about what had to happen now because of it.

His trolley cart and garbage skip were still where he had left them that morning by the dumpsters. He folded and laid the sealskin inside the skip before returning to the gear locker warehouse. From the low shelves just inside the entrance he got down three cans of marine paint in the primary colours and three cans of lead-based primer. At the back of the warehouse was a toolshed they kept open for communal use, and in one of the drawers he found a rivet punch and a hammer and that was all he needed. He put the paint cans and tools in the skip and pushed the cart down the dock, moving as slowly and painfully as Sisyphus pushing his rock. The workers were no longer on their smoke break and nobody noticed him. The tide was higher now and the marina water getting choppier as afternoon wore on. The gulls still circled ceaselessly, endlessly, indifferently.

As before he used the crane to manoeuvre the skip, this time angling it over the tug and lowering it directly onto the deck. He walked down the gangplank without hurrying and detached the skip from the crane. Only once did he look at the place where the seal had been; its blood was already going dark and tacky in the sun, like treacle. He turned away and gazed across the marina. From the tug he could see the Western Kraken and he could also see Rick plodding back and forth on deck, mindless and purposeful as a golem. Alex watched him for a few minutes, and then hobbled over toward the boat, deliberately accentuating his limp. Rick saw him approaching and stopped what he was doing and came to stand at the stern, facing the dock. In one hand Rick had a paint brush and in the other he had a pot of deck oil.

"What the fuck do you want?"

"Bill asked to see you."

"You ratted on me, you little scab."

"No. But he knows. I guess somebody saw. He called me in to explain my side of it and now he wants to hear your side."

"I got shit to do," Rick said, and spat a gob of black goo onto the dock at Alex's feet.

"Whatever. I'm just telling you what Bill said."

Alex turned and limped away, hoping he looked weak and defeated, and took shelter on his tug. In the wheelhouse he hunkered down to wait, feeling the burn in his back and side where he'd been beaten. From his position he was fairly well-hidden but he had a good view of the gangplank and wharf above. A few minutes later he heard the sound of boots on the dock, and then saw Rick lumbering up the gangplank. After Rick had passed, Alex counted to ten before he untied the tug, fired it up, and drove it directly to the north end of the marina. This time at the Kraken he docked with deliberate carelessness: grinding the prow right into the hull and scouring out a two-foot gouge. He lashed one tie-line loosely to a cleat on deck and lifted the cans of paint and primer one at a time, placing them on the portside gunwale, before he climbed aboard with the hammer and rivet punch.

The forward deck gleamed in the sun with the fresh coat of oil Rick had given it. Now that the newer planks were stained they blended in better with the older ones, but the contrast was still evident and always would be. The pot of deck oil was sitting on the deck; Alex kicked it over casually and got down to work. He took the first can of paint – the red can – and rested it upside down on the portside gunwale. Placing the rivet punch against the bottom, he brought the hammer down on the punch and drove it through the tin. As he worked the punch back and forth to free it, red paint started pumping out in arterial spurts. Picking the can up, he held it between his palms by the lid and base and shook it in front of him as he walked methodically around the deck. The red paint slopped and spattered across the newly-oiled planks, leaving coloured arcs like slashes of blood, as well as blotches of various sizes, from large spots down to tiny speckles. When the spurts of red dwindled to a trickle he let the can drop and started on the next. This one was blue and the brightness of the hue created an unreal contrast against the red. The red alone had looked like a mistake; two colours made it more meaningful and more like art. He added the blue judiciously, using the entire deck as his canvas. The paint had a chemical smell that reminded him of the model paints he'd used as a child, only stronger. He breathed it in as he worked and the heady stench made him giddy and dizzy and high. Then the last of the blue sputtered out, so he punted the can toward the prow and reached for the can of yellow.

He thought the result was becoming more beautiful with each coat, and he grew so engrossed in his project that he paid no attention to who might have noticed, or whether Rick could be coming back, until he heard a shout from the direction of the wharf. He looked up and saw the big man rumbling down the gangplank, his whole body rolling with the motion like a bull on the rampage. Alex dropped the half-finished can of yellow and left it to spill across the deck. In quick succession he punched holes in the remaining three cans of primer, knocking one overboard in his hurry. He left one of the others dribbling over the gunwale and bulwark and hull, and the last he lobbed like a grenade into the galley, where it landed with a clunk and began emptying across the linoleum.

Rick's footsteps were pounding on the docks, closer now, and Alex moved to undo his tie-line. As he did he glanced back and saw Rick's hands appear at the starboard gunwale, followed by his head, rising up like a baleful moon, his expression full of rage and hate and something worse, something murderous. Holding the rope in one hand Alex leapt down to the tug. Rick was screaming and rushing at him and Alex knew that he didn't have time to start the engine so instead he just shoved hard with his hands against the hull of the Kraken, pushing away from the larger vessel. As he did he felt something brush his head and looked up and saw Rick leaning out over the water, having lunged for him and missed.

"You son of a bitch," Rick was screaming, "you son of a bitch!"

His face had gone almost purple and he continued shouting and screaming at him, telling him he was going to kill him and

calling him a faggot and a cocksucker and a Newfie scab bastard, but all these insults sounded meaningless and empty over
the five feet of water between them. Alex stood and stared at
him like you might stare at a cougar snarling within its cage
at the zoo. Then Alex started to laugh. He laughed and continued to laugh as Rick shrieked and shook his fists and stomped
up and down the deck, going rabid, working himself into a
frenzy. Behind him, on the wharf, an audience had gathered.
Rows of packing plant workers stood gazing down, in their
white lab coats and face masks, observing the display like medical students who had come to witness some kind of strange
human experiment.

Rick was still ranting when Alex fired up the tug, drowning
the noise out. He did not say anything and did not look
back as he pushed the throttle forward and manoeuvred the
tug around the northwest corner of the marina. He headed for
the gap in the breakwater that he had always dreamed of passing through, and it felt like a dream as he did so for the first
and last time. Burrard Inlet opened up before him and the vista
of North Vancouver lay behind it. To the west he could see
the upright supports of the Lions Gate Bridge, and between
them the strands of the suspension cables were strung like thin
tensile wires that glistened in the sun.

He cranked the throttle further, as far as it would go, and
the tug lumbered forward, moving steadily and resolutely
into the oncoming waves, which broke across its bow and
crashed against its hull. He felt the concussions vibrating up
through the deck, and each wave exploded in a shower of white
spray, cool and light as snowflakes, that he felt flecking his face.
In the distance were a few sailboats slicing through the water,

as well as the slow, lumbering forms of trawlers and pleasure cruisers, but none of those vessels were near him. Four or five miles out, when he was midway between the North Shore in front of him and the shipyards behind, he cut the motor and let the tug drift, rocking like a cradle on the waves.

He went to stand on deck. It was mid-afternoon and the height of the day's heat, and in his coveralls he was broiling. He unzipped the front carefully, removing first one sleeve and then the other, having to peel the sweaty garment off like the skin he'd always imagined it to be. He lowered it down to his waist and pushed it further, to his knees, and then kicked off his boots so he could step out of it. From there it seemed only natural to peel off his tank top, too, and his boxers and socks, until he was naked beneath sun. Out there he could no longer smell the stench of rotten herring, only the richness of the sea air, which he inhaled in long and grateful lungfuls – as if he'd just emerged after holding his breath in a swamp.

The sealskin was still lying on deck. He picked it up and held it out at arm's length, studying it. It was a complete hide. They had slit the seal's belly and opened her up to her throat, leaving the back intact. The scalp, too, was intact, with its empty eye sockets and flaps to the left and right that would have been part of the jaw. He turned the skin around and draped it across his shoulders, cupping the scalp over his head and letting the tail hang down his back. It reached to just below his knees. He let go and found he could wear the hide like that without having to hold it in place. On his back it felt tough and comforting, a kind of armour, and he imagined himself as an Inuit or bush-man, inhabiting the hide of his animal totem. Dressed like that, he went to perch at the prow, with one leg on deck and the other propped on the gunwale, supporting his elbow, in the pose of a thinker. He studied the downtown shoreline and could just make out the shipyards he'd left behind. There was no sign of any boat coming from there and he guessed that meant they'd decided not to follow him but instead would wait for him to come back.

"I'm not going back," he said.

He did not know who he was talking to but it felt good to say the words aloud. After he did, as if in answer, he heard an odd, deep sound like a dog barking. He looked around. At first he saw nothing and thought he had imagined it. Then, off to the starboard side, he spotted a small, bulbous head. It made that unmistakeable dog-like sound again, and he made the same sound back at it, or his best imitation of it. At that the seal fell silent. It seemed to be regarding him with skepticism, as if it sensed he was an imposter but wasn't quite sure.

Then the moment passed; the seal lost interest in him and dipped beneath the waves and didn't resurface. Alex got back behind the wheel and fired up the engine. Instead of turning around and heading for the shipyards, he kept going toward the North Shore, his home, wearing nothing except his seal-skin cape, feeling aloof and alone and untouchable.

ANDREW MacDONALD

FOUR MINUTES

My twin sister is wearing a lace bra and lace panties that don't match. She expects me to know which one will turn on her boyfriend. She believes a combination of two separate styles is something he will find enticing.

"I don't know, they all look the same," I say, which is true. Underwear is a language I've never been able to speak properly.

Women in the underwear store are looking at us. A hefty employee occasionally comes over and asks if we need help. Zelda says no, the woman's opinion isn't the opinion she wants. It's my opinion she wants.

Or, actually, my ex-girlfriend's opinion.

"What would Emily want?" Zelda asks.

She comes outside, to the area between the change rooms and the store proper, wearing the mismatched underwear and tapping a kind of Morse code on her stomach.

This is common Zelda behaviour. Nudity as a concept is less confusing to her than the necessity of always being dressed.

"Put some clothes on, please," I say. "Or at least go over there so nobody else can see you."

She rests her head against the wall and makes a burbling sound.

"Tell me what Emily would wear."

I lie. I tell her Emily never wore underwear. The truth is, I don't remember what Emily wore, and this disturbs me. This fact disturbs me more than discussing what underwear my sister is going to wear when she loses her virginity. The imminent event is marked on the calendar beside the fridge.

Emily and Zelda always got along. Emily took Zelda for gelato and tried to teach her to read Russian, even though Zelda really can't even read English past a fourth grade level. They used to practise their signatures together, filling up page after page in the living room of the apartment. While Zelda's signature is a free-range farm of looping parabolas, Emily's has the tightness of a compressed accordion. According to an Internet website on graphology, Emily's small signature means she has good career aims and doesn't waste time or effort. Zelda's means she cannot face criticism.

"I like Emily," Zelda used to announce.

"Emily likes Zelda," Emily would say, making a mallet out of her hand and bonking it on Zelda's skull in a Three Stooges routine they'd worked out.

When Emily left me for her old college roommate's brother, Zelda asked why Emily didn't love me anymore.

"I don't know," I said. "People fall out of love some-times."

"Are you going to fall out of loving me?" Zelda asked.

We were watching a movie about penguins and for the first time since the baby penguins head-butted their way out of their shells she looked away from the TV and fixed her big baby blues on me.

"No, Zee," I said, pausing the penguin movie so she wouldn't miss a second of the birds sliding down ice dunes on their stomachs. "No, the love we have is a forever thing."

Culpability is a difficult concept to process. Zelda has drawn pictures of it. In some of them, me-as-fetus wears a cowboy hat and lassos her-as-fetus around the neck. According to the possibly inaccurate studies easily accessed on public library databases, thirty seconds of restricted oxygen can cause six per cent brain damage. When we were born, my umbilical cord choked her for four minutes.

The disability pension Zelda gets is enough to cover the apartment, while my job at the call centre, part-time for the time being, pays enough for our expenses. How Zelda saved up the money for her fancy underwear and her condoms and makeup is something I can't understand.

"Show me how to use the rubber thing again," Zelda says.

"I've already showed you three times," I say.

Then she frowns and flops on the couch, turning her back to me. I can tell she's pouting, making a show of it. We don't have any more bananas, so I use a carrot. She chastises me about using my teeth to open to condom wrapper.

"You said never to do that, since it could break the rubber thing."

"Good," I say, fumbling with the carrot. "You've passed test number one."

While putting the condom on the carrot, pinching the top like they say in the pamphlets you get at Planned Parenthood, the end of the carrot accidentally pokes through the rubber. Zelda laughs, I laugh, and suddenly the world isn't a place where terrible things arrive in waves. It's a nice, wholesome place where vegetables are responsible enough to use protection.

In the car Zelda wants me to tell her about my first time again. She thinks it was with Emily because I didn't have the heart to tell her it was with a person I didn't know, someone I met at a bar when I first came of age. Zelda believes people mate for life, just like swans.

"Did it hurt?" she asks.

Zelda's like baroque painters in this regard, obsessed with the human capacity for suffering. The drawings she makes suggest losing virginity is right up there with waterboarding on the Harvard pain scale. The faces of her mating stick-creatures are corkscrews of agony. They end up on the fridge with the rest of her crayoned artwork.

Once, when I was drunk, I told her the details and now I can't leave anything out or she'll get mad. Sex was so new to me I actually tore some of the skin on myself and bled everywhere. I wonder if there's a particular recliner in hell for brothers who tell their sisters things like this on the night they're supposed to lose their virginity.

"Do you think Marxy is like that?" Zelda asks. She sounds out every word. "Circumcised? Was Dad circumcised?"

"'Unknown' to both questions."

I turn on the radio, hoping Zelda gets that I don't want to talk anymore.

She walked in on Emily and me having sex once. At that particular point in our relationship, things had only just started to acquire the mist native to polluted relationships. The time we spent together was like a pre-op phase that preceded to the white picket fence. We talked often of down payments for condominiums in those days, of future advancements made in the name of our relationship. I'd found a ring made of endlessly folded Canadian silver topped with a speck of diamond that was delicate seeming but sturdy, an understated geological wonder that reminded me of Emily. I'd squirrelled away almost eight grand to pay for it.

We had been watching a documentary, Emily and I. I'd put Zelda to bed and could tell from Emily's eyes that amorous activity was on the horizon. She'd been inspired partly by the beauty of a pair of snails mating on the *Planet Earth* DVD, the one about rainforests. The things oozed out of their shells, turning an almost crystal blue as they hung from a tree on an ever-stretching teardrop of goo and coiled around each other until the body of one was imperceptible from that of the other.

"Shit, that's romantic," I said.

One had to acknowledge it: for invertebrates with underdeveloped nervous systems, they sure knew how to fornicate.

"It's been a bit," Emily said, lifting up my shirt and making a pink mess of my navel with her fingernails. "I think it's time we got like the snails and synthesize."

In long-term relationships, what excites must be cherished,

be it the muse wing-tipped garden clogs or gobs of mating snails. We went at it with a kind of brutality, a violence of entwining limbs. Normally we used rubbers. This round we didn't seem to have time. Our lovemaking became a thing so grand neither of us noticed Zelda awestruck under the door's arch. She caught my eyes and waved.

"Howdy," she announced, snapping me out of rhythm.

"What did we say about fucking knocking?" I shouted. I threw a shoe that damaged her cornea so severely we had to take her to the hospital.

"What were you thinking?" Emily kept asking.

They were both in the back seat of the car, Emily cooing soothingly in my sister's ear. Every so often she dabbed at a mark I'd left on her neck, a cross-hatch of blood vessels popped under the skin by my sucking lips.

I told her I didn't know, even though I did know: even then, I could feel her turning to air. If pressed to triangulate the exact moment Emily stopped loving me, all signs pointed here.

Occasionally, Emily still calls to ask how Zelda is doing. The other day we had a conversation about Zelda and the Marxy kid making their own two-backed beast. My reasoning is this: if Emily thinks the sex shouldn't happen, she can tell Zelda and nobody will have to go through with anything.

"I don't follow your lingo, Scotty. Is two-backed beast an arts-and-crafts activity?"

Zelda liked making things out of other people's waste. She spent every Tuesday at the local community centre, with people a third her age, surrounded by mountains of multi-coloured construction paper spaghetti.

I still fall into thinking of her as a child, something Emily endlessly chastised me about.

"She has a right to be sexually active. It's going to happen whether you consent or not. At least this way you'll be there."

"Like those needle containers in public libraries," I say.

"Come again?"

The public library downtown has this fluorescent container in one of its bathroom stalls, a hazardous waste sticker stamped on the side. The idea is, if you're up to any intravenous activities, say plucking your arm with a heroin needle, you can dispose of whatever's punctured your veins in these safety buckets.

Emily makes a chortling spit sound into the phone.

"It's for diabetics, fool."

"Or addicts. Have you ever seen a diabetic shooting insulin in the library? Not I. But I've seen junkies wiping their asses with encyclopedia pages when a fresh roll of toilet paper is in the next stall. It's the idea that you should facilitate something potentially problematic, say a drop box for dirty drug needles, which could just increase the problem and encourage more junkies to do more drugs. On the other hand, the library ostensibly would be a safer space, since there ostensibly would be less needles lying around for toddlers to swallow and the like."

"Ostensibly."

"Correct."

At this point I feel partially redeemed for being disgusting. Emily repeating my words back to me had always signified a solidarity of opinion, especially when it came to words that she didn't use much herself in her everyday life. In the two years we were together, plus the year of courting, plus the four months since we'd parted ways, I have never heard her say "ostensibly."

"I love you still," I say.

"It's not even remotely the same thing," Emily says. "If you're arguing that they're the same thing, what you're doing is saying that Zelda having a sex life equals junkies shooting up in public and leaving their diseased fucking needles everywhere. Which is a complete and utter bullshit thing to say about your sister, Scott."

She stops.

"And don't ever say that again."

"About Zelda?"

"About loving me still. Now I have to go. It's your decision as to what to do. But if she calls me and asks me to help her, I will help her. Sex can actually be beautiful and an expression of love."

Emily hangs up. In between punching the wall and regretting punching the wall, I notice Zelda has been doodling pictures of naked four-limbed upright creatures that could, ostensibly, be taken for humans engaged in various gravity-defying acts of sex.

"Emily says hi," I say, stepping over the pornography in search of a Corona. "And FYI: it doesn't look like that. Just so you know. It looks like this." I make my fingers into a gun and blow my own brains out. Zelda laughs and mimics the movement before falling on her back. The gun in her hand becomes a fist she starts licking. It's a joke Emily taught her, a parody of an old me who used to overrate the use of the tongue while kissing.

I crack open my Corona on the edge of the dining room table, thwacking off a small spear of wood. Zelda has stopped laughing.

"We all miss Emily," she says to one of her drawings, this one incomplete – a pair of headless, legless torsos sporting capes and breasts.

The clerk at the motel swivels around in his chair lazily. His fingers shine with the dust of potently flavoured Cheez Doodles, the sheen glowing when he licks each pad individually. His name tag is something incomprehensible, either *Pat* or *Tat* or *Clat.*

"Is there some kind of convention?" the clerk asks, clacking on the keyboard with his orange fingers.

"Pardon?"

"Of them."

He points his pen at Zelda, who's found an itch on herself that seems to travel from her ear to her neck to her shoulder. She walks around the lobby, examining the framed black and white photographic reproductions of Paris in the 1930s. Her dress already has a mystery stain on her ribs.

"If you are going to say 'retards,' or gesture verbally in that direction, I think we're going to have a problem here."

The clerk shrugs, possibly stoned, possibly still thinking of saying 'retard' but not prepared to deal with the repercussions of doing so.

"I was going to say people dressed up for prom."

"Good." I hand him my credit card. "That's the correct answer."

We make our way down the motel's L-shaped corridor that winds around what could be a leisure area, the concrete pool cracked and empty, not much more than a gouge, discarded swimming paraphernalia scattered around the pool's gums.

We find our room on the second floor, right across from where Zelda's boyfriend and his mother are staying. After setting up base camp in our room, we cross the hall and Zelda slaps at the door.

Marxy participates in Zelda's biweekly social group for younger adults with developmental issues. He is taller than I remember, hair Brylcreemed to the left in a side part that belongs in the late fifties. Unlike Zelda, who could "pass" unless you really gave her a hard stare, Marxy wears his condition irrefutably, just enough features exaggerated to tip you off. Zelda had introduced us a few times when I picked her up from her group. Still, he's cleaned up nice and makes a passable Casanova, holding flowers out to Zelda when he opens the door.

"Well howdy, partner," I say, standing awkwardly to the side as Zelda kisses him in a way that approximates the techniques she's been practising on her fist. Normally, I would jimmy myself between them, a human prophylactic. A voice eerily similar to Emily's echoes in my brain, saying, What's the point? In two hours' time, things will have reached critical mass between them.

The woman I assume to be Marxy's mother appears behind him, nudging past them both to shake my hand.

"You must be Scotty."

She introduces herself as Pearl. Her fingers are clammy in my hands, though warm to the touch. From the way she wrote her emails I thought she might have been a teenager; no grown woman I've met indulges in that many emoticons and that many apostrophe-less contractions. But she's not a teenager. The best way to describe her would be: woman, fully grown and languid. I have trouble imagining Marxy being brewed in her uterus.

From an objective standpoint, factoring in age, Pearl is not bad looking. Her hair is blond and she has fairly high cheek-bones, which men are supposed to find appealing. A part of me is glad I'm taller than she is. The bow on her bra, the fringe of which I can see from under my sunglasses, is a different kind of fabric than the rest of the bra, some kind of fluffy stuff knitted together.

Marxy and Zelda quit kissing and we all migrate into the hotel room.

"Drinks, anyone?" Pearl asks, lifting a bottle of Jack Daniel's. Marxy raises his hand, so Zelda raises her hand. Soon I'm the only one not raising a hand.

"Maybe we should save that for later," I suggest, even though the fog of a good buzz might make the situation seem more reasonable. Zelda has never been drunk, as far as I know. She turns and pulls on the skin of my elbow, tugging the excess skin taut. With her other hand she holds Marxy's hand.

"Please?" she asks.

"One nip or two can't hurt," Pearl says, already pouring out four plastic cups.

Irrespective of one's gender, erections are a difficult thing to avoid staring at. As Marxy walks around, his penis announces itself against the fabric of his suit pants.

"I think it's cute," Pearl says. "It shows he's passionate, in love with your sister."

The television is tuned to one of those adult music channels that plays songs that are the audio equivalent of what lava lamps are to the eye.

Marxy and Zelda have started dancing, vaguely approximating a box step. Neither of them knows much how to lead. As they turn, Marxy's erection moves like the dial of a compass.

"Zelda's sweet," Pearl says, flopping down on the bed next to me. She kicks off her heels and starts massaging one of her calves. "She's a few IQ points over Marxy, but on the whole I think they're pretty compatible."

I swish the whiskey between my teeth and swallow the burning.

"Seems that way."

"She didn't get enough oxygen, that right? Some umbilical cord issue?"

I nod.

"It wrapped around her neck."

She puts back her drink and pours another few fingers into her cup. The song shifts to a slow, grinding song that confuses Marxy and Zelda. He wants to keep the old pace, while she's already adjusting to the change in rhythm. Eventually they synchronize, bumping against each other like billiard balls.

The deal was I'd pay for the room, while Pearl and I sit tight, make pleasantries, and wait for nature to run its course.

"Zelda and Scott," Pearl says. She's got a deck of cards and does a professional job of shuffling them, cards spitting from one pile to the other in a pink-checkered blur. "Why does that sound familiar?"

"Ever read *Gatsby*?"

"Not since high school."

"F. Scott Fitzgerald wrote it. The love interest in it's based on his wife, Zelda."

"Named after a married couple?"

Pearl deals out a handful of cards, sculpting them into two piles. I'm not sure what we're playing but fan the cards out anyway. Pearl flips over a card from the deck and snaps it on the bed between us.

Without meaning to, I start thinking about how it might feel to wakeboard my tongue down the contours of her chest. In the months since Emily parachuted into someone else's life I'd only made it with one other woman, as easy to recollect now as a window smudge. We'd been drunk and flailing, the last two people at a martini bar with a jukebox that played only Brit pop. The number she left sat unnoticed in my pants for days. By the time I'd remembered it, the washing machine had smelted it to gummy paste.

"I'm drunk," I say, putting my cards down, slurping the booze through the filter of my teeth.

"Figured as much. You've been putting those back like you mean it."

Instead of crumpling, the plastic cup splits into the shards when I give it a squeeze.

"How do you suppose they're doing over there?"

"Fine, I imagine. I gave Marxy a two-hour lecture on how to treat a lady, how to put a condom on, how not to neglect the sweet spots on a lady's body."

"Jesus."

I stand up and scan the room for another plastic cup. Pearl leans back, using her arms to buttress herself. A slug of a vein pokes up from under her skin, right near the elbow.

"One of the things I learned straight off, having someone like Marxy, someone who'll never be like other people, is that you need to accept the reality while doing your best to improve things. Do I think it's completely normal for a mother to be teaching her son how to do finger tricks to please a woman? The pope would not approve. But if I don't show him, who will? He can't even spell his own name right more than thirty per cent of the time."

The glow coming from the half-lit sign outside the motel hits Pearl's face in a strange way, and for a minute she could be made of freshly blown glass. In that glow I reach out for her thigh. We both seem surprised when I make contact.

"We should probably put the brakes on," she says. "I told my therapist I'd stop doing this kind of thing."

She doesn't elaborate on how I went from very good brother to a thing.

She gets up, flicks on the TV, and sits over in the other bed. A laugh track pulses from the channel. Pearl messes her hair.

"Are you a fan of improvisational comedy?"

"She died a horrible death," I say.

"Who?"

"Zelda Fitzgerald. Was in a mental institution waiting to be zapped by electroshock when a fire broke out. She was caught inside and got burnt to a crisp."

The look on her face is like a photograph of the look I'd seen a hundred times on Emily's. Am I trying to be funny or am I secretly praying for locusts to descend over the evening and make the sky black.

"Aren't you a ray of sunshine this evening," Pearl says, flopping back on the bed.

—

Sometime while watching skits on television I fall asleep. No dreams come to me, just jets of colours – par for the course when I've been into the drink. Blue, purple, red, my brain projecting for me a buzzing panorama. None of them make it clear to my dream-self that my sister is in another room, making love or screwing or fucking someone.

I've never owned a cat, but they say the awful creatures have modulated their howls to replicate the sound of babies wailing, a Darwinian trick that makes them impossible to ignore even when you're asleep. Something about babies and crying hard-wired into the circuitry of our brains, a secret code delicately folded into the meat of our limbic systems.

Waking up, I can think only two things are happening: either a cat's fallen off something very tall and landed on its head, or a particular kind of sicko is doing a very bad thing to an infant.

"Just relax, honey," Pearl is saying, ushering in a haze of nakedness I come to recognize as my sister. Her body shivers, hiccups. She's got tears making a glimmering mess of her face. Soon Marxy rumbles into the room, a towel around his waist.

"Stay a ways back, Marxy," Pearl says.

Marxy's hair is still stiff to one side. He's crying, too.

"I did what you said, the way you said," he announces to the air.

"It's okay, just sit over there."

Pearl wraps a blanket around Zelda. Marxy doesn't even notice me. For all I know, I'm just a figment of his imagination. Zelda rolls up into a little walnut shape, squeezing her legs together around her hands. This is the shape of something that's suffered, I decide.

And it occurs to me, just then, that Marxy's face might

make an ideal landing pad for the ridges of my fist. I complete the operation quickly, the interaction of our bones echoing the sound Tupperware containers make when they're opened very quickly.

And so I see red. The sound of my fist hitting Marxy's nose is the only external stimulus that makes it through to my brain.

Instantly I understand that there has been a kind of miscalculation here. Pearl turns herself into a human shield, using the hem of her untucked blouse as a cork to stop the blood coming out of Marxy's nose. Marxy whimpers, curling into a nautilus shell.

Something has gone wrong. Brothers do things for their sisters. They take action when action is required. Should a bullet whistle through the air, on a trajectory heading for the sister's forehead, brothers must react in such a way as to negate the bullet. They must discover gaps in the theory of relativity. They must thwart Newton's laws. There is a theory that once every eleven billion times you drop a pencil, the pencil will rise instead of fall.

"No," Zelda starts up. She's yelling not at me but to various objects around the room. She sweeps the coffee machine onto the carpet. She throws the remote into the ice bucket, where it bobs like the carcass of a long-dead sea creature.

Zelda falls onto Marxy, a shawl expanding over him. Her back has Marxy's handprints on it. I can see the chorus of pink fingertips from my end of the room. From here, they are each very distinct, and each very far away.

KEVIN HARDCASTLE

OLD MAN MARCHUK

Two narrow beams of halogen light crisscrossed over the black prairie, found the warped and weathered sideboards of old man Marchuk's barn. An eerie blue round settled over the chained and padlocked barndoor handles. Up into the light rose a three-foot boltcutter. One man held the flashlight steady. One man slid the cutter-blades over the padlock shackle and squeezed hard on either handle. He had to reset twice before he'd cut through. The man with the light fussed with the lock until he freed it and could pull the chains clear. Then he pocketed the flashlight in his coveralls while he dragged the great barn doors open, his face lit like a jack-o'-lantern.

The cutter man had gotten to their one-ton pickup and he was backing it over toward the barnmouth, pushing a tow trailer by the hitch. He stopped short enough for the other man to loose and unfold the ramp to the trailer. The man in the truck waited while his partner hotwired a pair of four-wheelers and drove the first up the ramp onto the trailer bed, engine growling high. He parked it and went back for the other. Drove it into place and shut the engine off. The driver of the truck drummed the windowframe and watched, red cherry of his smoke glowing in the black. The other man raised the trailer ramp and fixed it shut. He started for the passenger side of the truck and froze three steps out.

They'd not heard the squelching of bootfalls in the thaw-mud near the barn. Not until the old man was right on top of them with his twelve-gauge raised high, stock pinned against his shoulder. Marchuk pulled and sprayed the driver's door. Muzzlefire showed him briefly against the outer blackness. The driver barked like a dog, ducked low and tried to cover up. Marchuk took aim again. The young man at the rear of the truck pitched his flashlight and it flew end over end past old man Marchuk's wild-haired head. Marchuk spun and fired blindly at the spot. The young man dropped to the muck and shrieked. He'd taken a shot in the side and through his upper leg, but he managed to clamber onto the trailer and fall in behind the last four-wheeler just as his buddy punched the gas and sent the truck tires spinning. The old man had shucked his spent shells and set about reloading the firearm. Marchuk emptied both barrels on the truck and its trailer as the vehicle sped off serpentine through his fenceless backfields.

He came upon the trailered vehicle not ten miles down the county road. The driver sped just slightly and held the road straight. Marchuk drove an old Dodge pickup and he had his running lights turned off. He drifted up alongside the larger truck until he could see both men sitting stung in the cab. When the driver turned and saw the old man coasting along beside him he panicked and swerved wide, caught the edge of the roadside drainage ditch and pulled back. The trailer nearly jackknifed before skittering back in line on the weatherbuckled asphalt. Old man Marchuk cut into the other lane and the driver of the one-ton chickened out and slammed his brakes, went too far wide this time and ended up ploughing sandied ditchturf for about a hundred feet before the vehicle shuddered to a stop. Marchuk got out with the scattergun and pumped holes through the driver door.

Constable Tom Hoye got the call from dispatch and had to floor it from two townships over. He saw four red eyes in the road and then felt a series of little thuds on the car's undercarriage. He drove on. The constable had lately been stationed at the lonely RCMP detachment that served the county, with its three-man rotation and one dispatch to cover four barren townships. They got calls of gunfire a few times a week and heard gunfire every night. That night was the first they'd gotten a call from the man who actually fired the shots, and that man went by the name of Marchuk. Hoye took the details as he drove.

"What's he sayin' he shot at?" Hoye said.

"Two men tryin' to steal his ATVs," said the girl at dispatch. "But he's not sayin' he shot at them. He's sayin' he shot them."

"What?"

"How far out are you?"

"Seven or eight minutes. Where's the EMT?"

"They won't be a minute behind you if at all."

When constable Hoye pulled up to the scene he saw the one-ton tipped over in the ditch, shrapnel and shards of windowglass that shone like stars by the light of the cruiser's headlamps. Marchuk was leaning up against the side of his own truck, one foot crossed over the other, cradling his shotgun in the crook of his arm. The old man put one hand up against the headlights. Constable Hoye got out of the car with his hand on his pistol. He flicked the safety off as he stood. Marchuk just waited there, taking the air as the constable came over. Plains wind travelled warm and gentle through the pass. The faint sound of ambulance sirens called out from afar.

"Set your firearm down on the ground and step away," Hoye said.

Marchuk frowned at him. Hoye had to pull his pistol and let it hang before the old man knelt and laid the weapon down on the tarmac. The constable waited until Marchuk stepped clear and then he gestured for him to keep going.

"Put your hands on the hood of your truck," he said.

"Son, you are wastin' my time," the old man said.

"Put your fuckin' hands on the hood I said. And stay put."

Marchuk sauntered over and did it, slapping his palms down like a showy child. He stood there in his coveralls, sandpaper beard and huge, crooked nose. Hoye passed him and stepped down into the ditch. Took his flashlight out of his belt and turned it on. When he shone the beam over the ditchhill he saw pieces of the truck's upholstery scattered across the turf like cottongrass, a full section of door siding with thin furrows in the mould. Then he saw the two shot men. One was on his side in the ditchbasin, his legs shuffling. The other lay starfished against the hillside in his bandit-blacks and he didn't move at all.

"Jesus fuckin' Christ," Hoye said.

He started to go for the men and then he stopped and lev-
elled his pistol at Marchuk. The old man took his hands off the
hood and put them up until Hoye barked at him to put them
back. The constable came back into the road and took out his
cuffs and braceletted the old man's bony wrists.

"Just what the fuck are ye doin', son?" said Marchuk.

"You shot those men?"

"They were robbin' me."

"Your farm is fuckin' three miles thataway," Hoye said,
nodding south.

The old man stared at him sourfaced. The back of his
scraggly head lit up in colours. An EMT wagon crested a rise
in the roadway and coasted toward them. Hoye stepped out
into the lane and waved it down.

He came home an hour before sunrise, the sky paling to the
east. The constable and his wife had rented a two-storey
brownstone with no house number. Just their name stencilled
on the mailbox. Their nearest neighbour was a gravel quarry
some three miles away. Hoye parked the cruiser on the driveway and went into the house through the side-porch entrance.
He hung his keys and undressed, hung his jacket and his
Kevlar over the back of a wooden dining table chair. Laid his
pants overtop, flat to the crease. Then he went to the fridge
and knuckled up two bottles of beer. He sat on the living room
couch with the TV on but nearly inaudible. The bottles were
empty after maybe five pulls so he got up to grab another.

Hoye's eyes had turned to slits when the stairwell groaned
behind him. He stood up and saw his wife descending slowly,
tiny bubble of tongue bit between her lips as she concentrated

on landing each footfall. She followed a dogleg near the stair-bottom and made her way down the last three steps. The young woman stood maybe five-foot-three with copper hair and a round, round belly pushing up the cloth of her nightie.

"Hey," she said. "Nice outfit."

Hoye stood there in his gitch, his blues unbuttoned and his undershirt showing. He had the legs of a quarterhorse.

"What time is it, Jenny?" he said.

"It's not morning and it's not night," she said.

He watched her shuffle past the couch and she eyed him sidelong as she went. She started smiling, deep dimple at her right cheek.

"If you sneezed I think you might pop," he said.

"Are you gonna go to bed or what?" she said.

"I didn't really think that far ahead."

"What happened out there?"

"That old fella Marchuk pumped about six rounds of buck-shot into two city boys who were stealin' his ATVs."

"My God," she said. "Are they alive?"

He nodded.

"Somehow."

"How was he when you took him?"

"He didn't think he did nothin' wrong."

She went into the kitchen and he heard the cupboards open-ing and closing. He came in to help her but she shooed him. Hoye got behind his wife and put his arms around her shoul-ders, held the belly in his big hands, his chin pinned to her shoulder blade. She reached up and cupped his cheek.

"Get off me you big oaf," she said, but she didn't move. Finally he kissed her neck and stood up tall, let her loose.

"Go to bed for a couple hours," Jenny said. "I'm not going anywhere."

So he did.

The two young burglars didn't die but came about as close to it as they could. The driver lost one of his feet and the meat of his right triceps and he had nerve damage throughout. The other burglar flatlined three times during surgery and that was after he'd almost bled out in the ambulance. They were under police guard and would be until they were fit for trial. But not their trial. They had pled guilty by proxy and were sentenced to community service and probation. The trial they awaited was Marchuk's. The old man had been arraigned and pled not guilty before cussing out the court and the sitting judge.

The old man had lands and money enough to post his bail-bond, high as it was, but some folks from that township and those that bordered somehow anted up the cost and posted for him. On a pretty autumn day Marchuk left the station-house shaking his head and then he drove back to his farm in his old Dodge. There he took back the tending of his property from cousins who had driven in from north-interior British Columbia. They didn't go back. Instead they shacked up with him and awaited the trial.

The first attack against Hoye was no more than the rude spray painting of the words "Eastern Pig" on his garage door. He managed to acetone the graffiti clear before his wife got a chance to see it. Hoye heard rumblings of who might have done it and he let it be known that the drinking age in that county was about to be enforced nightly. Fines to be given out

and liquor to be confiscated. Two weeks later somebody tore
up the sideyard of his house by spinning doughnuts all over the
crabgrassed turf. It happened when he was out on patrol and
when he got home he found Jenny on the porch steps with a
pump shotgun on her lap. Shells in a line on the wooden planking beside her. He had to talk a long time before he could get
his gun back. They went inside and sat together in the kitchen.

"What, are they retarded or something?" she said.

"They just ain't accustomed to having someone tell them
no. But they're gonna figure it out real quick."

Jenny sipped at a glass of water, the fingers of her right hand
lightly stained with gungrease.

"He nearly killed those kids."

"They think it was justified."

"We don't live in Texas."

"If we did he'd still be locked up. They would've had to be
inside his house for him to open fire."

"How much longer do we have before you can pick a new
station?"

"One year, three months, and eighteen days."

Jenny stood up slowly. Took up his empty beer bottle and
carried it over to the counter. She got him another from the
fridge and set it down.

"I just hope they quit it."

Hoye pulled hard on the bottle, set it down on the kitchen
table and stared at it. At the rough hand holding it.

"They will," he said.

Jenny Hoye drove over an hour to get to the nearest big-box
store. She took trips there weekly to load up on diapers and

formula, toiletries, other household necessaries. From those narrow, sunbaked roads she saw miles and miles of short-grassed dunes, low-rolling plains with not a pond or trickle of river. Rare sightings of stunted trees with their barks dried and sloughing. Remains of groundhogs and coyotes on the macadam or otherwise strewn in the roadside gravel. Once in a while a lonely oil-field pumpjack with its counterweight turning anticlockwise and its steel horsehead dipping low and rising again. There was a base and barracks in the town and on her visits she would see men in army camos trailing their wives down the aisles, some upright and solemn and others leaning down heavy to the carthandles as they shoved along.

She filled her cart and pushed it to the checkout line. When she rung through a young stockboy with a hairlip asked her if she needed a hand getting out. Jenny told him thanks but she'd be okay. He smiled shyly and went on. She wheeled the cart out into the lot and found her parking spot. As she was loading the trunk she heard someone calling her name. Jenny turned to see a young woman hailing her from across the lot.

"Fuck," she said.

On the way home she saw a four-door pickup in her rear-view mirror and it stayed there. Monster tires and a heavy steel grillguard. Mud and muck on the hood and windshield. Jenny drove through town and took a turn that she didn't need to take and the truck kept on straight. She snaked home through the county roads and there on the last length of dirt lane the jacked-up truck stood idling at an intersection, not a half-mile from her house. It pulled into the lane behind her and followed close. She could see sunburned forearms hanging thick on either side of the vehicle. There were at least four men, two in front and the rest in back. She nearly drove on past the house but cut a hard right at the last second and skittered onto the gravel driveway. The truck slowed but kept on. Four sets of eyes on the woman as she got out and studied the vehicle and the muddied British Columbia plates. A gun rack had been fixed in the back window of the truck and all the brackets were full.

Hoye pulled into the farm's frontlot at dusk with two cruisers trailing him. He saw lamplight through the thin-curtained upper windows. Brighter lights in the kitchen. The sound of country music and raised voices travelling raucous from an open side door. There was no proper driveway, just a ruined patch of land in front of the house filled with vehicles. Battered pickups and rusted-out car frames on blocks and a gargantuan RV parked sidelong to the house, power cables running between the two like tentacles. A raised, extended-cab pickup with B.C. plates. Hoye pulled in first and the other cars followed. Each cruiser rode two officers and they got out armed and armoured and Hoye took two of them toward that kitchen side-entry. Hoye was certain that there would be dogs to give them away early, but there were not.

When they walked in through the kitchen screen door it squealed on its springs. Four men sat at a massive oak-slab table with bottles of beer and whiskey staining the lumber. Two women were tending the stove. One middle-aged and greying, stout and squarejawed. The other young and dirty blonde and very pretty, a scattering of old pox-scars on her cheek and forehead. Hoye and his two constables came into the room and spread out, eyeballed the foreign men, hands on the heels of their pistols. A door shut somewhere in the back of the house and soon enough the three other constables filled the doorway at the other side of the kitchen. Hoye knocked a stack of papers from a nearby chair where it sat below a wall-mounted rotary phone. He spun the chair to the table and sat. Across from him sat old man Marchuk and he tried to stare a hole through Hoye. Black, biblical hate in his eyes. Hoye just stared back.

"You know that there's warrants out for your cousins here, from B.C., and they're to be escorted to the border and placed in custody there."

"That is a load of horseshit," Marchuk said. "What for?"

"I've got 'Fight Causing a Disturbance' for a Bretton Marchuk and 'Cultivation of Marijuana' for Gary Myshaniuk and Mark Oulette. The rest can just go in for assisting wanted fugitives."

"They're my guests and they aren't goin' anywheres. So you can go fuck yourself. You ain't got no warrant or cause to come into my house."

"We don't need a warrant to seize the wanted men. But I'll be kind and give them a chance to drive their asses outta here to the border under escort. Or they could get shot instead in this fuckin' kitchen for all I care. Seems to be a way of life for you folks."

Marchuk tried to get out of his chair and Hoye stood and sat him back down by the shoulder.

Old man Marchuk was taken into custody and locked up in the station holding cell while his cousins were driven west, handed off from detachment to detachment until they were released to officers from Golden. Bretton Marchuk had a broken nose plugged with bloody tissue when he was put under arrest inside British Columbia. The other men were marked with facial lacerations and contusions along their forearm and shinbones. The elder woman, wife to the cousin Marchuk, spat at one of the b.c. constables and then watched her husband take a baton to both of his knees. She held her spit from then on. The constables released the younger, blonde woman alone, and let her take the truck back to their lands in the foothills.

Marchuk saw his bail rescinded and spent his days and nights in holding at the Red Deer Remand Centre. He got letters and visits from townsfolk. Few people would speak to Hoye or his wife, any of the other officers or their families, even those born in that township. Hoye did not mind. One day he found their lawn staked with dozens of "For Sale" signs. He pulled them and stacked them in the garage.

On shift near Daysland, Constable Hoye had his radio flare up and the dispatch told him that his wife had been taken by ambulance to the hospital in Red Deer. Jenny Hoye had gone into labour nearly a full month early. The constable lit his sirens and drove those black nightroads with the gas pedal pinned. He pulled into the hospital lot just before midnight and found triage, took directions to the labour and delivery rooms.

Hoye wore scrubs over his uniform and they let him into delivery. Jenny gripped his hand hard. Her hair had gone dark with sweat and stuck to her forehead. She had taken no epidural and had just begun to crown. Hoye bent to better see her face. He wiped her brow with a wet cloth and tried to get the hair from her eyes.

"It's alright, Jenny," he said.

"Oh, fuck this," she said.

The doctors had her breathe and push. She hollered and swore and gritted her teeth. Again and again until the baby's shoulders cleared. The boy was born blue with the umbilical wound tight around his neck and upper arm. The doctors went to work unwinding the cord. Jenny had gone pale and stared at the little shut eyelids and the soft skin of his discoloured arms. Blood and mucous on her gown and at her inner thighs. Constable Hoye could barely stand and he waited cold by the hospital bed. It took four minutes for the baby to breathe and when he did he spoke in a wail and reached out with his tiny arms, cycled his feet in the air.

The constable watched his wife and son through the night and spoke to the attending doctors. The boy had no ill effects from the tangled cord and he'd been born heavy for a premature baby, had a strong heart and lungs to cry with. Hoye left in the morning and he hadn't slept at all. He went to the house with a list and gathered things for his wife. He stood over the patch of kitchen floor where Jenny had been when her water broke. He didn't know whether to clean it or not. After passing it by a few times on his rounds Hoye filled a bucket with soapy water and bleach and started mopping the tile.

Jenny stayed with the baby in the maternal and newborn unit of the hospital for the better part of two weeks. Constable Hoye came every day between shifts or he had another constable cover while he left his watch for an hour or two. He spoke to his son in whispers while Jenny slept.

The Marchuk trial had been set for a neutral, closed court in Calgary. It started on a Tuesday morning and did not look like it would last a week, so shoddy was the defense. Hoye gave testimony on the third day of the trial and when he came home he found his mailbox rent apart, pebbles of buckshot rattling around inside the deformed container when he pried it clear from the post. He flung it into the garage and drove to the hardware store in town.

The clerk limped slightly as he took Hoye down the shelf rows. A tall man of nearly seventy with a white moustache and short-cropped hair. He had no glasses but seemed to need some more than a little. He showed Hoye toward the mailboxes, most of them antiquated and covered in light dust. Hoye picked out the plainest one and followed the old man toward the buckets of screws and fasteners.

"Heard you had a boy," the man said.

"We did."

The clerk offered his hand. Hoye took it. Hoye was of the same height and wider by a foot but the old man's hand outsized his by far.

"You gonna raise him here?"

"Likely not," Hoye said.

The clerk smiled a little and stood with his knuckles to his hips, picked a stray bolt from a bin and put it back where it belonged. They started back toward the register. Hoye held up.

"Hang on a minute," he said.

Hoye went back to where he'd been shown the mailboxes and he came back to the counter with a second. The clerk had set the first on the woodtop beside the till. Hoye handed him the other and the man nodded and started to tally it all. He found a cardboard box behind the counter and filled it with the goods. Hoye paid him in cash.

"I suppose I don't have to tell you to be careful out there," the clerk said.

"No. But I appreciate it."

"It's not the whole town that's sided against you, young man, or even the half of it. But those that have are awful loud. If you know what I mean."

Hoye nodded and shook the clerk's hand again.

"If you run through those two just come back and I'll get you another, on the house."

Hoye laughed. Waved at the clerk as he went out the door. Wind chimes jangled where they hung from the lintel.

On a dry and sunbleached afternoon Constable Hoye pulled up to his homestead with his wife and newborn son. He'd been given a week's worth of leave. A cruiser waited at the roadside near the house. Hoye stopped to say hello and the constable in the other cruiser made faces at the baby in the backseat, the little boy in a safety chair beside his mother. The other constable shook Hoye's hand.

"How're you all handling it?" Hoye said.

"They got a fella from up near Viking that makes his rounds a little further south. He don't seem to mind. Shifts go long they're givin' us OT."

"Well, thank 'em for me will ya."

"Sure," the constable said. "Keep your radio nearby. Anything comes up I'll squawk at ya."

Hoye nodded and drove on, turned onto the width of gravel in front of the house. The cruiser crept out and took off down the county road. Hoye parked and came around the car to help Jenny. He wore her many bags and bundles on his arms as if he were a clothes maiden. Jenny took the boy up in her arms and swaddled him to her chest and neck. She turned him slow so that he could stare out goggle-eyed at the fields and fence-wires and hovering birds.

"We get a new mailbox?" she said.

Hoye stood there with the bags dangling. He nodded.

"Old one sort of blew in. So I got another, pegged it down a little sturdier."

Jenny studied the box some more and then she kissed the baby on his pale and peachfuzzed head and went down the walk to the house. Hoye kicked the car door shut with the toe of his shoe.

Hoye lay in the bed until they both slept. When he got up he went quiet as he could, clicking sound in his knees and his left ankle joint. He turned at the door and saw the dent in the mattress where he rested his bones of a night, his tiny son but inches from it, curled up and pinned to his wife. It hurt his heart just to look at her there, wild haired as she was in sleep, snoring lightly, so much bigger than their boy. It flooded hollows in him. Cold travelled along his spine and short ribs. He didn't want to leave but he did. He'd found cargo shorts in the laundry hamper and put them on, along with a clean undershirt. He went through the dark house and he knew it less by touch than he should have.

—

Out on the driveway he sat, garage door open to a tiny night-light and a fridge of cold beer. Crickets had gotten into the garage and they trilled from their hiding spots. He had an old poker table set up with cans of beer in every cup holder, a bottle of Irish whiskey standing quarter-empty on the felt. The Remington pump lay on a wooden crate beside his chair, five cartridges in the magazine. Chinook wind blew warm across the prairie, slowly spun a crooked weathervane that had been long ago fixed atop the high front gable of the house. Hoye had his Kevlar on over his cottons and the shirtcloth clung to his stomach and lower back. He heard distant reports of riflefire. High whine of small engines. Coyotes whooping at each other in a nearby field. Hoye sat there and watched either end of the long, country road. His portable CB radio sat on the table, silent except for sparse chatter between the dispatch and the constables as they roamed the territories.

CLEA YOUNG

JUVENILE

When Mia spots Pete on the ferry, seated in the forward lounge, she shouldn't recognize him – the shaved head, the golf shirt tucked in at the waist. She should glance at him without slowing (God help her, without stopping) and keep moving. She should be on to the next, next, next thing, not pouring toward him like water down a drain.

"Howdy-doody," Mia says.

Pete closes his magazine but doesn't stand to greet her. In fact, he doesn't even say hello. He offers the salutation's diminutive cousin: hi. Two letters. Bones on a plate. Mia notes the magazine in his lap, an entertainment weekly, the cover a collage of gowned celebrities. A feverish pink headline asks, Plastic Surgery?

"Funny," Mia says. "I'm always bumping into someone on this thing." She gestures wildly, throws her hand out into the aisle and smacks a kid's bony shoulder. "Sorry, I'm so sorry," she says to the kid, an unshakeable looking boy buried beneath a black fleece. He shrugs, keeps walking. Mia turns back to

Pete. What was she saying? But he offers no encouragement, no prompt. And then the captain is speaking, welcoming passengers aboard BC Ferries and promising whales off the starboard side.

"Well," she says, backing away slowly at first, then hurriedly. She's said too much already. Her right hand pops up to perform a little finger-dance, an idiotic toodle-oo.

Pete is flattered. It's been ten years but she's still flustered in his presence. His limbs grow warm, barbiturate-heavy. In high school Mia wrote him notes with scented markers and folded the foolscap into a series of triangles and tucks, which was what girls did then, before text messaging. Even now he half expects her to return and offer him one of her origami declarations, press it into his reluctant palm as if they're between classes, passing in the halls. He rarely read those notes but always granted his friends the pleasure. He liked to watch their eyes scanning for the good bits, the pathetic admissions – that Mia had skipped out on her mother's birthday at a downtown restaurant because he'd said he'd call – which his friends read aloud with a mixture of awe and disdain. Mia's devotion elevated Pete in the eyes of his peers. Outwardly they pitied him, she was such a cling-on, they said, but inwardly he knew they were jealous. The fact that she was always turning up, that his coldness didn't deter her, was testament to some power he possessed and the rest did not.

Pete returns to his magazine, the cover story featuring an actress's tanned and hefty cleavage. So what if they're fake? He thinks of his last girlfriend, a compact Asian woman with immaculate grooming. Every pore plucked of hair, every nail painted with professional artistry. She was mischievous and giving in bed, and, perhaps most incredibly, she didn't object when he hit on her friends. They'd dated close to a year and the end had only come about because he'd grown itchy for confrontation. Yet even at the party where he'd recklessly shepherded her younger sister into the bathroom, she'd maintained a hostess's anesthetized calm. Her resignation had reminded him of Mia. The time he buried her in his dirty laundry, two weeks' worth of sweaty ginch and rank socks. She'd actually stayed there while he showered. When he returned to dig her out, he found her pretending to be asleep.

Pete shifts in his seat, reaches inside his boxers, and brushes away the sand trapped beneath the waistband, those itchy but glorious grains leftover from Oyster Beach – the site of the long-weekend party where he ate pills and erected driftwood structures. Where he and his boyhood friend, Josh, danced frantically to severe music and patrolled the crowds with arms around one another's shoulders. Even Angie, Josh's fiancée, hadn't managed to stunt Pete's stride. After Josh was marshalled off to his tent, Pete continued, a lone wolf, grinding up against revellers who sometimes ground back.

The curiosity is killing him. Pete sacrifices his window seat and follows Mia down the crowded passageways. Even with the careful distance he maintains between them, he can see she's filled out in ways he would never have predicted. A waif of a girl, she now exudes permanence. Her ass is round and strong. She must run, or do yoga. Pliable, he thinks, recalling how he bent her body for his pleasure. She was awkward but always game. Now, watching her limbs whip through the crowd ahead of him, he marvels at how he once manipulated that body.

The ship's whistle sounds as the boat swings masterfully into Active Pass. On the outside deck, passengers belatedly protect their ears. Mia stops abruptly before one of the aquarium-sized windows as the Gulf Islands zoom into view; Pete dips into a stairwell to avoid being seen. He pulls his phone from his pocket and calls Josh. You'll never believe it, he wants to say, but Angie answers with a snide, "What do you want?" Pete hangs up. What the fuck? She probably checks Josh's email, too. Never, he tells himself, never will that happen to me.

Mia veers off in the direction she should never have strayed from, toward the cafeteria, located mid-ship. She clips around the slow-moving tourists, a local with intimate knowledge of the ship's amenities, the less-frequented washrooms, the best seats in the house. The engines have begun their throttle out into the Strait of Georgia. The surefootedness of land is behind her. It's not exactly a new sensation but it's been a while since she last experienced it: moving in the direction opposite the ship, backwards, makes her feel as if she isn't moving at all.

It's true, she thinks, she is always bumping into people on this thing. Once she inadvertently sat next to her grade six teacher who, sparing no details, told her of the nervous breakdown he'd suffered because of her class. Another time she found herself standing beside her grandmother's estranged sister before a bank of sinks in the washroom. Chance meetings, close encounters, until now they'd elicited only mild surprise, but this time, as she joins the cafeteria line, nausea bubbles up like reflux inside her and her hearing dampens; the din of the food service – the ladle falling back against the steel rim of the clam chowder bucket, the attendants conveying orders to the cooks – grows distant and flattens into two-dimensional natter. Mia slides her tray past the fountain pop and stops before the hot beverage station. What does she need? She plants her hands on the tray, still warm from the dish-washer, and tries to really consider this: the even keel of chamo-mile or the drop-kick of caffeine? The thrill of having Pete in her vicinity, of being able to walk past him and possibly exchange words, it was what she'd lived for. As she pulls the tap on the coffee urn she sees the paper cup in her hand shaking.

Pete had made her feel disgusting, too. The time he con-vinced her it was okay to have sex with a tampon still inside and she'd had to deliver herself to a clinic, into the exceedingly gentle hands of a medical student whose difficulty lay not in dislodging the cotton plug but in fathoming the circumstances that had seen it forced there in the first place. And here is Pete on the same boat, possibly remembering the same disgusting things. And here is her hand, shaking. Howdy-doody? Without a blip of warning, the world roars back to life. The line of customers behind her is a riot of ill manners. Suddenly she's starving. She craves starch. Mia abandons her tray and back-tracks toward the dessert fridge. Standing before the tidily packaged pieces of carrot cake and Nanaimo bars, she's bowled over with yearning. She sets her purse on the steel counter and slides open the zipper; the metal teeth separate with amazing complicity. With one hand she reaches inside her purse for her ChapStick, with the other she selects a Danish, a glossily pre-served apricot at its pastry heart. The two items switch hands. It's not so complicated, a little bit of smoke and mirrors. She presses the balm to her lips. Confident or reckless, she's been called both before.

Mia slings the purse across her chest and moves to claim her abandoned tray with its lone, steaming coffee. She will drink it outside on the upper deck as if she was a tourist, taking in the naturalist's presentation on marine life. Praise the salmon, their iridescent predictability, their homeward thrust. Give me science, she thinks, sweet quantifiable truths. Anything not to dwell on that slippery juvenile version of herself. Except she doesn't really have a choice, that girl's been resurrected.

There she is, slight, underdeveloped for fifteen, wandering the mall on Saturday afternoon with a list, Pete's list. She was such an exceptional shoplifter precisely because she didn't look the part: angelic, skin that glowed pinkly in her cheeks and revealed blue veins cross-hatching her temples. She plucked earrings and sunglasses from department store racks without looking askance. "Shoplifters Will be Prosecuted" warned stickers adhered to the change room mirrors, the same mirrors before which Mia hooked herself into promising push-up bras (sometimes two at once), slithered into designer jeans, then proceeded to pull her less snazzy clothes on over top. This was just before alarm-activating security tags, in the days of security guards, of whom there were never enough to police all those bored and covetous girls. Mia capitalized on her childish looks. And she wasn't dumb. Unlike other girls, she did not flaunt her booty in the mall food court. Nor did she spend a gratuitous amount of time in the change rooms. And she was genuinely polite to the older, wary sales girls. On occasion, she purchased something. A cassette for Pete. A cowrie shell necklace for herself. But the sports jerseys embossed with team logos, she took. The baseball caps, she took. A fortune-telling eight-ball, astronaut ice cream, sex-wax. Took, took, took.

Mia pushes her tray toward the cashier who announces the total owing. She pulls some change from her pocket and hands it to the girl.

"That's everything?" says the girl, still cupping the change in her palm. She's younger than Mia, smug in her union job and non-regulation eye makeup. She wouldn't, Mia thinks, she wouldn't dare.

"Yeah, thanks." Mia lifts her coffee from the tray, leaving it for the girl to deal with.

"You're sure about that?" the girl says to Mia's back.

Waiting for her at the condiment bar is a man in a militarily pressed shirt. He jerks his head for her to approach. Mia feels her insides fall slack. She thinks of the British slang for acute disappointment: *gutted*. Until now it has always struck her as over the top.

"Go ahead, fix your coffee," says the man.

She tears open a packet of sugar and empties it into the cup.

"I'd let this slide," he says, "but a couple of kids saw you and, well, there's protocol."

Mia sips her coffee and tries to pick out the tattletales. Easy enough: two ponytailed girls huddle against their mother, watching from a distance. She salutes them, raises her coffee in their direction. The mother glares.

Pete peers out of the stairwell to find Mia has moved on. He hurries after her, toward the cafeteria, and soon spots her at the coffee bar in conversation with one of the ship's workers. She's swept her hair into a loose ponytail to reveal what some might call a graceful neck but one that, to Pete, suggests surveillance, all those years it craned in his direction. He watches as Mia hoists her purse onto the bar and extracts a plastic-wrapped item from inside. The man turns it over in his hands as if he expects there to be more to it, and in that moment Pete knows what Mia has done.

In the chief steward's office, Mia's captor, Frank, hands her the Danish. "You must be hungry," he says, drawing out a form with many boxes to be checked and blank space to be filled in. Mia has always been curious about the chief steward's office. A set of keys has been found in the arcade, to claim them please come to the chief steward's office.

"Are you?" Frank asks.

"What?"

"Hungry."

"No."

It's disappointing, really, the office, like any bureaucratic space – desk, computer, filing cabinets – though the walls are stained a warm cherry and there's a showy compass mounted behind the desk.

"You wanted to be caught, is that right?" Frank asks.

"Nobody wants to get caught," Mia says a little too sharply. "Sorry, but I've never bought that theory." She can see the outline of an undershirt beneath Frank's shirt. Men wear undershirts, boys do not. Men are generous, and boys? Boys enlist girls to do their dirty work.

While Mia patrolled the Sports Emporium, Pete and Josh waited for her on the granite steps of a cenotaph dedicated to soldiers who'd fought in the First World War. The monument was the focal point of an inner city park and abutted Christ Church Cathedral. The place was shady with chestnut trees. Sour with pigeon shit. A row of mossed tombstones stood like rotten teeth along the north border. Pete nick-named the park the Dead Zone for the homeless men who loafed – one on each of the four green benches facing the cenotaph – like leisure-stricken princes, shopping carts parked alongside. Occasionally a wedding party wafted out of the church and into the park to pose beneath a chestnut tree's weighty green tiers. The understanding was if Mia didn't return within an hour she'd been caught.

"I'll need your driver's licence," Frank says.

"You're taking my licence?"

"I just need some information."

Mia hands Frank her wallet. She unwraps the Danish and bites into the dry pastry. It must have had something to do with timing, their emotional immaturity when they dated. Even Pete's toes had tasted teenaged. Fungal. They were stubby and sprouted black hairs. He wriggled them forcibly inside her mouth, once slicing her palate with his big toenail.

Pete lingers outside the chief steward's office. It has a counter for receiving people and beyond that an administrative area. Mia is seated with her back to the counter, before a desk. Pete thinks of the last time he saw her: a beach party, the night of their high school graduation. He remembers a massive bonfire, an impressive display of teenage disregard. Josh ran back and forth across a log through the flames. That night Pete, too, had felt reckless and in love with his peers. Soupy nostalgia warmed his chest and groin. He'd gone looking for Mia and found her squatting behind the stack of logs where girls disappeared to pee. She didn't see him at first – he stood in shadow, on slightly higher ground – and for a moment he simply observed her. She'd done something different with her hair, stabbed it through with pins so that it sat in a fluffy mound on top of her head. She looked defenceless in her crouch, and happy. He remembers the tide was high and all the bloated sea could manage was a continuum of breathless little waves. There was a moon, too, and the wet stones beneath Mia sparkled. She was humming a tune, some perky summer hit even he recognized, and for some reason this infuriated him, it soured his whole mood.

"Pete? Is that you?" Mia had said and tried to stand. But before she could hoist her jeans up over her slim hips, he'd stepped forward, thrust the heel of his hand against her forehead – that broad, sincere forehead – and pushed her down on her ass. Oof! The song went out of her then.

Thinking back, he feels almost badly. He can say now, with perspective, that there aren't enough women like Mia, a general prudishness about most single women his age. Or is prudishness just something that happens to women as they get older, as they become less obliging? Not since Mia has a woman been quite so indulgent of his whims.

Pete steps up to the reception counter. "Excuse me," he says, drawing the attention of the man behind the desk.

Mia can't bring herself to turn in her chair, to face him. The apricot is a lump of coagulated sugar sliding down her throat, nearly choking her. The loudspeaker chimes: Thank you for sailing with BC Ferries. If you are boarding a bus on the ferry, please return to the vehicle deck now.

"Can I help you?" Frank asks.

When Mia was finally caught, with a pair of slinky basketball shorts tucked into the waist of her jeans, she didn't rat Pete out, refused to tell the security guard, her parents, the school counsellor, who she was stealing for. Her punishment was a hundred community hours to be served at the Glengarry nursing home. Every day after school for three months she offered tea and digestive biscuits to the Glengarry's residents. She crawled around at one end of the common room arranging and rearranging plastic bowling pins for the geriatric to knock down. And for what thanks? The last time she'd seen him was at their high school graduation. He'd held her hand down the rickety stairs to the beach at Mile Zero, tightened his grip to help her over the tangle of logs and kelp at the bottom. That brief window when wild roses are in bloom, the cliffs knotted with them, their Victorian scent making her near faint with hope. Mia winces now, recalling the peak of her happiness, how later that same night he'd sought her out where she'd disappeared to relieve herself of the apple cider she'd consumed. He'd come looking for her, finally. She was ecstatic, there was no other word for it. Backlit by the moon, she couldn't read the expression on his face but was confident it was changed. All around them, the ocean's ceaseless applause. She said coyly, "Fancy meeting you here," then tried to stand. He was too close, towering over her like some kind of late-night evangelical preacher. Hallelujah! The heel of his hand against her forehead, forcing her down.

There's also a framed map on the wall of the chief steward's office, one charting what appears to be a fairly tricky route through the islands. Mia has always thought of the ship, its passage, as rather benign. Until today, her view has always been the same: oceanfront cottages, private beaches, the lives of the charmed. Often the water is the most striking green.

Often there are seals basking on rocky headlands. Sometimes there really are whales. On the outside deck the naturalist tells her audience that to avoid inbreeding Orcas will seek out a mate from a pod whose language of clicks and whistles is most varied from its own. Isn't nature brilliant? Isn't it appalling?

Pete isn't sure what he's doing, what he's going to say, but he feels compelled to bail Mia out, or at least soften the blow. The corridor behind him has grown busy with passengers preparing to disembark.

"Is this urgent?" says the man behind the desk.

"It was a dare," Pete blurts. "A stupid dare. I didn't expect her to go through with it. We were just joking around."

Mia doesn't start at the sound of his voice, doesn't even turn in her seat. Pete's face grows hot. The ingratitude. He wants to take it back. Need he remind her of a time when she arranged each footstep to arrive at him?

Frank looks expectantly at Mia across the desk. She can see he hopes what Pete has said is true, that it was just a prank. Somehow this will change everything, put an end to the paperwork. The metallic coffee has made her jittery, but outwardly she sits very still. Somewhere, from someone, she'd heard Pete worked in a bank. How appropriate. Miserly. She has since known men generous enough to throw a pillow beneath her hips before moving down between her legs. Mia reaches for the document at Frank's fingertips and signs her name.

Vehicle passengers may now return to their cars. Foot passengers may disembark by way of the overhead walkway.

"I don't know what he's talking about," she says. It's obvious

Frank wants to let her go without incident. Behind his head, Mia observes as the compass needles settle on their coordinates. She looks him in the eye and says, "I'm sorry, but I've never seen that guy before."

ROSARIA CAMPBELL

PROBABILITIES

Men go to Bowring Park at night to be with other men in the darkness. For a few short summer weeks in St. John's it is warm enough to be out at night and the darkness welcomes them, hides all the things that matter in their daytimes: the colour of their hair and the clothes they wear to work, the scar on their cheek and the place they are from. These things don't matter in the park because they slip into the shadows with the men, disappear into the grass and the trees next to the statues where the men gather at night. Sometimes certain words are exchanged and they go someplace more hidden, to the bushes or to a car, but often in the darkness the park just lets them rest or talk, get high, borrow money, sip Southern Comfort. There is a certain peace for them there in the company of other men, with the summer dampness and the smallness of their world punctuated only occasionally by a hesitation or a newness, a voice that no one's heard before.

You may think these are strange things for a straight woman to know, but Jeff told me all about the park, even took me

there a few times one summer. I can't say I was entirely comfortable but it was Jeff's world and after he told me I went with
him because I wanted to be open-minded. The park has always
been a constant for him, although he stopped going for a time
when he moved to Toronto and has been through a number
of phases in his life since his first days there – the bars, the
resorts, the four years with Allan, the four years after Allan.
Even after he was diagnosed he went there sometimes. He said
he could smell the life, his life, that lived there, that had adapted
to the darkness and flourished somehow, that laughed and
loved and fucked despite the occasional basher and the cops
who ignored the bashers.

Jeff went to the park in August right after his first bad flu,
the one that took him three weeks to recover from. He went
there on a Saturday night just to sit in the warmth and the darkness and to listen to the back and forth of male voices and the
sounds of the men who came to the park to look for other men.
But he stayed too long and ended up getting drunk and high
for the first time in nearly five years. He forgot the odds, put
his faith in the familiar smells under the cloudy St. John's sky,
thought that just once wouldn't matter. He said when he heard
the voice he thought that he knew the voice and that he
shouldn't be doing this, but by then he was drunk and stoned
and he hadn't been near another man since he was diagnosed,
so he followed the voice into the last hours of the August night.

In a different world Jeff should have been able to go back
and follow up the connections until he found that voice, to
explain what happened and to make sure the person belonging
to the voice got tested right away. In his heart he knew who it
was, even if he couldn't be sure, so he spent two weeks asking

around, checking the park and the bars, trying to make contact. But he got nowhere, and just as he was beginning to convince himself that he hadn't recognized the voice in the park he heard it again, in his second year stats class on the first day of the fall semester. He was calling names to get a feel for who was who and when he got to Wayne Whitten, the student who was sitting in the third row toward the middle said "Right here." There was no mistaking that voice, and even if Jeff couldn't be sure of those two words or of the name that went with them, he was sure of the face that looked up from the desk where its owner was doodling on a notepad, challenging the pause after his name while the rest of the class sat wondering why Jeff wasn't finishing the list in his hands.

At the end of the week Jeff calls me and on Saturday I have a late supper with him and Allan, who takes care of the helpline. Allan has been involved with every committee and support group and lobby you can name and nothing surprises him. But he's cautious with this one, even though he understands what it's like to wake up one day and find out that your whole life has been changed by something you can't even see. He sips his wine and listens quietly while Jeff tells him about getting drunk and stoned and about picking Wayne up, not because he was drunk and stoned, but because he could feel time there in the park: his time, closing in on him. Jeff knows that if anyone can give him a straightforward opinion on this it is Allan, and he leaves nothing out. He knows too that the damage is done, and that there is only one sensible thing to do, but he needs to talk about it because there are so many things to consider that he can't think of where to begin. There's Wayne for one thing, and the implications for Jeff's job, the connections to his past.

Jeff says that by the second class of the week he had pulled himself together, going ahead with his lecture on averages and probabilities, calculations based on the flip of a coin or the roll of the dice. He was glad for the simplicity of the material and for the in-class exercises that kept the students busy while he tried to get his thoughts in order, giving them more time than they needed to complete their work. He spent this time watching and listening, confirming what he already knew: that this is the man who picked him up in the park, that he is also Eddy Whitten's son, and that both their lives have now become very complicated.

"You're sure it was the same guy, Jeff?" Allan is chopping tomatoes and cucumbers for a salad now.

But Jeff doesn't let himself get drawn in by this easy possibility. "Not only the same guy, Allan, but Eddy's son. If you'd ever been to Black Bay you'd know what I mean. It wasn't just an accent that the Whittens had. Their everyday speech had something that went beyond how they pronounced words or how they made sentences. It was like a song almost, or like they were always on the verge of a story of some kind." I have no trouble remembering this, no doubt that Jeff was sure about who it was in the park that night.

"And besides," he says, "I got someone I know at the registrar's office to look up his home address. I'm not taking any chances that it wasn't him." Jeff spins lettuce in a plastic drier and none of us talk for a while. I think about how complicated this must be for my brother, how anything I say would sound trivial and simplistic, how obvious and hard the choices must be for him.

But Allan turns to him now and says, "You'll have to tell him, Jeff." His voice is kind and even and I imagine this must be the voice that talks to the just-checking and the I-may-have-a-problem and the near-desperate on the helpline every Wednesday night.

"Yes, I know." Jeff is no stranger to the realities of his condition. "I just don't know how to bring myself to do it. If he were out someone would have seen him by now, but I made a few calls and asked around, and I came up with nothing."

"Is there anyone else who could make contact? Someone from home maybe?" Allan's voice is still kind and even, trying out the unlikely for Jeff.

I look at Jeff now and I see the Jeff who has not been home in over twenty years, who even went to our grandmother's for Christmas every year so he could see the folks without going back. He rarely talks about Black Bay, not even to Allan or to me, who grew up there two years behind him. Tonight he just says that he doesn't think he could do it that way and Allan lets it rest because he's mostly here to listen – that's what Allan does best. By this time the lasagna is done and Jeff and Allan make garlic bread together. I settle back on a kitchen stool and watch them talking, glad that Jeff still has Allan's experience and compassion to rely on even though they have been split for over four years. Allan passes no judgements or opinions and he offers no easy solutions to Jeff. Other than pointing out the possible complications for Jeff's job at the university, there is nothing new or concrete he can offer, so as the garlic bread browns he and Jeff catch up on the news and bring each other up to date on their separate lives.

After supper Allan leaves and I call home to tell Jessie I'm staying with Jeff for the night. He's due to go on shift in a few hours anyway so he just says he'll see me sometime tomorrow and we say good night over the phone. We've been together long enough that we're used to having a certain amount of room to do things on our own. We rarely get involved in other people's lives, but for the past year Jeff has been an exception for me and I think Jessie understands why I need to spend time with him. So on the nights Jessie is working I sometimes stay over with Jeff because it gives us a bit of time to chat, or just to watch TV together. One of the perks of cooking at the bar is that there's no night work so once the grill is cleaned you can get away before the fifth version of "Great Big Sea" and still have a semi-normal social life.

Jeff takes some folders into the living room and digs the remote out from under a cushion, tries to lose himself in some class preparation while the remote manoeuvres through the channels, looks for an old movie or something not too heavy. It finally finds a late-night talk show on channel eight and I settle into this, every now and then watching Jeff as he goes over his lectures for next week. I worry about him constantly these days, although he doesn't like me dwelling on the details of his diagnosis. "When I need you I'll let you know," he says, if he catches me worrying about something, and I have no doubt that he means this. He doesn't hide things from me but there's a line that he doesn't want me to cross and I have to acknowledge it, even if I do cross it from time to time.

As adults Jeff and I have always kept in contact with each other, but we've never felt the need to talk about Black Bay, preferring to believe that your adult life is more important than any ties to the past or the place you are from. So there's a lot I don't know about him, even though we grew up in the same house, because I didn't really put things together about him until after I left home. But tonight I'm curious about Jeff and his last year at home, about the absolute silence that seemed to follow him everywhere he went that year.

"Where would a guy like Wayne go if he wanted to talk to someone?" I ask him. For all the openness between us I'm still not entirely comfortable asking him directly about it. "I mean, if he's going to the park he must have found out about it somewhere."

Jeff puts his pen down on the coffee table and stares at the TV for a while. "I doubt he'd really be able to talk to anyone," he says after a bit. "Not back there." He is about to say something else but the talk show host breaks for a commercial, a collection of hits from the seventies. Jeff and I recognize them all, bare feet tapping the hardwood floor along with the music. When he turns to me I see in the light from the TV screen some of the constant strain that is his life now, so I take the remote from the coffee table and turn the sound off, ask him if he wants to go to bed. But he says to just turn it down a little and we talk until the show is over, because that music was Black Bay and Saturday nights, and because until tonight I'd never really thought about what it was like for him growing up there, going to house parties or to the takeout with the guys, trying to pick up girls in Eddy Whitten's F150.

For some reason the clearest memory I have of Jeff as a teenager is in a neighbour's living room where the coffee table is pushed back and someone is banging out "Me and Bobby McGee" on an acoustic guitar. He is dancing with a neighbour's wife, shuffling his feet and staying well back from the woman, who tries to get him to jive and who makes rude jokes about her friend and the plastic bananas on the dining room table. The husbands are standing around in the kitchen with their backs to their wives, drinking Labatt Blue and smoking Export "A" cigarettes, talking about fish and motors and hockey until they drink the right number of beers. Then they dance something slow like "Matilda" cheek-to-cheek with their wives, fight with them over the keys to drive home. These parties were where we went when there was nothing else to do, where we learned to drink behind the houses, to talk crude talk about sex and real talk about the world that we had to fit into. Jeff is sixteen years old and I think that he is like the rest of us in Black Bay: a little quieter maybe, and not as sure of himself, but happy enough as he slowly grows into the body of an adult, waiting for the rest of his life to catch up.

All the new bodies were starting to take their places in Black Bay then, moving as a group mostly, going to dances or just hanging out, bouncing off each other in the limited space they had around them. Black Bay is small, so by necessity my little group of friends sometimes overlapped with Jeff's little group of friends, and I can remember hanging out on the rocks by the wharf or in the empty gravel pit, wherever we could get cover from passing cars. The guys would skip rocks and smoke borrowed cigarettes while they tried to outdo each other's lies about the weekend and it seemed at the time that for them everything came down to the piece of ass that either would or wouldn't put out for them on Saturday night. None of them had much to do except Eddy, who was two years older and who had quit school to fish with his father. Eddy was a bit of a hero to them because he had a truck and his own money and because he sold a bit of drugs on the side. He bought their beer for them and gave them a deal on their hash, took them to the takeout for refried chicken and chips.

Jeff always stayed a little removed from this, drinking some beer with the guys but never really getting drunk or out of control. And he tells me he hardly ever toked with them because he says he got too paranoid when they sat around laughing and pointing, trying to make him more paranoid like teenage guys do when they're stoned. This is the other Jeff then, the one he is telling me about tonight: the Jeff who grew up inside the Jeff I saw in Black Bay, pushing and shoving against the sides of the shell, never really sure what he was pushing against. It is the Jeff who could never completely hide his embarrassment when the guys told jokes and then punched one another for proof of something he didn't understand, who could only hang out with them so long before he'd have to go off by himself. He says he'd sit in the woods with his head in his arms for hours sometimes, crying and never knowing why he was crying. He would later recognize those first pains for what they were of course but this would take years. All he knew at the time was this strange, sad core of heat that never seemed to leave him, that was always there somewhere in his chest or just below the surface on the left side of his throat. He knew something was different for him, but he had nothing to think about it with, and certainly nothing to talk about it with.

Tonight he seems happy and at ease with these two younger Jeffs, laughing with me at how he fantasized about living at home with Mom and Dad for the rest of his life, teaching grade nine forever, like Albert Walters. Or about how he was always uncomfortable when he went to weddings and saw the men dressed in the pale blue or beige tuxedos that their fiancés had picked out to accent the colour of their eyes or their wind-burned skin. I'm fascinated with Jeff's look at Black Bay and with how he talks about it, so I ask him how and when he knew.

"I always knew," he says. "I just never knew what it was that I knew." He laughs at this, but his face is serious, tired almost. "I actually heard that on the new sitcom the other night, and it occurred to me at the time that we're out there now, and that this must make a difference to someone like Wayne." I can see what he means. Right now at work if I don't hear at least one line from that show in a night it isn't a good night.

"But it was never that simple," he says then, and his voice is quiet on the other end of the couch. I turn the volume off now so I can hear him better and he starts talking again about Black Bay and growing up there, telling me in the flickering light of the TV screen about the things that can almost destroy a fifteen-year-old and yet still end up on a prime-time TV show.

One day Jeff visited our cousin in St. John's and discovered that people there tacked notices onto telephone poles. On one of the notices was a word that he'd never heard anyone say before – even in the jokes the boys told when they'd had a few beers – and today he says he can still remember the phone number even though he would not actually use it for another five years. For no clear reason he could think of at the time he went home and looked up the word in the encyclopedia in the school library, making sure he kept a finger on the page with "horses" for a quick escape in case someone he knew came by. After that he kept the word and its meaning with him, even trying it out loud once or twice when he was alone in his room. It was an odd word, unfamiliar and hard to say, like a word someone had invented without trying it out first. A word that popped into his mind at the oddest of times and sat there on the edge, as if it were watching for something or trying to speak to him.

But it was the numbers in that encyclopedia passage that meant the most to Jeff, and he says he sat there in the corner where no one could see him, reading and rereading those numbers that told him he was not alone, that he was probably just one of the thirty per cent, and that he would one day get married like the other sixty per cent and forget all this. He memorized the passage and left the library with this new-found mathematical courage, certain that the anxiety he felt when he was riding around with Eddy and the guys could now be explained scientifically. Jeff believed in those numbers because they were his only hope, especially since he wasn't even sure if he was pronouncing the word correctly.

There was a time, though, when he was finally able to make firm the connections between that word and his numbers and the world around him in Black Bay. It happened one day when the guys left to hitchhike into town to look for girls and Jeff stayed with Eddy to help him put some gear away. This was the third time in a row Jeff had skipped the trip into town and he was standing in the middle of the shed watching the muscles on Eddy's back when Eddy just turned to him and said, "Not turning into one of them queers now, are you, old man?" Jeff says the sentence changed his life forever, even more than the word on the telephone pole or the numbers in the encyclopedia, because it's one thing to hear it in a joke or see it in a book, another thing when all of a sudden it's there in the air, a part of Black Bay bouncing around with Eddy's voice in the smells of diesel and fish in the shed where you're working. He swears he could see it that day and that it turned around and looked straight at him, so he dropped the piece of gear he was carrying, pretending not to pay attention.

"What was that, Eddy?" he asked, coughing to hide the redness in his face and the sound of his heart pounding under the muscles of his chest.

"Nothing, old man. Just joking. Get back to work now, so I can get into town too." And Jeff says Eddy went right on working, never giving it a second thought that he had maybe just changed Jeff's life forever.

But Jeff gave it a lot of thought and about two weeks later he got himself a girlfriend named Roberta who was shy and religious and the rest of the guys tormented him about poking her after mass on Saturdays. In fact everyone made a joke or a comment about it, and Jeff felt like he had finally fixed something that had been broken. What no one noticed was that Jeff was never really happy and that he was often nervous, like he was afraid of something. And there was that other number too, the ten per cent that whispered even more quietly to him that he was not alone. But there was no one he could talk to and nothing that he could check the encyclopedia's tallies against, so Jeff says he just kept on taking Roberta to the takeout and when he was alone at night he would total up all two hundred and fifty of his neighbours and relatives in Black Bay, trying to guess which of them were the twenty-five the book said were there.

—

"It really does look like freedom out there," I joke with Allan and Jeff. We're sitting behind a glass window in a room at the back of the bar and even though it's only eleven o'clock the floor is going wild, arms waving, screaming for Dolly. I take in the feel of a Friday night on booze and bennies and my professional side envies the lineups at the bar and the drinks being pushed across it. It's different here than in the park and we all know we're slightly out of place, too old or too straight or too something for the energy that's in here. Both Jeff and Allan have let their memberships go and tonight the guys at the desk had to get someone to sign us in.

"When I first came here it was total freedom to me," Jeff says, and I look out at the dance floor again. "It was totally foreign and unreal and I didn't know any of the rules, but it felt like a freedom I didn't even dream could exist."

My first time here with him he hadn't said anything beforehand, just told me where it was and that they had the best music in the city. "Years ahead of everyone else," he said. He was twenty-five and I was twenty-three and we hadn't really been in contact much until I moved to St. John's to take a job at one of the restaurants. He had left home before I did so it was natural that I'd call him up to see what was on the go on the weekends. He was usually a little vague and unspecific about his plans and his friends and for a long time we just went to the regular bars. But he always kept talking about this other bar and then one night he finally got enough nerve to take me there. He watched me for a while and when he saw I was probably okay with it he just leaned over and said, "Me too," followed some guy onto the dance floor. That was all that passed between us, all we thought was needed at the time. I wasn't entirely okay with it at that time but he seemed a hell of a lot happier than the Jeff who ended up in the hospital in his last year in school, and I was only too glad not to have to talk to him about anything too deep. It took a while to get used to the place but he kept bringing me back, and after a year or so I was like one of the regulars and Jeff and I hung out together a lot after that.

Tonight I doubt there is much chance that I'd recognize Wayne but I scour the faces in the crowd anyway, trying to guess if any of them might belong to Eddy Whitten's son. Jeff is doing the same, and so is Allan. The dance floor is surrounded by mirrors and the guys who don't have a partner dance with themselves in the mirrors. Those who aren't dancing circle the floor or stand at the side bars, watching. It's pure motion out there but you can still pick out the little groups, and the little corners for the little groups – that hasn't changed much since the first time I was here. There are corners for torn jeans and muscle shirts, corners for bare skin and corners for leather and corners for drag. There are rules too: rules about how to dance and how to ask someone to dance and about who you can ask. And, depending on which group you belong to, there are even rules about whether or not you should dance.

"He'll show up here someday," Jeff says. This is a given in his world. It's Friday night and if Wayne's not here it's probably because he still has to find his corner, just like the Jeff I saw leaving home twenty years ago did. The DJ ratchets up the sound and the lights and jams the tunes one after the other and I realize it was a mistake for me to come here after working in a bar all week. Jeff is sweating in the heat and I worry about him being in here where the air is so close and where the crowd is packed in well beyond what I guess to be regulation for the size of the room. The speed of the circling around the dance floor has picked up now and I watch someone try to go against the flow, give up, join the crowd going the other way. It's getting too loud to talk, even behind the glass, but no one comes here to talk anyway. They come here to get drunk and high and pack the dance floor, to circle the crowd and leave with someone and then to come back the next week and do it all over again. So I catch Allan's eye and we look over at Jeff, who signals that he is ready to leave, and the three of us walk out past the bar and the sign-in desk, into the fresh air and the release of not having to be there on a Friday night.

On Saturday evening of the third week of classes I sit with Jeff at his kitchen table while he marks assignments. Jeff always did well in school, always had either the highest or the second-highest marks in class, especially in math. So it was natural that he would go into mathematics – statistics, actually. When he was in the hospital he missed so much time from school that he nearly failed, but he had a teacher who put in extra time to help him catch up and he was still able to graduate with everyone else, even though he never went to his graduation. He went further in university than anyone else from home ever had, paying his own way with student loans and part-time jobs, later as a graduate student. After his PhD, he taught part-time in Toronto for a while, then came back to take up a full-time position at the university.

His class has moved on to something called distribution curves and the assignment is to construct a series of what he tells me are "histograms." They are using data for adult height and when he takes a break he shows me how the histogram for the data they are working with is patterned, how if you fit a curve to it the result is a bell-shaped curve with a hump in the middle and a tail on either end. "This is what we call the 'bell curve' or the 'normal curve,'" Jeff the statistician tells me, the cook. "You can find all kinds of things in there if you know where to look." He then explains how all data varies and how the average – or the "mean" as he calls it – is the least interesting of anything in statistics, how statisticians always look for some measure of variation as well. He shows me the curves as if they were pieces of art, pointing out the things he sees in them, how the shape is different for each one even though the averages are all the same. He's lost me by now but I listen to him anyway, because it's the first time in nearly a month that I've seen him this relaxed.

He is the only one in his department who always marks his own assignments, the others preferring to use hired markers whenever they can. I ask him about this and he tells me he likes to see first-hand how his students are doing, likes to watch each class quantifying difference and graphing life in the same old ways. Jeff loves to teach and he says he won't give up working until he absolutely has to. I know that if he seems exceptionally calm and rational about his problems it is because teaching means so much to him and because he is desperate to hang on to that calmness and rationality in the classroom, even though everything around him is caving in. And I know too that he is losing sleep and that he thinks of nothing else but Wayne and what has happened.

Jeff has always tried to keep some distance between his work and his personal life, and after he was diagnosed he drifted apart from most of his friends. So Allan and I are pretty much all he's got now, and tonight he tries to explain to me what it's like to have Wayne in class every week, to see in front of him the past and present they now share.

"All I can think of is that his face won't be fading into the usual oblivion at the end of the semester, and that sooner or later I will have to sit down with that face and explain a very different type of probability." The assignments are piled on the table between us, but he seems to have lost all interest in them now.

"This is so complicated," he says, "that tonight I could just walk away from everything." I turn my head and try to concentrate on the title page of "Janet Anthony – Assignment 2," because if there is anything I would wish for my brother it would be that things would be less complicated for him. But I know that this will never happen so I tidy the table a bit, and then as I look at the pile of curves and calculations that connects him to Wayne, he tells me about the last time he spoke to Eddy.

They are in a horseshoe-shaped dip in the beach, burning the end of an old dory, and Jeff is drunk for the first time in his life. Roberta's dumped him for some guy with a dirt bike, and the guys are teasing him about not being able to give her enough but he doesn't care because Roberta's let him off the hook, made him one of the guys. Eddy's rolling hash while the rest of them pass a flask in the shelter of an overhang and every time the blaze explodes into the night sky they drink to this and pass a joint. The batteries on the tape recorder die on the first verse of "Mamas, Don't Let Your Babies Grow Up to Be Cowboys," but Eddy continues the lines anyway and the rest of them join in on the chorus. They stay there all night, taking turns passing out, throwing up, and falling down, and when day breaks they all piss on the dying fire before thanking Eddy. They say things like "Good hash, man" and "Best fucking drunk in a long time," arms reaching out to grab a shoulder or punch another arm. They disappear one by one into the morning then, leaving Jeff and Eddy alone on the beach with the sun coming up and the moon going down on opposite sides of Black Bay.

Eddy is smoking one last joint before he goes home and the air smells of wet fire and coals and Jeff is drunker than he's ever been in his life. He leans over to say, "Right on man," crooks his elbow around Eddy's neck, hauls Eddy's head through the space between them. But at the last second something changes, and what starts out as a joke aimed for the temple becomes something more tender, on the cheek right next to Eddy's lips. Jeff's arm stays there too long – just a few seconds really – and Eddy doesn't move. Then Eddy jumps up and drops his joint in the rocks and Jeff stumbles to his feet too, weaving in front of him.

"What the fuck you doing?" Eddy pushes Jeff now, who stumbles in the unevenness of the rocks.

"Nothing man. Just joking. Fucking joking." Jeff's words are slurred and flat and when he tries to snort a laugh he ends up spitting on Eddy.

"Well fuck off with the fucking joking then." Eddy is walking across the beach now, and Jeff sinks down into the rocks again. He's too drunk to realize that his jogger is on a live coal, because he's watching Eddy climbing the bank, turning into two Eddys as Jeff starts to pass out. He can taste rye whiskey and salt and Eddy's lips in the morning and the wood smoke: his first real kiss. Then he passes out on the beach for what was probably the last easy sleep he ever had in Black Bay.

At Jeff's kitchen table I shuffle the student assignments, look at the different writing styles, and read Jeff's comments. Jeff is doodling on his marks sheet.

"I know I've been avoiding talking to Wayne," he says, "but it's got nothing to do with Black Bay."

This is bullshit, of course, because I know it has everything to do with Black Bay and with Eddy, and with two words spoken at a takeout over twenty years ago, what I now know must have been about a week or so after that night on the beach. It was all Eddy said and most likely all Eddy knew how to say, but it was all that was needed there. I don't say anything and across the table Jeff looks back through the pile until he finds Wayne's assignment. He looks at it for a long time and then finally he puts a Post-it Note on the first page, asking Wayne if he could please drop by during office hours on Tuesday.

Later, when I'm soaking in the tub, I see Jeff as a young man again. He's just home from the hospital and we've come out for a smoke on the edge of the bank where it hangs over the beach. You can see most of the houses in Black Bay from that point and Jeff has his back to all of them. It's the first smoke we've had together since he came home and he's dropped a pile of weight, taken on the colour of the hospital in his face.

"Are you leaving?" I ask him. I'm afraid to say much else because I don't know what he's thinking. None of us really understand what's going on with him so we've all just kind of backed away and left him alone.

"As soon as school is finished," he says after a bit. We finish our cigarettes so I light the last two I have and hand one to him. The waves are smashing against the rocks below, cleaning the beach out of the cove again, and we both stand there on the edge of the cliff watching this. There is nothing between us but the wind, even though I know there should be something more, and when our smokes are finished we walk back to the house together. By the end of June he's gone, heading out long before university starts in the fall with nothing but a suitcase full of clothes and what I remember now as an odd kind of certainty. He's never been back there for anything.

Jeff comes by for a late lunch and a beer on Friday and tells me about his week and Wayne's visit while I sit at the table and work out the details of the next menu changes. The manager has asked for this a couple of times now, and this is the last day I can put it off. Our menu allows us enough flexibility to take advantage of the fads and the seasons and this means you have to redo the specials on a regular basis, which takes a bit of time. The bar attracts a mix of university students and faculty, tourists and permanent downtowners, and if you don't have the right blend of the new and the predictable they don't come back after the first few times.

I'm up to Saturday on the menu and Jeff is telling me that in class Wayne still works away quietly at his desk, his fingers careful and precise around his pencil and his mind apparently on the numbers in front of him, even after their meeting. Before he showed up at the office Jeff had spent almost thirty minutes thinking about what he was going to say to him, even making a few notes about some things to talk about – courses, university life, the fishing, the takeout and if it's still open. He normally likes this back and forth of question and answer with his students and the chance to get to know a little bit about them and their lives, but this was a delicate balance for him. He had about five minutes to guess how out Wayne is and to look for some kind of hint of how to approach him, a place where either he or Wayne might feel they could acknowledge or pursue the connections between them.

Wayne had shown up on time and had been polite and casual, but when Jeff invited him to take a seat he refused and leaned against the filing cabinet instead. Jeff started by telling Wayne that he recognized his name on the class list and there was a shift in Wayne's posture then, a small movement of the head until he was staring directly at Jeff. Jeff says he is used to seeing students and how they react outside the classroom but that the gaze from Wayne across the office that day had trapped him in its perfection. This is how he describes it to me as I work away on the daily specials and I look up when he says it. I see that he is dead serious and over the noises of the bar he tries to work out exactly what it was that he saw in Wayne's face: part invitation, part challenge, part fear, and part need. And so different from every face that's ever looked back at him from across that office. He had to look at his notes before he spoke to Wayne again because by then he was struggling to breathe inside the membrane he had once touched this man so intimately through. These too are his words, how he sees the space that surrounds him and Wayne, the predicament they have found themselves in.

At first their conversation was just a set of routine questions from Jeff – things like how Wayne liked the university and what courses he was taking – followed by a set of just as routine answers from Wayne, who never once looked away from Jeff or broke what was between them in that space. After a few minutes Jeff moved on to more relevant questions, like where Wayne lived in town, when he had left Black Bay, and if he got home often. Wayne answered each question without hesitating, his head sometimes moving a little but the gaze never shifting or backing off, telling Jeff nothing other than that he was ready for the next question. Jeff says he was thinking how Wayne was already practised at this – that he probably could have guessed each question and the answer he was supposed to give – but he continued anyway. He asked Wayne if he had any roommates, the safest way he knew how to ask this, and Wayne told him just one and stood there waiting for the next question. So Jeff took his time before asking this last one, ignoring the notes on his desk and refusing to break the eye contact between them as he put into words the one question he knew Wayne would not answer automatically.

"How is your father, Wayne?" The question was quiet and deliberate and it caught Wayne off guard, left him vulnerable for a few seconds while Jeff watched from the other side of the room. Jeff says he had expected some kind of rupture from the question and its obligations to the past, the difficulty for Wayne in seeing his father there with Jeff in the world they now share. But for the first time the gaze across the room slipped a little and the voice hesitated before it spoke, and Jeff was unprepared for the face that looked back at him then, just as he was unprepared for his own response as he watched Wayne and waited for him to recover.

"The same as ever," Wayne said eventually. He was looking straight at Jeff again but the perfection was gone now, damaged by this simple question about his father and the reminder that he will never again belong completely to the place he was born into. Jeff knew that this was as far as he needed to go so he let it rest there, told Wayne he wouldn't keep him any longer and thanked him for his time. Wayne left without saying anything else and after he left, Jeff called me to see if I was free for a late-week lunch and a chat. I give him a few minutes now and then ask him what he plans to do next, but before he can answer the manager comes by the table again for the menu changes. I know I have to finish them for her so I come up with something for Saturday that's made with browned pork and steamed clams and watch Jeff while she reads it. I can see that he still wants to talk but the manager says she wants something a little more exotic, so I read what I wrote again and add a bit about fresh cilantro and a choice of fall greens or a spinach salad. She's satisfied with this, just changes *browned* to *gently sautéed* before taking it back to the office. Jeff has finished his lunch now so I turn to him and apologize for having to ignore him.

"It's okay," he says, but he doesn't continue right away and I order a rare lunchtime beer. We people-watch for a few minutes and talk about the changes in downtown St. John's, about the bar business and how tough it is to keep up. The waitress comes by with his bill and after she leaves he takes his card out, taps the edge of the table with it.

"I'm going out to Black Bay for a trip on Sunday," he says. He's stopped tapping the table now, focused all his attention on the conversation between us. "Do you think you could come with me?"

In the corner a folk-rock band is doing an early sound check and at the big table near the window there is the routine confusion of a crowd of students taking their places for wings and beer. We wait while the bass player runs through a few passing lines from the latest bar version of a tune I half remember and then I ask Jeff if he thinks it's a good idea, say something about what a narrow-minded little shithole it was, probably still is. But when he answers I realize that I'm just saying what I'm expected to say, and I'm a little ashamed at having expected it of him too.

"After Wayne left I sat there thinking about his being Eddy's son, carrying Eddy's voice into the park, the bars, other men's beds. About how that must be for him – for both of them." He looks around at the crowd that is gathering and finishes the last of his beer.

"I don't think it's so unusual for someone in my situation to want to go back," he says, and I wonder what it must be like for my brother to always have nowhere to go but forward. He's nearly forty and he's never driven the sixty-seven miles it takes to go back to the place he grew up in and I'm thinking that it deserves something more than the sound of a bar getting ready for the weekend. But the waitress is taking orders from the students and this is all I have time for before I have to go back to the kitchen. I give him a quick kiss and tell him that I'll go with him, and then I call Jessie and we argue a bit over the loss of our first Sunday off together in nearly two months. But I'm firm that this is something I have to do for Jeff and in the end he understands this, tells me to say hello for him.

The lunch crowd really packs it in then and it's a long, hot afternoon. I don't have time for anything except keeping up with the crowds and the downtown frenzy over the last few days that feel like summer.

So I take Jeff back to Black Bay and on the trip out it's as though we'd never left there. Jeff watches for moose while I drive and we talk about how the communities along the way have or haven't changed over the years. When we get to the spot where the takeout was – about a mile down the road from where we lived – he doesn't say much, and I don't expect him to. We drive by our old house, where a young couple is putting a flower bed to rest for the winter, then park on the wharf and get out of the car. The wind is off the water today and Jeff is dressed in a sweater and windbreaker, taking no chances with colds and flus. He looks around at the postcard where he spent the first sixteen years of his life, then stares for a while at the kelp moving back and forth at the bottom of the bay. I watch the waves hitting the shore below the cliffs, let the wind wash away the noise of downtown St. John's and the strain of the last few weeks. I lose myself in the pattern of large and small waves, thinking about Eddy and Wayne, about Jeff twenty years ago, and then I hear him speak for the first time since we parked the car.

"When I looked at Wayne in the office the other day I couldn't help seeing myself trapped there with him." He's looking at Eddy's house now, built by Eddy himself not fifty feet from the one he grew up in, a blue and white longliner resting on a trailer by the side of the house.

"But it was one of those times when you can see everything – the mistakes you've made, the few successes you've had, a night or two that you remember – right there in a single moment." On the road in front of the houses the cars are slowing down for the same potholes they did twenty years ago, and he turns back to me before he speaks again.

"It was good to still be able to feel that," he says, and I see him again when he was sixteen, leaving here to make a life out of a few numbers and a word he had never heard anyone say before, exiled by that one word yet still following it, straight to a voice he heard on a summer's night over twenty years later. The wind picks up a bit so he zippers up his jacket and the two of us stand there on the wharf with what I know now was the one possibility for my brother's life. After a while he says, "Let's go home," and we get back in the car. I get the heater going and when the car warms up he stops shaking, unzips his jacket.

"I'll think of some way to tell him," he says, and I don't say anything about doing the right thing because I know he's thought of nothing else for over a month now. I just drop a suggestion that probably won't change much, other than it might get the message to Wayne and give Jeff some piece of mind: get his St. John's address from the registrar's office and have Allan send him something anonymously, with the phone number for the centre if he wants to talk. I close my hand over Jeff's for a second and then put the car in reverse, manoeuvre out onto the road, and head back to St. John's.

Every Saturday that I have off now I pack a thermos of tea and go to the park with Jeff. He goes there a lot still, waiting to see if Wayne will maybe show up where the ground is more neutral. Sometimes I think that he should just stay home and take care of himself and try to forget about everything, but he won't hear of it. He's getting treatment and holding his own as far as his condition goes, and he says he still finds a kind of peace in there, in spite of everything. So most days I try not to say too much. I just sit there with him and pour tea and feed the pigeons in the rare St. John's sun, trying to enjoy what little time we have before the weather turns cold again.

LEONA THEIS

HIGH BEAMS

Two nights before the date printed in silver italic on her wedding invitations, Sylvie's old friend Erik from high school called, the guy she'd ridden with through all those dust-hung after-darks on country gravel grids in his mom's long Meteor, boatlike in the night. He was on his way through the city, he said. They should have a drink. In her left hand Sylvie held the clunky weight of the phone receiver, and in her right she held a half-made yellow wedding flower. Begin by stacking half a dozen sheets of coloured, see-through plastic. Pleat the stack accordion-style, then bind it at the middle. Spread each side into a fan; fluff. Repeat four dozen times. Get married.

"Hang up the phone," said Margo. "Pay some attention already." She took the flower from Sylvie's hand and fluffed the unfinished side and handed it back. Among the rules for nuptials in 1974: decorate the wedding car with flowers the colour of the bridesmaids' dresses. Or, in Sylvie and Jack's case, decorate the wedding truck. They might have used

Jack's Corolla, but rust had made macramé of its lower regions; the Dodge pickup Sylvie's dad bought December a year ago was the better choice, looking new except for a few pocks in the paint along the driver's side from stones and speed, his refusal to concede ample passage to oncoming traffic.

Sylvie angled the receiver away from her mouth. "I *am* paying attention."

"Course you are, it's just not all that obvious."

Sylvie held the flower to her nose as if she expected perfume. Somewhere in this city was Erik, also with a receiver in his hand and a cord leading away from it. Tug. She looked out the high, small window. Living in a basement suite, you see the lowest quarter of anyone walking around to the back door at the head of the stairs. She knew her friends by their legs, their shoes, the sizes of their feet. Here came Penny's sneakered feet now, Penny arriving to help with the flowers.

Things get away on you, the better part of a year goes by, next thing you know your mom's booked the United Church out home and made arrangements for the midnight lunch: cold cuts and buns and Uncle Ronald's special pepper pickles.

"Yes, let's," Sylvie said into the phone.

"Good," said Erik. "I'll meet you at that club, what is it – The Yips?"

"Sure, okay." Sylvie thought how he sounded like a hick, referring to Yip's as *The* Yips. Hello country bumpkin, with your definite article and your capital T. Sylvie hung up and said, "Let's wrap this up, Margo. I'm going out."

"Without Jack?"

"Without Jack."

"Who then?"

"Not your beeswax." She went up to meet Penny. "Thanks for coming, Penny," she said, "but it turns out this isn't a good night for making flowers after all."

"But Sylvie, you only have tonight and tomorrow and then that's it."

Yes, Sylvie thought, that's true.

They used to drive at night, she and Erik, along the back roads near Ripley, looking for parked couples. Once they found a vehicle, they'd train their high beams on the rear window for a bit, and then they'd back up and turn around and take off to find another car, laughing to think of Shelley or Beth or Serena struggling to do up her blouse, the buttons so big and the buttonholes so small and the fingers so suddenly fat.

Sylvie and Erik called their game birth control. Let's go do some birth control tonight. Let's go do some *backseat interruptus* in Ripley, Saskatchewan, Playground of the Prairies. In those days Sylvie's Grandma Peterson had in her living room a green satin cushion that dated from the forties. It was silk-screened with the "Playground of the Prairies" slogan and pictures of babes water skiing and men golfing and fishing. In the real-life Ripley, there was no lake where a person could launch a boat or put on water skis. There was no fishing hole, no river. There *was* a nine-hole golf course that would flood in the spring, and for a week or so kids would put on rubber boots and go out and sink the rickety rafts they knocked together out of branches and tail-ends of lumber. These days, Grandma Peterson's satin cushion sat on the couch in Sylvie and Jack's basement suite, a slippery joke.

The day after tomorrow Sylvie and Jack would get up and have breakfast, take their finery sheathed in plastic bags, and drive out to Ripley, where they would tape the yellow flowers to the Dodge and have the ceremony. Tonight the boys had come to pick up Jack. Took him out to party with them. Not that the girls hadn't given Sylvie a special night: there was the bridal shower last Thursday, where they made her wear a tin pie plate with an orange pot scrubber stuck over to one side, supposed to look like a bow on a bonnet. They played parlour games. Margo won a Tupperware orange peeler for having in her purse the item voted most unlikely to be found in a purse, specifically, a moo-cow creamer from the truck stop south of the city on Number 11. Tea and instant coffee were the beverages on offer, so with Erik calling up this way it was no wonder the thought that came to Sylvie's mind was, You have to make your own fun.

"Okay," said Erik as they sat in Yip's and raised their bottles of Boh and brought them together in a clumsy kiss of glass. "Okay, you're already living with this guy anyway, and day after tomorrow you'll drive out to Ripley for the wedding, and then what?"

"What do you mean, then what?"

"Then you just come back to your same place?"

"No."

"No?"

"Too far to drive. We stay overnight at the Capri in Foster and don't drive back till the next day."

"And you get up Monday morning and go to work, same as always?"

"Yes."

"Is there a point?"

"Anyway," Sylvie said, getting out of her chair, "this place has a dance floor."

They would drive barefoot in the long dark car, shoes and socks stripped off and thrown in the back. They took turns at the wheel. When Sylvie drove, the hard rubber ridges of the gas pedal and the brake pedal pressed into the sole of her naked foot, patterning her skin. When she was the passenger, she'd sit on her heel, switching legs when her knee cramped. They never once parked as a couple, though one night, after backing away from Paulie's old Buick and laughing at the idea of Paulie with his trademark white pants around his ankles – and he wore them pretty tight and it wouldn't be an easy dance to pull them up in a hurry, wiggle waggle, and would he even care or would he simply carry on? – after turning around and a few miles later driving slowly past Panchuck's grain bins and seeing that no one had rolled the signal tire out to the middle of the lane to show that the spot was taken for the evening – Sylvie and Erik did each press a look on the other across the wide space between them in the front seat. Sylvie, sitting on her heel, allowed herself to grind against the bone. She wanted him to notice, and she wanted him to not. She told herself the rush and flush were no more than heightened feelings from the game. She and Erik were each waiting for the single, right match, the ones they'd be willing to be exposed with through all of it – jobs and kids and grandkids and the old folks' home. They'd talked about this.

The band at Yip's was midway through Proud Mary. Erik leaned in close and said, "You didn't invite me."

"I don't hear from you for ten months. I don't know where you are. I'm supposed to invite you?"

He waved to show it didn't matter and said, "This guy then, you're fine about being naked in the headlights with him, yea unto glory-be?"

"Yea in the when and the what?" she said, stalling, standing on the dance floor, her hand palm up, a blank where she dared him to put the specifics.

"You remember."

"Is this a test?" she said.

"Come on. First the babies, and then all the way through to the nursing home."

She was annoyed with him for mentioning babies. It was only a wedding; they were only going to see how it went. The band sang for Proud Mary's big wheel to keep on turning, and Sylvie began a slow three-sixty on the dance floor, arms in the air, moving only to every second beat in order to prolong the attention her movement called to itself. She was somewhat on the skinny side, but she was pretty sure Erik appreciated skinny, and what's a little appreciation between friends? By the time she'd finished her first revolution, though, she was thinking less about the look of her hips under the strobe light and more about the image of the wheel that came to her as she revolved. She put herself at the centre of the wheel, and from her spot on the dance floor, spokes radiated. She could set out and step her way along any one of the spokes, say, two over to the left, all the way to the other end of her life. Or she could turn one-eighty and head off directly opposite. Her wheel of fortune. If only there were more Sylvies, to try out the different directions. The further she went, the further she'd be from herself. She could end up clear on the other side of the wheel, so far away from the first Sylvie, the Jack-marrying version, that all she could do would be to wave, and hope to be seen.

There was only one Sylvie, and she was only having a dance with an old friend. Over the music, she said, "I guess we considered ourselves pretty important back then, to think anybody would be watching what we did. Nobody's exactly training their headlights on us, on me and Jack."

"Not even yourself?" Erik said. "Even you're not watching?"

"You think too much."

He shrugged, which was infuriating.

"Erik, just dance."

When Yip's let out they drove across town, she in the rusty Toyota, he following in the Meteor, which he'd bought from his mom. His lights bounced off her rearview mirror and into her eyes and made her squint. They parked on Fourth Street in front of the bungalow where Sylvie and Jack lived in the basement.

Erik reached across in front of her and opened the front gate. "You lurch a lot," he said.

She saw he was barefoot, carrying his shoes and socks. She said, "I'm not good with a clutch. Jack won't have an automatic." She slipped out of her sandals. The grass teased her naked arches. "Wet," she said. "There's dew." The pattern on the concrete tiles that led around back pressed into the soles of her feet. She unlocked the door. Inside, down the stairs, past the washing machine and into the suite.

"Bathroom?" he said, and she pointed the way. He touched her shoulder as he passed. It's the wedding coming up, Sylvie told herself as she waited for him to come out. Only tonight and tomorrow, and that was it. They didn't bother with drinks. They stood with their bare feet inches apart and ignored the half-finished heap of flowers on the table. Behind Sylvie was the stove. Beside the stove was the water heater and beside the water heater was the bedroom door, open. Erik looked up at the little kitchen window. "You live underground," he said as he moved his gaze from the window to the bedroom doorway. Those were the actual words, but he could have strung together any old combination of syllables and the meaning would still be, There's a bed in there.

"Hold on a sec," Sylvie said, and she went into the bathroom and closed the door. She sat to pee and said to herself, Think this through. But it wasn't the time of night for in-depth thought. She ran a powder blue movie that featured Erik. How his hardness would press into the hollow beside her hipbone, how his bare shoulders would feel new under her hands, like something she'd saved up for. Different from Jack's, whose deep-slanted shoulders might be her least favourite of his physical traits; the shoulders and the fact that one of his earlobes was weirdly long, which wasn't his fault, but still.

She flushed. Ran the tap.

"You get swamped by a motorboat in there?"

"Just a *sec*," Sylvie said, turning the slick bar of soap between her palms. There must be an equivalent, in Erik-terms, of the weird earlobe. Yes: the way his left knee angled outward when he walked – something you stop noticing in a friend once you've known him awhile, but that knee, in a lover, would be more than itself. It would be the single thing you wanted to change and couldn't. Along with all the other single things.

His inherited weakness of eyesight. Erik's eventual wife would be leading him and his white cane around before he turned sixty. Sylvie took a moment to dry her hands.

She came out of the bathroom and took Erik's hand and led him into the dark bedroom. He looked toward the small window where the light from the street came in, high above the bed. He pointed to the bell-shaped red decal stuck to the windowpane. "What's that thing?"

"The fire department gives them out to mark the windows where they might have to come in and rescue someone."

"How would they get in through a little wee window like that?" he said. "And how am I gonna get *out* through a little wee window like that when your old man comes down the stairs?"

"He won't be home tonight," Sylvie said. She knew about these stag parties. He'd sleep where he passed out, and she wouldn't see him before two in the afternoon.

Erik guided her onto the bed. He took her foot in his hand. "This part's already naked." He began to massage – his thumb inside her arch, his hand traveling from her ankle, up inside the leg of her jeans, his finger wiggling its way between the tight fabric and the back of her knee. Lordy, who knew the back of a knee could start a quiver that would travel out so far from the source.

She heard the scuff of shoes against cement. Erik's hand pulled out *interruptus* and came to rest on her heel. Sylvie opened her eyes and saw in the pale glow from the streetlight three pairs of running shoes passing the bedroom window. Alex, shuffling along backwards; two other pairs of feet – Benj and Cyril? – shuffling forward. Clueless damn bozos. There was heat on the back of her knee in the shape of Erik's finger.

Cooling. Gone. She put a hand to Erik's shoulder and the two of them held still.

She heard Alex say, "Lemme find his keys here." They were a noisy crew, shuffling and grunting and letting the screen door slap behind them. Then an uneven rhythm, step-thud-step, thud-step-step. Sylvie pictured them in the stairwell, Alex with Jack by the armpits, below him Benj and Cyril, each with an ankle in hand. Jack's inert body hitting the walls of the stairwell side to side. She looked at Erik, who was looking up at the emergency decal on the window. "Stay put," she said. "He'll be out cold and the others don't need to see you."

She went to open the door at the bottom of the stairs. "Why didn't you let him sleep it off?"

Cyril said, "We thought he might be needed here tomorrow."

"Thanks a million." Sylvie pointed to the couch and they lifted him there and arranged him on his side. He groaned and rolled off, onto the unforgiving floor, cold tiles overtop of concrete.

"Ouch, jeeze," said Benj.

"We could put him in the bedroom," said Alex.

Sylvie shook her head.

"I don't suppose he's feeling any pain," said Benj.

"All the same," said Alex, looking toward the bedroom. When Sylvie shook her head again, Alex lifted Jack's floppy-doll head off the tiles and slid the satin Ripley cushion underneath.

Once the three of them had tromped back up the stairs and the door had slapped shut, Erik came out from behind the bedroom door. Sylvie let him take her hand and together they stood looking at Jack's oblivious face. Sweet, she thought. Sweet, but she'd seen him like this a dozen times and she knew he wouldn't be sweet tomorrow. Not horrible, not mean, but far from sweet. For a moment all her doubts attached themselves to his long, limp earlobe and the less than attractive line of his shoulders. But the earlobe and the slopey shoulders, those were nothing. Once you'd focused on them, you had to dismiss them, because it doesn't do to be shallow. You couldn't blame a guy for having a saggy bit of skin to one side of his face.

Erik squeezed her hand.

"What was it we thought we were doing?" she said.

"Drastic times, drastic measures." He wrapped her in a hug. "He's not your man for the headlights."

"Don't go thinking *you* are." She wished he wouldn't talk as if her life from here to forever rested on what would happen the day after tomorrow. It was only a wedding. A party in the lit hall, little girls in ruffled dresses dancing past their bedtimes and half the town bellying up for their free drinks. It was what you did. It was what they all did, Shelley and Beth and Serena, and now herself.

"Oh, Sylvie," Erik said, "I know I'm not the one. I know that." But when she started to ease out of the hug, he pulled her close and said, "Don't, not yet."

"Everybody's got their faults," she said, her cheek against the green plaid softness of his shirt.

"That's a fact."

"You have to back up now and drive away."

"That is how the game goes."

She stayed inside his arms for the moment. The strain in her head was like the strain she felt when Jack would interrupt a drinking party to get out The Riddle Game; people reading brain teasers off cards in their palms, and you couldn't muddle through to an answer and you'd think, At this time of night, who cares? There were the flowers on the table there, and the girls would be back to help finish them come morning. Things were in *place*. There was the hall booked, and the church, and the ladies baking buns, and Other Grandma coming from Alberta.

Erik pushed his toes underneath her naked arches and she stepped up and stood on his feet, skin over skin. They began a lumbering waltz, slow circles, each step coming down bare inches from where it originated. On the floor, Jack drooled onto a silkscreened babe on the Playground of the Prairies. Sylvie felt the odd fit of her right leg with Erik's left where his knee angled outward. She felt the upward press of his foot against her arch, then the moment of release, then the settling of weight with each graceless landing.

AMY JONES

WOLVES, CIGARETTES, GUM

Annalise and her mother dress exactly alike. Short denim skirts with fraying hems, pink tank tops, platform sandals: too old for one, too young for the other. They stand in line at New York Fries, looking out over the food court in opposite directions, one chewing on nails, one chewing on hair. From the back, at this distance, it's actually hard to tell them apart.

Annalise's hair is crimped like it's the eighties, which she told me is back in style, according to all the magazines. She doesn't have a crimper though, so every night she goes to bed with tiny wet braids that make her pillow wet. I imagine haphazard geometric patterns crisscrossing her skull, red marks on her neck where the elastics have dug into her skin while she sleeps.

Annalise's mother's hair is in a ponytail, her bangs curved up in a preposterously high inverted C shape plastered into place above her forehead. Red with large swaths of platinum running through them. Gravity-defying bangs.

"Bangs you could shatter a bottle over," Troy says, like he's given this a lot of thought.

It's hard to believe Annalise's mother has even seen the inside of a bank, let alone robbed one. She just doesn't look like a bank robber. She looks like she might be able to hold up a Mac's, maybe, a balaclava pulled over her freckles, a dirty syringe waving in the air, maybe rip an old lady's purse out from under her arm at a bus stop, maybe even a smash-and-grab at a mom and pop electronics store. Something street-level, no security, no finesse. But not a bank robber. Those are not the bangs of a bank robber.

"It was actually a credit union," Troy tells me, taking a bite out of his sub, wimpy shreds of lettuce falling out onto the tray from between two slabs of bread as hard and white as styrofoam. "She used a paintball gun. No one got hurt."

"They just got . . . what, decorated?" I ask. Troy just stares at me, gives me that *You're so dumb, Robin* look, a dollop of mayonnaise smeared across his lower lip. He still doesn't get why I'm pissed. I pick up a piece of fallen lettuce and pop it into my mouth without thinking about it. Then I think about it all at once: *When was the last time they washed those trays? What kind of cleaner did they use? What was on there before? Whose fingers? Which bodily fluids?*

I stick my tongue out, let the lettuce fall.

———

Troy met Annalise's mother, whose name is either Joy or Joyce or maybe just Jo, at the bowling alley. Troy is very serious about bowling. He is on a team called The Gutter Sluts and they play in a league every Tuesday and Friday night, talk about their scores the way other people talk about their kids. Annalise's mother worked at the bowling alley bar until she got caught stealing bottles of Wild Turkey and selling them to kids in the parking lot on her smoke break. Shortly after, she robbed the credit union.

"No one suspects her, because she looks so trashy," Troy told me this morning, smoking cigarettes in bed even though I keep telling him he's going to burn the building down. Secretly, though, I like it, the way the sun comes in through the slatted blinds and makes a pattern on his bare chest, the way the smoke flickers in and out of the light. But I'd never tell him that. He'd just take it as permission to ash on the floor.

"So what are you going to do?" I asked, fiddling with the drawstring on his pyjama pants. I wasn't nervous or anything, just curious. I'm never nervous for Troy. There is something about him, the way he licks his lips or juts his chin forward that makes you feel like he knows what he's doing all the time. It's comforting, being with a man who makes you feel that way, even if it's not entirely true.

He swatted my hand away, taking a long drag on his cigarette. "Drive the car, mostly," he said.

"Mostly?"

"I might be providing some of the firepower."

"I'm guessing you don't mean paintball guns."

He looked at me through narrowed eyes, that look that he gave me when he wanted me to remember the distance between us. "You don't want to know."

He was right. I didn't want to know. I didn't want to know what he meant by firepower, just like I didn't want to know why suddenly he had the need to progress from breaking and entering to armed robbery. I also didn't want to know if he had slept with Annalise's mother, this random Jo-Joy-Joyce he was ditching me for. Instead, I tried to think about how much I missed his goatee, that surprised O of hair, the little bristly wreath framing his mouth. He shaved it off a few weeks ago, and now it was like I was kissing a different person. A smoother person, someone who didn't care about hiding any part of his face, like, *Look at me world. Here's my fucking chin. Deal with it.*

"And why can't I come, again?" I asked.

Troy didn't say anything. He just stubbed out his cigarette and let the last bit of smoke curl away from his lips in a slow, thick stream, his eyes closed, one hand rubbing over his smooth, hairless chin.

———

Annalise and her mother come back to the table with their tray, a giant container of fries and two oversized cups of soda. "Holy Christ," says Annalise's mother, sitting down next to Troy. "How hard can it fucking be to get french fries, right?"

Annalise sits down next to me, earbuds shoved in her ears, fingers flying across her phone's touchscreen. Without slowing down, she leans forward and takes a sip from one of the giant cups, then makes a face.

"That one's yours," she says to her mother, stopping her texting just long enough to exchange cups and shove a handful of fries in her mouth. She looks like she hasn't eaten in weeks – and mows through that handful of fries like it, too – but doesn't eat any more after that.

Her mother picks through the fries like she's trying to find a four-leaf clover in a field of corn. She finally decides on one and bites down delicately on one end.

"I fucking hate these things," she says, dropping the fry back in the container. "Annie, where's our fucking ketchup?" She kicks her daughter under the table. Annalise kicks back, eyes still focused on her phone.

I try to make eye contact with Troy. This should be something we do, as a couple – make eye contact in meaningful ways when other people around us are batshit crazy. But Troy ignores me, reaching around Annalise's soda cup and grabbing three little packages of ketchup.

"Here ya go, geniuses," he says. Annalise takes a package and rips it open with her teeth, then squirts the contents directly into her mouth.

I can't help it; I gag.

Annalise stares at me, then opens her mouth and sticks out her tongue, ketchup smeared like blood across her teeth. She reaches for the other two, but I grab her hands and we have a little slap fight until I finally tear the packages away from her, holding them up over my head so she can't reach. Eventually, she rolls her eyes and sits back down with a huff, grabbing her phone and typing again.

"Ugly skank," she says. Tap tap tap. I try to imagine what she's texting. *This bitch at the food court won't let me eat fucking ketchup. I'm probably going to starve.* I look at her mother, but she's digging through her ugly red sequined purse for something. I wonder if she keeps the gun in there. I wonder if it's heavy.

"Troy," I say. "I can't do this."

Troy balls up his sub wrapper with one hand. "You can't do this? Fuck, Robin. You've got the easiest job of all." One leg bounces under the table, his eyes shift from the top of my head to a point in the distance, restless and unfocused, and I know it's too late. There's no pulling him back from this, not now. Not this time.

Annalise's mother pulls a tube of lipstick out of her purse and runs it over her mouth. Cherry red, like her purse, caking into little globs the minute she applies it. She looks at me for the first time since we arrived at the mall. "Don't let her into Claire's," she says. "She'll steal everything she can get her hands on."

———

Troy and me, we burgled for love. At first. I just wanted my diamond ring back. Percy had taken it when I broke off our engagement, forcibly ripping it from my finger while crying like a little girl. We broke into Percy's house when I knew he was away on business, a smashed basement window, our black hoods pulled up over our hair, taking not only the ring but some gold cufflinks, a watch, an iPod, some antique coins, and a wad of cash we later discovered was Canadian Tire money, schlepping it all back out the window in a garbage bag that might as well have had a giant dollar sign painted on it. Then we ran, until our hearts stopped and our lungs exploded. We ran until we collapsed against a park bench fifteen blocks away, giddy and coughing, our lungs screaming for air, our vision blurred with euphoria, our skin sparking with electricity, and Troy pushed me down against the cold wooden slats and fucked me right there under the streetlight, the animal desire on his face backlit by the soft yellow glow.

The next weekend, we sat on our couch and watched a

movie and drank beer and tried to forget about it. But both of us were antsy. We couldn't sit still. We couldn't concentrate. We couldn't even agree on a movie to watch. We should have seen it coming. How could we go back, after that first rush of the window breaking?

"You wanna do it again?" Troy asked.

I nodded.

We were so stupid in those early days, so reckless. We didn't stake out. We didn't track the neighbours or scope out security systems. We didn't even wear gloves. We just smashed windows and hoped for the best. That we were never caught is still shocking to me. That we never felt guilty about it, possibly less so. When you're in the middle of it, when you're standing in a stranger's house and everything is dark and silent and there are things everywhere – all this stuff that someone has because they traded some little pieces of paper for it, stuff they don't even use anyway, which just sits around being looked at, being owned, not fulfilling its true destiny as a functional object – it doesn't feel like you're doing anything wrong. It feels like the way it should be: that everything belongs to everyone and that you are just making it right. We restored the balance to the universe. We took other people's stuff and we felt like goddamn fucking superheroes.

And now, somehow, I've become nothing but a babysitter.

———

"Wolves, cigarettes, gum," Annalise says to me, suddenly, one earbud hanging out of her ear.

"Huh?" I'm slumped over, one ear down, listening to the beat of the piped-in music reverberating through the plastic of the table, the muffled sounds of people talking around me. It's oddly soothing. Troy and Annalise's mother have been gone for twenty minutes. Twenty more minutes to go before we leave the mall to meet them at the rendezvous point at Mission Marsh, where we divvy up the money and go our separate ways. This is the part of the plan I am most excited about, the part that I have been looking forward to ever since Troy told me what we were doing.

"Don't you know anything?" She sighs, tapping away on her phone. "Wolves, cigarettes, gum. It's a game. What do those three things have in common?"

"Uh . . . they're all things that you shouldn't swallow?"

Annalise rolls her eyes. "Like there's anything *you* won't swallow."

I look down at my own phone. Nineteen minutes. "I'm going to get a coffee," I say. "Stay here."

There's no one in the line at Tim Hortons except for two fat women in front of me, who can't make up their mind about what kind of muffin they want. And when they do, the cashier runs out of the little paper squares they use to pick up the muffins and has to go in the back. "I think I should have a bagel instead," one of the fat ladies says while she's gone.

On my way back to the table with my double-double, I don't think about Troy, but about Percy, my ex, and how he used to make up little songs about his food before he ate it. He thought it was cute, that it would make me laugh. *Macaroni and cheese, macaroni and cheese, nothing else can fill me up like macaroni and cheese*, he'd sing, to the tune of "Winnie the Pooh," and I would roll my eyes, or ignore him, get up and leave the room. Thinking about it now, Percy and those stupid little cheerful songs, it just, I don't know, makes me want to cry.

Stupid Percy loved me with every soft round part of his heart. Troy loved me with all the sharp, jagged edges.

I mean loves. Loves me with all the sharp, jagged edges.

When I get back to the table, of course Annalise is gone.

———

Troy and I fell in love over burgers and coffee at the Coney Island Westfort on a Friday afternoon. I had just got off my shift and was counting my tips when he came in and sat down at the counter. He had his work boots on, splotches of paint over all over his Carhartts, his cheeks windburned and shiny. He'd been in before, ordering takeout, and I'd watch him open the greasy brown paper bag on the sidewalk, rip into the burgers like a starving animal right there in front of the window. This time, though, he ordered two burgers and two cups of coffee and when I asked him if there was someone joining him he said, *You are*, with this wide grin, and in that instant I saw both the boy he had been and the man that he would be and I wanted all of it, all of him.

So even though I was supposed to go grocery shopping with Percy, I folded up my apron and sat down beside Troy. His legs were open wide and I had to tuck mine to the side to make sure they weren't touching his. He wiped his face with a napkin and swivelled his stool to face me, his eyes resting on my left hand.

"Nice ring," he said.

———

It isn't Claire's, like her mother said it would be, it is The Body Shop, her Hello Kitty purse weighed down with little tubs of lip gloss, smooth, cool vials of perfume, bars of glycerine soap wrapped tightly in plastic. I can smell her fruit salad stench the moment I step into the security office.

"Who are you?" the security guard asks. He is round, rosy-cheeked, bored. It occurs to me that he has gone through this with Annalise before. Annalise sits in front of the security desk, texting. For some reason, the fact that she is still doing this infuriates me. Why would he let her do that? Why wouldn't he take her phone away?

"I'm her babysitter," I say.

Annalise makes a little puff of air through pursed lips. "No she's not," she says, without looking up. "I've never seen her before in my life."

"Of course you haven't," I say. "You've been looking at that phone the entire time I've known you."

"Whatever," says Annalise, slouching down in her chair. One of the straps of her tank top slips down her arm. She pulls it back up and scratches her shoulder with so much force I feel like she must have ripped through the skin, but when I look, there's nothing but a light pink streak across her tanned skin.

The security guard hands me some papers to sign. I sit down on the chair next to Annalise and search through my purse for a pen. The security guard hands me one. It's a blue ballpoint that skips when I try to write with it. I want to stab the security guard's eye out with it.

"Can I go now?" Annalise asks.

"No, you can't *go now*," the security guard says, mimicking her tone. "This is the fourth time we've caught you shoplifting. The cops are on their way."

Both of us go rigid, and even though Annalise rolls her eyes and gives another "Whatever," I can see it in the tips of her fingers turning white against her phone's keyboard, in the sudden straightening of her spine: terror. I know, because I feel it, too. The security guard turns to his computer, shaking his head. That word, *cops*, clangs around in my brain for a good thirty seconds before I'm leaning in to Annalise's ear, my mouth nearly on her earlobe before I whisper.

"Run."

———

It's not the way I remember running. In the gas station parking lot across the street, I stop the car and close my eyes, my hands shaking on the wheel. The windshield is still partially frozen, thick blades of frost reaching upward from the tiny half-moon of defrosted glass above the dash that I had to lean forward to see through as I drove. My breath comes in tremendous gulps. Maybe running is different when there's someone chasing you. Maybe it hurts more, somehow.

Annalise seems unfazed, of course. She turns on the radio, flips to a Justin Bieber song. Stares out the window for a moment, her phone forgotten in her lap.

"They all come in packs."

"What?"

"Wolves, cigarettes, gum. They all come in packs." She shakes her head. "Jesus, Robin, keep up." She turns to me, and the sudden sight of her eyes is startling, wide and blue and utterly hopeless. She opens her hand, and I see she has held on to one of the glycerine soaps, red and glistening in her palm. "Wanna smell it?"

I take the soap, sweaty from Annalise's hand, and press it to my nose. It's strawberry, or a soap company's interpretation of strawberry. But it smells good. I breathe deeply, then pass it back to Annalise, who has already turned back to her phone. When the song on the radio ends, I realize I can hear the distant wail of sirens, and I wonder if they're for me and Annalise, or if they're for Troy and Annalise's mother, or if they're for someone else stealing something from somewhere else, or if it really even matters, if we're all just moving stuff around.

"Bagels, buttons, blue whales," I say. Annalise is silent for a while. "Annalise?" I say. "Bagels, buttons, blue whales. They all have a hole in them."

Annalise sticks her earbuds back in her ears. "That's stupid," she says, eyes down even as the cop cars race through the intersection in front of us, cherries flashing. "Everyone has a hole in them."

ABOUT THE CONTRIBUTORS

Rosaria Campbell is a fiction and essay writer who also tries her hand at poetry. She studied Creative Writing at St. Mary's University, and has participated in the Writers' Federation of Nova Scotia's mentorship program and the Maritime Writers' and Great Blue Heron workshops. She won *The Fiddlehead* short fiction contest in 2002 for "Reaching," and the *Prairie Fire* short fiction contest in 2013 for "Probabilities," and both stories were subsequently published in *The Journey Prize Stories*. Originally from Campbell's Creek, Newfoundland, she now lives and writes in Wallace Station, Nova Scotia. She is currently working on a collection of pieces about the decades of the twentieth century.

Nancy Jo Cullen's short fiction has appeared in *The Puritan*, *Prairie Fire, Grain, Plenitude, filling Station, The New Quarterly*, and *This Magazine*, where "Hashtag Maggie Vandermeer" was first published. Her short story collection, *Canary*, won the 2012 Metcalf-Rooke Award, and she was the 2010 winner of the Writers' Trust of Canada's Dayne Ogilvie Prize for LGBT Emerging Writers. Her story "Ashes" appeared in *The Journey Prize Stories 24*. She holds an MFA in Creative Writing from the University of Guelph.

M.A. Fox's "Piano Boy" is one of her gossip-based *Stories for the Left Ear*. Her novel *The Bones of Time* is a portrait of a Hemingwayesque young writer in 1920s Paris, and she is completing a dystopian revolutionary trilogy, *Band of Comrades*. She has a doctorate in English from the University of Toronto, a checkered past as a rock singer and lay midwife, and is the founder and principal of The Dragon Academy.

Kevin Hardcastle is a fiction writer from Simcoe County, Ontario. His work has been published in journals including *The Malahat Review*, *Little Fiction*, *The Puritan*, *PRISM international*, *EVENT*, *The New Quarterly*, and *Shenandoah*. His story "To Have to Wait" appeared in *The Journey Prize Stories 24*, and was a finalist for that year's prize. "Old Man Marchuk" will also appear in *14: Best Canadian Stories*. Hardcastle is at work on a collection of stories, forthcoming from Biblioasis. He lives in Toronto.

Amy Jones is the author of the short fiction collection *What Boys Like* (Biblioasis), which won the 2008 Metcalf-Rooke Award and was shortlisted for the 2010 ReLit Award. Originally from Halifax, she now lives in Thunder Bay, where she is currently working on a novel and a collection of short stories.

Tyler Keevil was born in Edmonton, grew up in Vancouver, and moved to Wales in 2003. His short fiction has won several awards and appeared in a wide range of magazines, literary journals, and anthologies. His debut novel, *Fireball*, received the 2011 Media Wales People's Prize, and his second, *The Drive*, has been shortlisted for the 2014 Wales Book of the Year. *Burrard Inlet*, his first story collection, was recently published in the U.K. Among other things, Tyler has worked as a landscaper, tree planter, and ice barge deckhand; he now lectures in Creative Writing at the University of Gloucestershire.

Jeremy Lanaway lives in Vernon, British Columbia, with his wife and daughters. He writes fiction in blinks between teaching English at Okanagan College and writing and editing textbooks for Pearson-Longman Hong Kong, where he and his wife lived for three years in the early 2000s. He also writes a hockey column for *The American*, an arts and culture magazine based in London, England. He has published stories in Canada, the United States, and Hong Kong, and is currently working on a novel and short story collection to be anchored by "Downturn," the story that appears in *The Journey Prize Stories 26*.

Andrew MacDonald won a Western Magazine Award for Fiction and the Deborah Slosberg Memorial Award. His story "Eat Fist!" appeared in *The Journey Prize Stories 22*. He lives in Toronto and New England, where he's writing more stories and a novel.

Lori McNulty's fiction and non-fiction have appeared in *The Fiddlehead*, *The New Quarterly*, *PRISM international*, *The Dalhousie Review*, *Descant*, and the *Globe and Mail*. She holds an MFA in Creative Writing from the University of British Columbia, and an MA from McGill University. She is currently completing a collection of short fiction and at work on a novel. Africa is next on the horizon for this Vancouver-based digital storyteller. Please visit www.lorimcnulty.ca.

Shana Myara's writing has won fiction prizes sponsored by *subTerrain*, *PRISM international*, and *Geist*, and been short-listed for two CBC Literary Awards. She is the artistic director of the Vancouver Queer Film Festival, and is ever so close to completing her first collection of short stories.

Julie Roorda is the author of three volumes of poetry and a collection of short stories. Her fiction has appeared in periodicals across Canada, including *The Fiddlehead, Room of One's Own,* and *The New Quarterly.* She has completed a second collection of stories and is currently working on a novel, while supporting herself with other freelance writing and editing projects.

Leona Theis is the author of the story collection *Sightlines* (Coteau) and the novel *The Art of Salvage* (Coteau). She won the 2006 CBC Literary Award for Creative Non-fiction. "High Beams" just might become the first chapter of a novel-in-stories. The story that might become the second chapter, "How Sylvie Failed to Become a Better Person through Yoga," was longlisted for the Vanderbilt–Exile Award. Recently, Leona completed work on a second novel, *The Originals.* The protagonist of *The Originals* has posted her thoughts on what it's like to be a character, subject to an author's whims, at AlwaysUnderRevision.com.

Clea Young's stories have appeared in *EVENT, Grain, The Fiddlehead, The Malahat Review, Prairie Fire, Room,* and *Coming Attractions.* In 2012, she was shortlisted for the CBC Short Story Prize. This marks her third appearance in *The Journey Prize Stories.* Clea received an MFA from the University of British Columbia. She is currently Artistic Associate at the Vancouver Writers Fest and lives in Vancouver, British Columbia, with her husband and son.

ABOUT THE CONTRIBUTING PUBLICATIONS

For more information about the journals that submitted to this year's competition, The Journey Prize, and *The Journey Prize Stories*, please visit www.facebook.com/TheJourneyPrize.

Descant is a quarterly journal, now in its fifth decade, publishing poetry, prose, fiction, interviews, travel pieces, letters, literary criticism, and visual art by new and established contemporary writers and artists from Canada and around the world. Editor: Karen Mulhallen. Managing Editor: Vera DeWaard. Submissions and correspondence: *Descant*, P.O. Box 314, Station P, Toronto, Ontario, M5S 2S8. Email: info@descant.ca Website: www.descant.ca

EVENT features the very best in contemporary writing from Canada and abroad, from literary heavyweights to up-and-comers. For over four decades, *EVENT* has consistently published award-winning fiction, poetry, non-fiction, notes on writing, and critical reviews – all topped off by stunning Canadian cover art. Recent stories first published in *EVENT* have gone on to win both the Gold and Silver National Magazine Awards in Fiction in 2012 and 2011, and the Western Magazine Awards in Fiction in 2012 and 2010. *EVENT* is also home to Canada's longest-running annual non-fiction contest and a reading service for writers. Editor: Elizabeth Bachinsky. Managing Editor: Ian Cockfield. Fiction

Editor: Christine Dewar. Submissions and correspondence: *EVENT*, P.O. Box 2503, New Westminster, British Columbia, V3L 5B2. Email (queries only): event@douglascollege.ca Website: www.eventmagazine.ca

The Fiddlehead, Atlantic Canada's longest-running literary journal, publishes poetry and short fiction as well as book reviews. It appears four times a year, sponsors a contest for fiction and for poetry that awards a total of $5,000 in prizes, including the $2,000 Ralph Gustafson Poetry Prize and the $2,000 short fiction prize. *The Fiddlehead* welcomes all good writing in English, from anywhere, looking always for that element of freshness and surprise. Editor: Ross Leckie. Submissions and correspondence: *The Fiddlehead*, Campus House, 11 Garland Court, University of New Brunswick, P.O. Box 4400, Fredericton, New Brunswick, E3B 5A3. E-mail (queries only): fiddlehd@unb.ca Website: www.TheFiddlehead.ca Blog, with original content: TheFiddleheadNews.blogspot.ca

Grain, *the journal of eclectic writing*, is a literary quarterly that publishes engaging, diverse, and challenging writing and art by some of the best Canadian and international writers and artists. Every issue features superb new writing from both developing and established writers. Each issue also highlights the unique artwork of a different visual artist. Editor: Rilla Friesen. Associate Fiction and Non-fiction Editor: Kim Aubrey. Associate Poetry Editor: Adam Pottle. Art Editor and Designer: Betsy Rosenwald. Submissions and correspondence: *Grain*, P.O. Box 67, Saskatoon, Saskatchewan, S7K 3K1. Email: grainmag@sasktel.net Website: www.grainmagazine.ca

The New Orphic Review is a semi-annual literary magazine that publishes fiction and articles up to 10,000 words in length and poetry ranging from sonnets to free verse. It is listed in *Poet's Market, Novel & Short Story Writer's Market, The Pushcart Prize, Best American Short Stories,* and *Best American Mystery Stories.* It has featured poetry, fiction, and essays by authors from Finland, Switzerland, Italy, Ireland, Britain, Chile, Canada, and the United States. Editor-in-chief: Ernest Hekkanen. Associate Editor: Margrith Schraner. Submissions and correspondence: *The New Orphic Review,* 706 Mill Street, Nelson, British Columbia, V1L 4S5. Website: www3.telus.net/ neworphicpublishers-hekkanen

The New Quarterly is an award-winning literary magazine publishing fiction, poetry, personal essays, interviews, and essays on writing. Now in its thirty-third year, the magazine prides itself on its independent take on the Canadian literary scene. Recent issues include The QuArc issue (a 290-page flip book on the interstices of science and literature undertaken with *Arc Poetry Magazine*) and The TNQ Extra (writers on their collections and obsessions), and more exciting projects are in the works. Editor: Pamela Mulloy. Submissions and correspondence: *The New Quarterly,* c/o St. Jerome's University, 290 Westmount Road North, Waterloo, Ontario, N2L 3G3. E-mail: pmulloy@tnq.ca, sblom@tnq.ca Website: www.tnq.ca

Prairie Fire is a quarterly magazine of contemporary Canadian writing that publishes stories, poems, and literary non-fiction by both emerging and established writers. *Prairie Fire*'s editorial mix also occasionally features critical or personal essays. Stories published in *Prairie Fire* have won awards at the National Magazine Awards and the Western Magazine Awards. *Prairie Fire* publishes writing from, and has readers in, all parts of Canada. Editor: Andris Taskans. Fiction Editors: Warren Cariou and Heidi Harms. Submissions and correspondence: *Prairie Fire*, Room 423, 100 Arthur Street, Winnipeg, Manitoba, R3B 1H3. Email: prfire@mts.net Website: www.prairiefire.ca

PRISM international, the oldest literary magazine in Western Canada, was established in 1959 by Earle Birney at the University of British Columbia. Published four times a year, *PRISM* features short fiction, poetry, creative non-fiction, and translations. *PRISM* editors select work based on originality and quality, and the magazine showcases work from both new and established writers from Canada and around the world. *PRISM* holds three exemplary annual competitions for short fiction, literary non-fiction, and poetry, and awards the Earle Birney Prize for Poetry to an outstanding poet whose work was featured in *PRISM* in the preceding year. Executive Editors: Sierra Skye Gemma and Andrea Hoff. Prose Editor: Jane Campbell. Poetry Editor: Zachary Matteson. Submissions and correspondence: *PRISM international*, Creative Writing Program, The University of British Columbia, Buchanan E-462, 1866 Main Mall, Vancouver, British Columbia, V6T 1Z1. Website: www.prismmagazine.ca

Room magazine publishes fiction, poetry, creative non-fiction, and artwork by and about women. *Room* was founded in 1975 (as *Room of One's Own*) to provide opportunities for emerging and established writers and artists who identify as women to publish their work in Canada. Contributors have included some of Canada's most celebrated writers, including Alice Munro, Jane Urquhart, Larissa Lai, Carol Shields, Karen Solie, Pamela Porter, Elizabeth Bachinsky, and Betsy Warland. Each quarter we publish original, thought-provoking works that reflect women's strength, sensuality, vulnerability, and wit. Correspondence: *Room* magazine, Box 46160 Stn. D, Vancouver, British Columbia, V6J 5G5. Submissions: roommagazine.com/submit Website: roommagazine.com Email: contactus@roommagazine.com

Taddle Creek often is asked to define itself and, just as often, it tends to refuse to do so. But it will say this: each issue of the magazine contains a multitude of things between its snazzily illustrated covers, including, but not limited to, fiction, poetry, comics, art, interviews, and feature stories. It's an odd mix, to be sure, which is why *Taddle Creek* refers to itself somewhat oddly as a "general-interest literary magazine." Work presented in *Taddle Creek* is humorous, poignant, ephemeral, urban, and rarely overly earnest, though not usually all at once. *Taddle Creek* takes its mission to be the journal for those who detest everything the literary magazine has become in the twenty-first century very seriously. Editor-in-Chief: Conan Tobias. Correspondence: *Taddle Creek*, P.O. Box 611, Stn. P, Toronto, Ontario M5S 2Y4. E-mail: editor@taddlecreekmag.com. Website: taddlecreekmag.com.

For more than four decades, **This Magazine** has proudly published fiction and poetry from new and emerging Canadian writers. A sassy and thoughtful journal of arts, politics, and progressive ideas, *This* consistently offers fresh takes on familiar issues, as well as breaking stories that need to be told. Publisher: Lisa Whittington-Hill. Fiction and Poetry Editor: Dani Couture. Correspondence: *This Magazine*, Suite 417, 401 Richmond Ave. W., Toronto, Ontario, M5V 3A8. Website: www.this.org

Submissions were also received from the following publications:

The Antigonish Review
(Antigonish, NS)
www.antigonishreview.com

Briarpatch Magazine
(Regina, SK)
briarpatchmagazine.com

carte blanche
(Montreal, QC)
www.carte-blanche.org

The Dalhousie Review
(Halifax, NS)
www.dalhousiereview.dal.ca

ELQ/Exile Literary Quarterly Magazine
(Holstein, ON)
www.exilequarterly.com

Found Press Quarterly
www.foundpress.com

FreeFall
(Calgary, AB)
www.freefallmagazine.ca

Joyland Magazine
www.joylandmagazine.com

Little Brother Magazine
(Toronto, ON)
www.littlebrother
magazine.com

Little Fiction.
(Toronto, ON)
www.littlefiction.com

The Malahat Review
(Victoria, BC)
www.malahatreview.ca

Maple Tree Literary
Supplement
(Ottawa, ON)
www.mtls.ca

Matrix Magazine
(Montreal, QC)
www.matrixmagazine.org

On Spec
(Edmonton, AB)
www.onspec.ca

Plenitude Magazine
www.plenitudemagazine.ca

The Prairie Journal of
Canadian Literature
(Calgary, AB)
www.prairiejournal.org

The Puritan
(Toronto, ON)
www.puritan-magazine.com

Queen's Quarterly
(Kingston, ON)
www.queensu.ca/quarterly

Ricepaper Magazine
(Vancouver, BC)
www.ricepapermagazine.ca

Riddle Fence: A Journal of Arts
& Culture
(St. John's, NL)
www.riddlefence.com

The Rusty Toque
(London, ON)
www.therustytoque.com

subTerrain Magazine
(Vancouver, BC)

PREVIOUS CONTRIBUTING AUTHORS

* Winners of the $10,000 Journey Prize
** Co-winners of the $10,000 Journey Prize

1

1989

SELECTED WITH ALISTAIR MacLEOD

Ven Begamudré, "Word Games"
David Bergen, "Where You're From"
Lois Braun, "The Pumpkin-Eaters"
Constance Buchanan, "Man with Flying Genitals"
Ann Copeland, "Obedience"
Marion Douglas, "Flags"
Frances Itani, "An Evening in the Café"
Diane Keating, "The Crying Out"
Thomas King, "One Good Story, That One"
Holley Rubinsky, "Rapid Transits"*
Jean Rysstad, "Winter Baby"
Kevin Van Tighem, "Whoopers"
M.G. Vassanji, "In the Quiet of a Sunday Afternoon"
Bronwen Wallace, "Chicken 'N' Ribs"
Armin Wiebe, "Mouse Lake"
Budge Wilson, "Waiting"

2

1990

SELECTED WITH LEON ROOKE; GUY VANDERHAEGHE

André Alexis, "Despair: Five Stories of Ottawa"
Glen Allen, "The Hua Guofeng Memorial Warehouse"
Marusia Bociurkiw, "Mama, Donya"
Virgil Burnett, "Billfrith the Dreamer"
Margaret Dyment, "Sacred Trust"
Cynthia Flood, "My Father Took a Cake to France"*
Douglas Glover, "Story Carved in Stone"
Terry Griggs, "Man with the Axe"
Rick Hillis, "Limbo River"

Thomas King, "The Dog I Wish I Had, I Would Call It Helen"
K.D. Miller, "Sunrise Till Dark"
Jennifer Mitton, "Let Them Say"
Lawrence O'Toole, "Goin' to Town with Katie Ann"
Kenneth Radu, "A Change of Heart"
Jenifer Sutherland, "Table Talk"
Wayne Tefs, "Red Rock and After"

3
1991
SELECTED WITH JANE URQUHART

Donald Aker, "The Invitation"
Anton Baer, "Yukon"
Allan Barr, "A Visit from Lloyd"
David Bergen, "The Fall"
Rai Berzins, "Common Sense"
Diana Hartog, "Theories of Grief"
Diane Keating, "The Salem Letters"
Yann Martel, "The Facts Behind the Helsinki Roccamatios"*
Jennifer Mitton, "Polaroid"
Sheldon Oberman, "This Business with Elijah"
Lynn Podgurny, "Till Tomorrow, Maple Leaf Mills"
James Riseborough, "She Is Not His Mother"
Patricia Stone, "Living on the Lake"

4
1992
SELECTED WITH SANDRA BIRDSELL

David Bergen, "The Bottom of the Glass"
Maria A. Billion, "No Miracles Sweet Jesus"
Judith Cowan, "By the Big River"
Steven Heighton, "A Man Away from Home Has No Neighbours"
Steven Heighton, "How Beautiful upon the Mountains"
L. Rex Kay, "Travelling"
Rozena Maart, "No Rosa, No District Six"*
Guy Malet De Carteret, "Rainy Day"
Carmelita McGrath, "Silence"
Michael Mirolla, "A Theory of Discontinuous Existence"
Diane Juttner Perreault, "Bella's Story"
Eden Robinson, "Traplines"

5

1993

SELECTED WITH GUY VANDERHAEGHE

Caroline Adderson, "Oil and Dread"

David Bergen, "La Rue Prevette"

Marina Endicott, "With the Band"

Dayv James-French, "Cervine"

Michael Kenyon, "Durable Tumblers"

K.D. Miller, "A Litany in Time of Plague"

Robert Mullen, "Flotsam"

Gayla Reid, "Sister Doyle's Men"*

Oakland Ross, "Bang-bang"

Robert Sherrin, "Technical Battle for Trial Machine"

Carol Windley, "The Etruscans"

6

1994

SELECTED WITH DOUGLAS GLOVER;
JUDITH CHANT (CHAPTERS)

Anne Carson, "Water Margins: An Essay on Swimming by My Brother"

Richard Cumyn, "The Sound He Made"

Genni Gunn, "Versions"

Melissa Hardy, "Long Man the River"*

Robert Mullen, "Anomie"

Vivian Payne, "Free Falls"

Jim Reil, "Dry"

Robyn Sarah, "Accept My Story"

Joan Skogan, "Landfall"

Dorothy Speak, "Relatives in Florida"

Alison Wearing, "Notes from Under Water"

7

1995

SELECTED WITH M.G. VASSANJI;
RICHARD BACHMANN (A DIFFERENT DRUMMER BOOKS)

Michelle Alfano, "Opera"

Mary Borsky, "Maps of the Known World"

Gabriella Goliger, "Song of Ascent"

Elizabeth Hay, "Hand Games"

Shaena Lambert, "The Falling Woman"

Elise Levine, "Boy"

Roger Burford Mason, "The Rat-Catcher's Kiss"
Antanas Sileika, "Going Native"
Kathryn Woodward, "Of Marranos and Gilded Angels"*

8
1996
SELECTED WITH OLIVE SENIOR;
BEN McNALLY (NICHOLAS HOARE LTD.)

Rick Bowers, "Dental Bytes"
David Elias, "How I Crossed Over"
Elyse Gasco, "Can You Wave Bye Bye, Baby?"*
Danuta Gleed, "Bones"
Elizabeth Hay, "The Friend"
Linda Holeman, "Turning the Worm"
Elaine Littman, "The Winner's Circle"
Murray Logan, "Steam"
Rick Maddocks, "Lessons from the Sputnik Diner"
K.D. Miller, "Egypt Land"
Gregor Robinson, "Monster Gaps"
Alma Subasic, "Dust"

9
1997
SELECTED WITH NINO RICCI; NICHOLAS PASHLEY
(UNIVERSITY OF TORONTO BOOKSTORE)

Brian Bartlett, "Thomas, Naked"
Dennis Bock, "Olympia"
Kristen den Hartog, "Wave"
Gabriella Goliger, "Maladies of the Inner Ear"**
Terry Griggs, "Momma Had a Baby"
Mark Anthony Jarman, "Righteous Speedboat"
Judith Kalman, "Not for Me a Crown of Thorns"
Andrew Mullins, "The World of Science"
Sasenarine Persaud, "Canada Geese and Apple Chatney"
Anne Simpson, "Dreaming Snow"**
Sarah Withrow, "Ollie"
Terence Young, "The Berlin Wall"

10

1998

SELECTED BY PETER BUITENHUIS; HOLLEY RUBINSKY;
CELIA DUTHIE (DUTHIE BOOKS LTD.)

John Brooke, "The Finer Points of Apples"*

Ian Colford, "The Reason for the Dream"

Libby Creelman, "Cruelty"

Michael Crummey, "Serendipity"

Stephen Guppy, "Downwind"

Jane Eaton Hamilton, "Graduation"

Elise Levine, "You Are You Because Your Little Dog Loves You"

Jean McNeil, "Bethlehem"

Liz Moore, "Eight-Day Clock"

Edward O'Connor, "The Beatrice of Victoria College"

Tim Rogers, "Scars and Other Presents"

Denise Ryan, "Marginals, Vivisections, and Dreams"

Madeleine Thien, "Simple Recipes"

Cheryl Tibbetts, "Flowers of Africville"

11

1999

SELECTED BY LESLEY CHOYCE; SHELDON CURRIE;
MARY-JO ANDERSON (FROG HOLLOW BOOKS)

Mike Barnes, "In Florida"

Libby Creelman, "Sunken Island"

Mike Finigan, "Passion Sunday"

Jane Eaton Hamilton, "Territory"

Mark Anthony Jarman, "Travels into Several Remote Nations of the
World"

Barbara Lambert, "Where the Bodies Are Kept"

Linda Little, "The Still"

Larry Lynch, "The Sitter"

Sandra Sabatini, "The One With the News"

Sharon Steams, "Brothers"

Mary Walters, "Show Jumping"

Alissa York, "The Back of the Bear's Mouth"*

12

2000

13

2001

14

2002

Jocelyn Brown, "Miss Canada"*
Emma Donoghue, "What Remains"
Jonathan Goldstein, "You Are a Spaceman With Your Head Under the
    Bathroom Stall Door"
Robert McGill, "Confidence Men"
Robert McGill, "The Stars Are Falling"
Nick Melling, "Philemon"
Robert Mullen, "Alex the God"
Karen Munro, "The Pool"
Leah Postman, "Being Famous"
Neil Smith, "Green Fluorescent Protein"

15
2003
SELECTED BY MICHELLE BERRY;
TIMOTHY TAYLOR; MICHAEL WINTER

Rosaria Campbell, "Reaching"
Hilary Dean, "The Lemon Stories"
Dawn Rae Downton, "Hansel and Gretel"
Anne Fleming, "Gay Dwarves of America"
Elyse Friedman, "Truth"
Charlotte Gill, "Hush"
Jessica Grant, "My Husband's Jump"*
Jacqueline Honnet, "Conversion Classes"
S.K. Johannesen, "Resurrection"
Avner Mandelman, "Cuckoo"
Tim Mitchell, "Night Finds Us"
Heather O'Neill, "The Difference Between Me and Goldstein"

16
2004
SELECTED BY ELIZABETH HAY; LISA MOORE; MICHAEL REDHILL

Anar Ali, "Baby Khaki's Wings"
Kenneth Bonert, "Packers and Movers"
Jennifer Clouter, "Benny and the Jets"
Daniel Griffin, "Mercedes Buyer's Guide"
Michael Kissinger, "Invest in the North"
Devin Krukoff, "The Last Spark"*
Elaine McCluskey, "The Watermelon Social"
William Metcalfe, "Nice Big Car, Rap Music Coming Out the Window"
Lesley Millard, "The Uses of the Neckerchief"

Adam Lewis Schroeder, "Burning the Cattle at Both Ends"
Michael V. Smith, "What We Wanted"
Neil Smith, "Isolettes"
Patricia Rose Young, "Up the Clyde on a Bike"

17
2005
SELECTED BY JAMES GRAINGER AND NANCY LEE
Randy Boyagoda, "Rice and Curry Yacht Club"
Krista Bridge, "A Matter of Firsts"
Josh Byer, "Rats, Homosex, Saunas, and Simon"
Craig Davidson, "Failure to Thrive"
McKinley M. Hellenes, "Brighter Thread"
Catherine Kidd, "Green-Eyed Beans"
Pasha Malla, "The Past Composed"
Edward O'Connor, "Heard Melodies Are Sweet"
Barbara Romanik, "Seven Ways into Chandigarh"
Sandra Sabatini, "The Dolphins at Sainte Marie"
Matt Shaw, "Matchbook for a Mother's Hair"*
Richard Simas, "Anthropologies"
Neil Smith, "Scrapbook"
Emily White, "Various Metals"

18
2006
SELECTED BY STEVEN GALLOWAY;
ZSUZSI GARTNER; ANNABEL LYON
Heather Birrell, "BriannaSusannaAlana"*
Craig Boyko, "The Baby"
Craig Boyko, "The Beloved Departed"
Nadia Bozak, "Heavy Metal Housekeeping"
Lee Henderson, "Conjugation"
Melanie Little, "Wrestling"
Matthew Rader, "The Lonesome Death of Joseph Fey"
Scott Randall, "Law School"
Sarah Selecky, "Throwing Cotton"
Damian Tarnopolsky, "Sleepy"
Martin West, "Cretacea"
David Whitton, "The Eclipse"
Clea Young, "Split"

19

2007

SELECTED BY CAROLINE ADDERSON;
DAVID BEZMOZGIS; DIONNE BRAND

Andrew J. Borkowski, "Twelve Versions of Lech"

Craig Boyko, "OZY"*

Grant Buday, "The Curve of the Earth"

Nicole Dixon, "High-water Mark"

Krista Foss, "Swimming in Zanzibar"

Pasha Malla, "Respite"

Alice Petersen, "After Summer"

Patricia Robertson, "My Hungarian Sister"

Rebecca Rosenblum, "Chilly Girl"

Nicholas Ruddock, "How Eunice Got Her Baby"

Jean Van Loon, "Stardust"

20

2008

SELECTED BY LYNN COADY; HEATHER O'NEILL; NEIL SMITH

Théodora Armstrong, "Whale Stories"

Mike Christie, "Goodbye Porkpie Hat"

Anna Leventhal, "The Polar Bear at the Museum"

Naomi K. Lewis, "The Guiding Light"

Oscar Martens, "Breaking on the Wheel"

Dana Mills, "Steaming for Godthab"

Saleema Nawaz, "My Three Girls"*

Scott Randall, "The Gifted Class"

S. Kennedy Sobol, "Some Light Down"

Sarah Steinberg, "At Last at Sea"

Clea Young, "Chaperone"

21

2009

SELECTED BY CAMILLA GIBB;
LEE HENDERSON; REBECCA ROSENBLUM

Daniel Griffin, "The Last Great Works of Alvin Cale"

Jesus Hardwell, "Easy Living"

Paul Headrick, "Highlife"

Sarah Keevil, "Pyro"

Adrian Michael Kelly, "Lure"

Fran Kimmel, "Picturing God's Ocean"

Lynne Kutsukake, "Away"
Alexander MacLeod, "Miracle Mile"
Dave Margoshes, "The Wisdom of Solomon"
Shawn Syms, "On the Line"
Sarah L. Taggart, "Deaf"
Yasuko Thanh, "Floating Like the Dead"*

22

2010

SELECTED BY PASHA MALLA; JOAN THOMAS; ALISSA YORK

Carolyn Black, "Serial Love"
Andrew Boden, "Confluence of Spoors"
Laura Boudreau, "The Dead Dad Game"
Devon Code, "Uncle Oscar"*
Danielle Egan, "Publicity"
Krista Foss, "The Longitude of Okay"
Lynne Kutsukake, "Mating"
Ben Lof, "When in the Field with Her at His Back"
Andrew MacDonald, "Eat Fist!"
Eliza Robertson, "Ship's Log"
Mike Spry, "Five Pounds Short and Apologies to Nelson Algren"
Damian Tarnopolsky, "Laud We the Gods"

23

2011

SELECTED BY ALEXANDER MacLEOD;
ALISON PICK; SARAH SELECKY

Jay Brown, "The Girl from the War"
Michael Christie, "The Extra"
Seyward Goodhand, "The Fur Trader's Daughter"
Miranda Hill, "Petitions to Saint Chronic"*
Fran Kimmel, "Laundry Day"
Ross Klatte, "First-Calf Heifer"
Michelle Serwatuk, "My Eyes are Dim"
Jessica Westhead, "What I Would Say"
Michelle Winters, "Toupée"
D.W. Wilson, "The Dead Roads"

24
2012
SELECTED BY MICHAEL CHRISTIE;
KATHRYN KUITENBROUWER; KATHLEEN WINTER

Kris Bertin, "Is Alive and Can Move"
Shashi Bhat, "Why I Read *Beowulf*"
Astrid Blodgett, "Ice Break"
Trevor Corkum, "You Were Loved"
Nancy Jo Cullen, "Ashes"
Kevin Hardcastle, "To Have to Wait"
Andrew Hood, "I'm Sorry and Thank You"
Andrew Hood, "Manning"
Grace O'Connell, "The Many Faces of Montgomery Clift"
Jasmina Odor, "Barcelona"
Alex Pugsley, "Crisis on Earth-X"*
Eliza Robertson, "Sea Drift"
Martin West, "My Daughter of the Dead Reeds"

25
2013
SELECTED BY MIRANDA HILL;
MARK MEDLEY; RUSSELL WANGERSKY

Steven Benstead, "Megan's Bus"
Jay Brown, "The Egyptians"
Andrew Forbes, "In the Foothills"
Philip Huynh, "Gulliver's Wife"
Amy Jones, "Team Ninja"
Marnie Lamb, "Mrs. Fujimoto's Wednesday Afternoons"
Doretta Lau, "How Does a Single Blade of Grass Thank the Sun?"
Laura Legge, "It's Raining in Paris"
Natalie Morrill, "Ossicles"
Zoey Leigh Peterson, "Sleep World"
Eliza Robertson, "My Sister Sang"
Naben Ruthnum, "Cinema Rex"*